vabfi
WEISS

Weiss, Kelly Fumiko, author
The stories we choose not to tell
33410015694278   03-02-2021

Valparaiso Public Library
103 Jefferson Street
Valparaiso, IN 46383

ALSO BY THE AUTHOR

THE CUBE

The Stories We Choose Not To Tell

a novel by
KELLY FUMIKO WEISS

The Stories We Choose Not To Tell

© 2020 by Kelly Fumiko Weiss. All rights reserved.

This book is a work of fiction. Names, characters, places, and incidents either are products of the author's imagination or are used fictitiously. Any resemblance to actual persons, living or dead, events, or locales is entirely coincidental.

All rights reserved. No part of this publication may be reproduced or transmitted in any form or by any means, electronic or mechanical, including photocopy, recording, or any information storage and retrieval system, without permission in writing from the publisher.

Please contact publisher for permission to make copies of any part of this work.

Windy City Publishers
2118 Plum Grove Road, #349
Rolling Meadows, IL 60008
www.windycitypublishers.com

Published in the United States of America

ISBN:
978-1-941478-96-7

Library of Congress Control Number:
2020906891

WINDY CITY PUBLISHERS
CHICAGO

For my grammy, Mary
For my mom, Sharon
For my sister, Julie

Author's Note

THIS NOVEL IS MOST CERTAINLY fiction. The names, the relationships, the sequence of events, all came about as most novels do, from an idea I couldn't let go of, to a draft (and another draft and another draft, etc.) to this book before you. However, it is grounded in truth. My Grammy was in the Japanese incarceration camps at Amache (she was a teenager at the time). Her family owned land and a business in California, all lost when they entered the camps. My family relocated to Chicago after being released from the camps. My Ojichan was in the MIS during WWII and I went to Washington DC in 2010 to receive the Congressional Gold Medal on his behalf. My mother married a white man before it was socially acceptable to do so and it did cause family tension. I have struggled with my mixed race identity for my entire life and still struggle with how to carry on our family's legacy. And, I did make a pilgrimage to Amache, to stand where my Grammy had once stood, while I was pregnant with my daughter.

Other than those core foundations, the rest of this book is entirely made up. Why didn't I just write my family's story? In part because my family is very private and many parts of my Grammy's and my mother's story were not mine to tell. In part because I wanted the flexibility to share certain events and feelings without being tied down to the exact things that happened. In part because I had other things I wanted to talk about that fell outside of what my family experienced. In part because I had characters in my mind and in my heart that I wanted to write about that aren't a part of my family's journey. And, in part because my family's story is actually a little too dramatic for a novel. I'm not sure anyone would believe it.

But I cannot say I wasn't thinking of myself and my family every step of the way. One of the legacies of my family is in this photo. This famous photograph can be found in so many places and is often used alongside news articles or even tweets. [Clem Albers, Arcadia, CA, April 5, 1942. (Photo No. 210-G-3B-414) National Archives]. I often find myself taken aback when randomly stumbling upon it and seeing my Grammy, aunties, and other family members. It emotionally affects me every time. Here we have added the names of my family members for the world to know and see. Remember their names. Remember their faces. Mary Kochi is my Grammy.

I've been fortunate enough to take my Grammy to many museum exhibits about the camps and when we see this photo of her, she is always overcome, flooded with memories. I cherish listening to her as she tells stories she didn't even know she remembered. In 2017, The Alphawood Gallery held an exhibit called "Then They Came for Me" and I was able to take her and take these photos of her in front of it. By 2017, her memory was really fading, but she still began to tell stories as she stood there, including why she wore that white hat—as she tells it—she thought it made her look cute.

I want the world to know the names of the people in this photo, the names of my family. While this photo has become a symbol of the time, to me it will always be a personal reminder of everything my Grammy has lived through.

As of the publishing of this book in 2020, my Grammy, born in 1925, is still alive and this photo hangs in her living room. Our connection to it was tucked away for many years, but now it is front and center. She is a part of history and due to the potency of this photo, she will be with me and us and the country for generations to come.

P.S.
You may notice that I use the term "incarceration camps" in most places in this book, but sometimes the word "internment" is used instead. Internment is the word that was used by the government during the war. The switch from internment to incarceration is relatively recent and one that I think is important to convey what actually happened. I stuck to internment when I felt it was generationally appropriate. For example, my Grammy and my mom have never used the term incarceration camp. They grew up with the word internment and still speak and think that way. I wanted to respect that in this text.

1 Angela

(CLICK)

Aiko: Pamela, tell me why we are doing this again?

Pamela: Mom, we've been over this a thousand times. I'm working on a project for school. I need to interview someone who's lived through a major event in American history.

Aiko: And how is that me exactly?

Pamela: Mom, you know how.

Aiko: I just don't see how my experiences in the camps are worth talking about.

Pamela: That's because you've spent the better part of your life pretending it never happened.

Aiko: You don't know what you're talking about.

Pamela: Mom, let's just start....

NAUSEA WASHED OVER ANGELA LIKE a wave, causing her to step back and lean up against the wall. Even looking at the trays of inari and sashimi made her shudder. Normally, she would have been the first one in line for the buffet, but nothing was going to allow her to eat today. Her morning sickness had worsened since yesterday. She was doing her best to play it off as grief, not pregnancy, but of course, it was both. No one could know that though. No one, not even her husband, knew she was pregnant. At times she tried to convince herself she was imagining all of this, that this buffet was for an anniversary or a birthday or that the whirlwind of the past couple weeks was something positive like a job promotion or a marriage. But that never lasted more than a second. Soon enough, the raw emotions of losing her Obachan would wash over her, followed closely behind by the recurring realization that her urge to puke all over the carefully laid out food platters was more than just heartache.

Some people say that the death of an older person isn't as sad. Many people had come up to her in recent hours and offered the consolation, "Your grandmother lived a long, full life," or similar platitudes. But to Angela, that was little relief. Her beloved Obachan was gone, and Angela already missed her. Angela looked around the room at all the little old ladies that were now filling her Obachan's living room. Some of them she recognized, but most she did not know. She knew that her Obachan was involved in the JASC—the Japanese American Service Committee—and that they had tons of programs for seniors that her Obachan loved going to. But, looking around at all these faces, guilt hit her like a ton of bricks. She had never really asked her Obachan anything about them. Even when the JASC started providing in-home care for Obachan, Angela didn't really pay much attention to the organization. Her connection to the JASC was their annual holiday party, the "Holiday Delight," where she would start her Christmas shopping with Japanese tchotchkes and nibble on some soba noodles and gyoza. Her connection to her Obachan was one of grandmother-granddaughter. Now, looking around this room at all these friends of her Obachan, she realized how one-sided that relationship really was. So many people were coming up to her like they knew her, obviously full of stories her Obachan had told them about her. She had nothing but a courteous smile to offer in return.

She needed a drink of water. As she made her way into the kitchen, she scanned the crowd. Her husband, Carl, was amiably chatting with an old man, another person Angela did not recognize. She wasn't surprised that Carl was at ease talking like nothing had happened. Her husband was characteristically charming and easy to make friends. Basically, the opposite of her. She saw her mother sitting on the couch, politely talking to their pastor, with her father right behind, on guard for her mother's needs as per usual. She looked around for her Auntie Pamela, one of the only people she wanted to see today. She noticed that Pam's partner Sheila was not there. If Pam was in her friend circle, she would have asked bluntly where Sheila was today. But Pam was her Auntie, so that question was off limits. Angela stepped into the kitchen and turned the faucet on, letting the water run for a few seconds until it became ice cold. She thrust a mug into the water stream and greedily drank every last drop before she had even fully turned the faucet back to off. *The baby is thirsty*, she thought to herself.

She hung her head down low, surprised at how quickly she had started to think of the world in terms of what the baby felt and wanted. She confirmed its existence less than two weeks before, mere moments after she had learned that Obachan had died, setting off a roller coaster of emotions that she had not yet recovered from. In those few minutes, her whole world had changed and tilted on its axis. And now, here she was, bent over a sink, her only primordial thoughts, *When will this baby let me eat? It must be as hungry as I am.*

She knew Carl would be thrilled. More than thrilled. He'd been wanting kids for years now. But she still couldn't bring herself to tell him. Part of her thought she was being magnanimous, not wanting to steal the thunder from honoring her grandmother. But, really, she just wasn't ready yet. She had resisted having children for so long. For her, having a child meant the end of something, not the beginning. The end of her life as she knew it. The end of her career as she knew it. The end of her marriage as she knew it. The end of her family heritage as she knew it. The thought of all of those endings at the same time as saying goodbye to her Obachan was almost too much to bear.

She placed the mug back in the sink and re-entered the living room, witnessing mingling, quiet sipping of tea, and eating of finger foods. She made eye contact with Carl and couldn't help but smile. He gave her a classic Carl wink, a wink she used to find incredibly annoying but now could only find endearing. It was her wink now, hers and his, a wink they shared forever. A new wave of nausea washed over her, a mix of morning sickness and self-loathing. *My gosh*, she said to herself. *How have I not told him yet?*

As she turned to avoid him, she noticed her Auntie Pamela walking toward the stairs to the second floor carrying a large wooden box. Angela had seen the box before but couldn't quite place where. Angela couldn't help but wonder why Pamela was carrying it around.

Pamela caught Angela's eye line and beckoned with a quick tilt of her head. Angela trotted over, greeted by her auntie, "Looks like you could use a little break."

"I really could," Angela said as she followed Pamela up the stairs. They made their way into the bedroom that time forgot, the bedroom that Pamela and Angela's mother, Judith, had shared growing up. It looked like Obachan hadn't changed or touched the room since the girls were kids, even though there was barely anything in it. It almost smelled like the 1960s, if that was possible. Pamela sat down on her old bed, gently touching the box with her fingers, delicately tracing its borders. Pamela was always quiet, so Angela knew not to push.

"Come, sit," Pamela said as she patted the bed. "I brought this downstairs, looking for you, but couldn't find you. This house is so small, I didn't think that was possible. But I'm glad fate brought us to the stairs, because there is something I want you to see."

Angela stayed quiet as she contemplated whether or not fate had anything to do with them running into each other. They were separated by a living room, not an ocean. Angela decided this was not the time for one of her usual snarky comments. She realized she was perfectly fine waiting to see what Pamela would say next, relieved that someone else was choosing the topic of conversation.

"As you know, many years ago I took it upon myself to play the role of family historian. It started with a school project and continued on rather ferociously for a time. I went around interviewing people, recording their memories and experiences. I even stole journals from your mother," Pamela paused with a light laugh, "salacious as they were."

"You stole Mom's journals?" Angela asked. Curiosity burned through her. There were so many things about her mother she didn't know.

"Yes, although I haven't thought about them in years. I kept everything in this box. And as soon as Mama died, I remembered it. I ran to the house to make sure the box was still here. That she hadn't thrown it out. That the recordings of her voice and her story were still safe. That we didn't lose all of her at once. Thankfully, it was fine. Just sitting here. In this room. Right where I had left it."

"You have recordings? Recordings of Obachan?"

"Yes. All on tape. It was state-of-the-art technology at the time," Pamela laughed. "And now I'm worried they will all turn to dust." She turned and looked at Angela. "So, I want to pass them to you."

"Sure, I can digitize them. I'd be happy to…"

Pamela cut her off. "No. That's not the reason. Although I suppose that would be nice," she paused. "No, I want you to have them because I want you to hear these stories from my mom and from yours. So, you can learn where you came from, so you can share it with your sons and daughters."

Angela took in a shocked breath. Could Pamela know? She must only be a few weeks along. Was it already that obvious?

Pamela lifted her hand off the box and placed it on Angela's cheek. "You are so much like me. So much inner conflict. Your life pulling you in too many directions. We both have a resistance to being who we are. It's hard to be defined by more than one thing."

"I don't think I know…"

"You have tried to prove yourself with your career, not knowing how to fully embrace that you are enough just as you are. Trust me, I know the feeling."

"Auntie Pam…"

Pamela held up her hand. "I never had kids. I suppose it was a choice, but mostly my own life circumstance. So, forgive me if I take some liberties of sharing some pearls of wisdom to you. It's my hope that these stories will help you. Show you."

"Show me what?"

"That your Japanese heritage, your English heritage, the shape of your eyes, your life as a hapa, who you are when you are at your most true self, is all a part of what makes you, you. It's so easy to try to live by one thing. It's taken me years to figure out the balance. But you are not your career. You are not your ethnicity. You are not your marriage or your hobbies. You are so much more than any one of your parts."

"Pam, I'm not…"

"One thing you are though…you are so much like the women who have come before you. Strong. Stubborn. Driven. Worried. Uncomfortable in your own skin."

"Is that really how you see me?"

"You don't have to pretend with me, Angela."

"I'm not pretending, I just don't understand."

"Maybe you're not ready, but I want to tell you this from the very beginning." She made eye contact with Angela in a way that made Angela want to look away but locked her in too. "Even if that baby you are carrying comes out with blonde hair and blue eyes like Carl, he…or she…even if she is nothing like what you expect her…or him…to be…your baby will be loved."

"How did you…?" Angela began to ask, but was rendered speechless.

""But if our family doesn't respond the way you think they should to this new life or we don't treat your baby the same way Carl's family might, I wanted you to know that there are reasons. So many reasons. And these tapes and journals will start to explain those reasons to you."

Pamela handed her the box. "Because I know you." She stood up and walked toward the door. "But don't worry, I don't think anyone else has noticed. Loss can mask a lot."

Pamela walked back toward Angela and held out her hand. Angela took it. "Congratulations. I am so happy for you." She squeezed Angela's hand and then turned around and walked out the door.

Angela sat on the bed, stunned, unable to move, the waves of fatigue the only indication that she was still in the moment. She looked down at the wooden box now on her lap. She traced her fingers along the top, just as her aunt had done, and slowly opened the lid. There, inside, were dozens of small cassette tapes, labeled with names and dates. On the side was a tape recorder. Below the rows of tapes, Angela could see the purple cover of one of the journals, presumably her mother's. How had she never known about these tapes before? Why had her mother never told her?

Angela shut the lid, placed her hands on top of the box, and closed her eyes to steady herself. She began to cry, lightly at first, and then openly wept. She did not know how long she cried for, but it was Carl that ultimately found her.

He kneeled down in front of her and tried to place the box aside. She gripped onto it tightly and wouldn't let it go.

He shifted and sat next to her on the bed, wrapping his arms around her. "It's going to be okay. I love you so much."

She sank into him, wiping her tears on his blazer, letting herself be calmed by the feel of his arms around her and the in and out of his breath. Loss *can* mask many things. He didn't even question why she was crying, assuming it was over the death of her grandmother. Now, gripping this box, feeling the rumblings of her stomach, she was feeling so many things, too many things, like a dam about to break.

She hugged the box closer to her chest and pushed her face further into Carl until her crying stopped. They stayed that way for several more minutes, closer than ever, and yet, in many ways, indelibly far apart.

2 Angela

AS SOON AS ANGELA GOT home from the wake, she laid down on her bed and thought she might never get up. She had taken a couple bereavement days off of work right after she found out her Obachan had passed, and then took a few more once the funeral and wake dates had been set, giving her only two more days before reentering the fast-paced world of TV production. Her coworkers didn't seem to care she was grieving though. She glanced at her phone. Twelve texts, three missed calls, two missed FaceTime calls, 120 emails. She worked as the deputy news producer for one of Chicago's major local news stations, meaning her work was her life most of the time. But just as she was about to tap on her messages, her stomach started to roll. This wasn't a wave of nausea. This was the real deal. She dashed to the bathroom and violently threw up until her vomiting turned into dry heaving. She flushed, brushed her teeth, and laid back down on the bed. "How is this going to work?" she whispered to herself.

She struggled with even taking the time off that she did. Since her promotion, she had never taken off more than a day or two at a time. She and Carl used to go on extravagant vacations—another perk of having no kids—but they hadn't done that in the past year either.

She picked up her phone again, waiting for the urge to respond to all of the messages to surge through her. Normally, her body would start buzzing with adrenaline to respond as soon as possible. To be on top of every question. To never miss the chance at a story. Today, nothing. She tossed her phone onto the end table, groaning as she rolled over and buried her face into a pillow. She could hear Carl downstairs, putting away all the casseroles and baked goods that had been passed onto them from well-wishers. They would have food to eat for days, if not weeks. Too bad this baby didn't want her to eat. That made her even more frustrated. She was ready to dive in. To eat her feelings. She was about to get fat anyways. Might as well eat some fettuccini.

She glanced over at her dresser, willing her earrings to take themselves off and place themselves on her earring rack. Next to the jewelry stand was one of her favorite photos, from the night Carl met her grandparents. It seemed like so long ago now, a bittersweet impossibility. She remembered how scared she was that night; how reticent she was to even bring Carl over. Her grandmother could be a formidable woman, never one to hold back an opinion, never one to concede even the smallest point. Before they arrived at her grandparents' house, Angela did her best to prepare Carl for the fact that Obachan would truly say anything that came to mind.

"I have seen her more than once tell white people that they smell bad," she warned.

Carl just laughed it off. "You know, white people have racist grandparents too."

"Just know that she's automatically going to disapprove of you. That she will be mean to you until you prove worthy."

"I'm in it for the long haul," he answered with confidence, so sure of himself, of their relationship.

As they pulled up to her grandparents' house, her heart was nearly beating out of its chest. Carl practically had to pull her out of the car, the cold winter air hitting her face like a shock wave of warning. "Maybe we shouldn't do this," she hesitated.

Carl merely smiled at her, threw his arm around her, and marched her right up to the house. As he rang the doorbell, he tossed her a quick wink.

It was her grandfather, her Ojichan, who answered the door. He was in his usual attire. No matter what the weather was like in Chicago, inside he was still Hawaiian, and in his own house he wore shorts, a white T-shirt, and a Japanese Yukata robe. "Please, come in," he said with a slight bow and a strong pat on Carl's back. Carl strolled in without hesitation with a hearty, "Thank you for having us, Mr. Oshiro," not noticing Angela lingering in the doorway for several moments.

To her surprise, Angela's grandparents pulled out all the stops for the meal including rolled maki and rice balls. There were homemade egg rolls and glazed chicken. There was a small bowl of spaghetti, presumably in case Carl refused to eat the other food. It made Angela more suspicious that they had gone to so much trouble. Throughout the meal, the conversation was so innocuous she almost gave herself an ulcer waiting for the other shoe to drop, waiting for her grandparents to dig in with an interrogation or say something inadvertently foul. But nothing happened.

As they were clearing the table, Carl leaned over to Angela and said, "I told you that would go just fine, they loved me!"

Angela was still skeptical. She stayed in the kitchen to help her grandmother start soaking the pots, waiting for the inevitable review.

"He's not so bad for a white boy," she started. Angela laughed, relieved the commentary had finally begun.

"Do you like the flowers he brought you?"

"They are pretty, a good color, but I can see he did not spend too much money on them. Probably got them at the grocery store right before he came over."

Angela didn't concede that her grandmother was right; that was exactly what happened. "Well, he really loved your food."

"Sure, he only ate two plates though. A tall man like him would have eaten three or four if he had really enjoyed the taste." She continued, "Perhaps he is too complacent, thinking he doesn't have to eat when he can, with his big fancy job. But he will know. One day. You can't buy, sell, hold, and trade without things going south. He probably knows very little about savings."

Even that comment surprised Angela. She did not see Carl's job at Bank of America as a potential downside. Leave it to Obachan to find a pro and make it a con. "He does quite well for himself, Bachan," she responded.

"I'm sure he does now, but where will this career be in five years? In ten years? And what kind of a last name is Campbell anyway? I half expected him to smell like soup. You need to think about your future."

Angela rolled back over in her bed, her grandmother's words from so long ago still ringing through her head. *You need to think about your future.* What would Obachan think of the future that laid before her? What would her reaction have been to the news they were having a baby? Would she have been happy for her? Would she have immediately told her all the ways she wasn't ready? Would she make a joke about how white the baby was going to be? What kind of great-grandmother would she have been?

Angela sat up and looked at the wooden box of memories, now resting in the corner of their bedroom. Carl must have carried it up, although she didn't remember him doing so. She dragged herself out of bed and walked over to it. She closed her eyes and took a deep breath as she opened it. She moved the tapes aside and reached for her mother's journals. What kind of *mother* had Obachan been? Maybe her Auntie Pamela was right. Maybe it was time she learned more about her past, so she would be ready for the future.

3 Judith & Angela

March 3, 1974

Well that's it. I don't have a family anymore. And you know what? I think I'm relieved. No more passive-aggressive dinners. No more constant critiques of my clothes of my schooling of my jobs of my life. I've gone and sinned the ultimate sin—I fell in love with someone who isn't Japanese. But, I mean, come on...of course, I did, right? THEY are the ones that wouldn't allow us to speak Japanese in the house. THEY are the ones that wouldn't even let us learn it. THEY are the ones that told us to dress like everyone else, to talk like everyone else, to show the world we are AMERICANS. They made us sing the Star-Spangled Banner and say the Pledge of Allegiance and bow to every holiday and pastime possible. Never has a family more enthusiastically faked loving the 4th of July, year after year, than ours. We barely even go to Japanese community events, except when they parade us around the Ginza Festival like we are up for market.

And when I brought Eddie home, they never said, "You can't marry him." They just said their usual crap—the ridiculous, judgmental comments they make about all of us. And of course, I'm the oldest. Little do they know Pamela will probably never get married. If only they knew the things about her that I do. But she will never tell them, so I'm first. I'm always the one to break the ice, to make my parents see a new way. Being the oldest sucks.

So yeah, my parents are traditional, so Eddie ASKED my father if he could marry me. ASKED him. And my father said YES. Because he thought it would be rude to say NO. And so, Eddie ASKED ME, because they said YES, and now when we tell them the good news that we are engaged, they tell us NO. My mom took me aside and told me that if I married a white man, I could no longer be a part of their family. She actually played the camps card. She's never done that before. Going on and on about how the white man took everything from her. About how the white man never gave it back.

I know what my mother and her family went through. I get it. And it was horrible. But things are different now. There aren't laws against congregating together anymore. There isn't the same level of overt hate of the Japanese. I mean, don't get me wrong, people are idiots. I get racist comments every single day. But not from Eddie. Or his family. They are different. And I love them. I can't wait to be a Garrington. Judith Garrington. It just sounds great, doesn't it? It's not like I won't be an Oshiro anymore. My face is my face. I can't hide it.

I just wish my parents could see Eddie for who he is. And understand that they laid this groundwork for me. I mean seriously, what did they expect?

Well, screw them. If they are going to disown me for following my heart, then so be it. Eddie and I will make our own life together, and there's nothing they can do to stop us.

ANGELA PUT THE JOURNAL DOWN. It was the luck of the draw that she had picked this particular entry. She had reached into the stack of journals and selected one, for its flowery exterior more than anything else. She opened it to the first page and found this rather explosive start. She had no idea that Obachan had disowned her mother, that there was an actual family rift over race. Is that why she was so sensitive to it? Had that somehow permeated its way into her consciousness?

March 7, 1974

I have officially removed all traces of my life from mom and dad's house. Although my room still has two beds, it might as well just be Pamela's. Only her things remain there now. And, if I did leave anything behind, I'm sure Pamela will bring them to me. Apparently, my sister is still talking to me at least. She says this will blow over, that Mom and Dad will cave. But it will have to be them. I'm not going to cave. I hope they are prepared for the fact that they will get what they want—and they will never see me again.

Angela flipped forward through the book. It covered the next year as her mom and dad moved in together and started their careers. She tried to remember if Ojichan and Obachan were in her parent's wedding photos. As she scoured her mind trying to think of any stories her parents had told her about their wedding, her "morning" sickness hit again. She rushed back to the bathroom, but with nothing left in her stomach to expel, she was back to dry heaving over the toilet bowl. She really needed to tell Carl. She got up and looked into the mirror. She looked tired. She craved Carl's comfort. His strength. But something stopped her. She couldn't tell Carl. Not just yet. She needed to talk to her mother first. Even though they had just gotten home, she willed herself to get up. She wanted to talk to her mother in person. And she needed to do it now.

Carl walked in as he saw Angela putting on her shoes and jacket.

"We just got home, where are you off to?"

"I just have to," she paused. "There's something I need to talk to my mom about."

"You're exhausted, babe, and I bet she is too. It can't wait?"

Angela looked at her husband. She had never kept a secret from him before and she couldn't bear to keep the baby from him much longer. "It can't wait. But I'll be home soon, I promise."

Carl kissed her forehead before she headed out of their bedroom and out the door. As she placed the key in the ignition, she wondered if she was too tired to drive. But she willed herself to keep going. As she pulled out of the driveway, she did as her mother had taught her. She put on a smile and said out loud, "Just keep swimming."

4 Angela

ANGELA'S PARENTS' HOUSE STILL FELT foreign to her. They had sold the Lakeview home she grew up in a few years ago, choosing a smaller two-bedroom ranch house in Sauganash instead. It always felt odd going to the new house, seeing knickknacks and paintings so familiar to her in a place that she barely knew.

She pulled the car into the driveway and turned off the ignition, sitting quietly for a moment, staring at the front door. She had been practicing what she wanted to say the entire drive over, but now the words seemed to be eluding her. She took a deep breath, pushed herself to get out of the car, and rang the front doorbell.

A look of surprise crossed her mother's face as she opened it. "Angie, what are you doing here?"

Angela walked inside and gave her mother a hug. Already a sign that something was off, as they did not hug often. The look on her mother's face changed from surprise to concern. Angela took off her coat, hung it on the nearest coat hook, and stepped out of the foyer and into the sitting room. She walked over to the coffee table and picked up a small, ceramic Daruma doll, with both eyes colored in. *Have I ever stopped to ask what wish this fulfilled?* she asked herself.

She turned to her mother. "Mama, can I see your wedding album?"

"What for?" her mom asked incredulously.

"Just…Mom," Angela took a deep breath. "Will you just show it to me, please?"

Her mom gave her a long hard look and then disappeared around the corner, presumably into her bedroom. She came back moments later with a thin, blue photo album. It seemed ancient, the photos locked behind cellophane, forever stuck to the cardboard pages that held them. Angela took it and sat down on the couch, flipping through it quickly, knowing exactly what she was looking for.

"They weren't there," she said quietly. "How did I never notice that before?"

Judith sat down next to Angela and placed her hands in her lap. "It was a long time ago."

"But didn't you want them there?"

"Of course, I wanted them there," Judith replied curtly. "But, at the time, they didn't want to be there. And I was young and angry and headstrong and most importantly, I was in love, so I went ahead anyway." She paused. "It was a different time, a different world, Angie."

Angela looked up at her mom. "How did you move past it? How did you get over it?"

"It took me a long time to realize it, but they never hated your father. It was hurt. My parents just didn't know there could be another way. You know everything Ojichan and Obachan went through. The struggles they had. The way they treated me and your dad, it was probably destined to be. They couldn't imagine a world where a white person would love someone like me."

It was the first time Angela had ever heard her mother use a phrase like "someone like me." Her mother had always been so annoyingly neutral about race, dismissing Angela's adolescent angst about being half-Japanese as the silliness of youth. For a large part of her childhood, Angela thought her mother didn't even care that they were Japanese at all. Angela looked at the Daruma doll again, second-guessing herself and thinking how short-sighted that might have been.

"Did you ever really forgive them?"

Judith raised her hand slightly off her lap, hesitated, and then slowly placed her hand on top of Angela's. "It's something your dad taught me. He still says it today: Love always wins. Love always wins."

Angela broke down into tears. She had heard her dad say that many times before. The optimism of the phrase reminded her so much of Carl it made her ache. It was also hard to hear as it was so contrary to her mother's normally stoic personality. Were they all being transformed by their grief?

She looked up at her mom. "Auntie Pam gave me the tapes," she hesitated, "and your journals."

Judith looked at Angela but her face was indecipherable. After a brief moment, she said sternly, "Listen to the tapes, Angie. Listen to them and know that nothing is black and white. Nothing is fair. But you come from a long line of very strong women," she paused, her eyes glistening wet. "Sometimes that puts us at odds with each other. But, overall, it means we keep going."

Who was this emotional mother that was now before her? She sounded like a stranger. It made her realize even more that she didn't know anything about her mother at all.

"Can I read your journals? Will you mind?"

Judith gave a light laugh, incongruous to her previous harshness. "Sure, why not, I guess. I haven't seen them or thought about them in years," she said, pausing ever so slightly. "Is that why you came over here tonight? You could have just called."

"It seemed like something I had to ask in person."

"What exactly are you hoping to find?"

"I'm not sure, but I need to start looking."

Angela could feel Judith's skepticism, and couldn't fault her for it. It was weird, to rush over here for apparently no reason. But Angela couldn't even explain it to herself yet, how was she going to explain it to anyone else? Maybe it was the journalist in her, but there were questions that needed answers and she felt an urgency to find out more, even if she didn't know what she was looking for.

Judith and Angela sat in silence for a few moments before Judith finally broke the pall. "I only ask one thing."

"What's that?" Angela asked, wiping a small tear off her own cheek.

"Remember, I was young. And when you listen to the tapes, remember that Obachan was young in the camps too. If Pammy gave you these, then there's something she wants you to learn. Try and find out what it is. Lord knows, Pammy has gone through more than most, even though she never talks about it."

Angela nodded her head that she understood and handed her mom the photo album back. She stood up. "I really should be going. I need to talk to Carl about a few things."

Judith stood up and placed her hand on Angela's stomach. "I love you, Angie."

Angela placed her hand on top of her mother's and squeezed. The intimacy and the outright expression of love took her aback, but she wasn't as surprised this time that someone had figured out she was pregnant before she had told them. Maybe Auntie Pamela had even told her mom after they talked. She was too tired to care that people knew. She just hoped Carl hadn't pieced it together yet; she wanted to be the one to tell him. Why was her family so good at keeping secrets? She walked toward the door and as she opened it, she turned back toward her mom. "Do you want to listen to the tapes with me?"

"No, thank you. I have made my peace with the past. It's time for you to do the same."

5
Angela & Aiko

WHEN ANGELA GOT HOME, CARL was already fast asleep and the next morning when she woke up, he wasn't in bed. She started wandering around their duplex looking for him. She looked by the front door and saw his running bag on the floor. He must've gone out for a jog. No matter what the weather was like outside, Carl could always run. When they had bought their condo, proximity to the Lake Michigan running path was a key factor for him. Angela had never really given the Edgewater neighborhood much thought before, but now she loved living there. One more small piece of joy Carl had brought into her life.

As she peered out the window looking for him, it dawned on her that she wasn't actively dry-heaving and sprang into action, making herself a quick sandwich to eat while she still could. She was already chomping on it as she took it upstairs. Normally she didn't like to have food in the bedroom, but she decided that this was an exception. She was pregnant, hungry, and she wanted to be on her bed. There were going to be a lot of exceptions over the next nine months. Her inner anal retentiveness would just have to get used to it.

After she ate half of the turkey on wheat, she pulled Pamela's box in front of her and pulled out all the tapes. She looked at the labels. They each had a main topic such as "School in the Camps" and each had two dates on them: the date recorded and the general date range that the conversation covered. Which chronology should she follow? Should she organically listen to how the conversation evolved between Auntie Pam and Obachan, or should she hear Obachan's story from start to finish?

Ultimately it was the title "Beginning" that drew her in. She picked up the tape recorder and popped the tape in. She leaned back on her bed and closed her eyes as she pressed play.

(CLICK)

Pamela: Mom, just start at the beginning.

Aiko: What beginning? My beginning here in Chicago? When I was born? How I grew up?

Pamela: Any of those would be fine.

Aiko: No, that's not true. There's only one beginning.

Pamela: Well, what do you think your beginning was then?

(LONG PAUSE)

Pamela: Mom?

Aiko: I could start when I got married or had kids. I could start when I was born. I was born in California in 1930. My last name was Matsuo then. I had two brothers and two sisters. I went to school. I worked and then I didn't.

Pamela: Okay, start there then. You were born in California.

Aiko: No. That's not really my beginning. It's what happened before.

Pamela: Before what?

Aiko: Before the war.

Pamela: Okay, well, let's make sure to get all the details. During the war you were in the internment camps, right, Mom?

Aiko: I was at camp from 1942-1945. I was twelve years old when I entered. I felt forty years old when I left. (soft laughter)

Pamela: Were you at Amache the whole time?

Aiko: No, at first, I was one of many that was taken to Manzanar when it first opened as an assembly center. Manzanar was not always a camp. First it was a place where people were stored like canned pineapple. Huddled together in stalls and makeshift rooms, waiting to be assigned living quarters.

Pamela: Was your whole family there?

Aiko: No, just my mother and my sisters. My father and brothers were not with us.

Pamela: Why not?

Aiko: My father was taken from our home in the middle of the night about a year before. We never saw him again.

Pamela: And your brothers?

Aiko: After my father was taken, my mother sent my brothers away, afraid they would be next. At the time, I didn't know where my brothers went. My mother didn't speak to me about such things. All I knew was that we were alone.

(LONG PAUSE)

Aiko: When I was a kid, I used to carry great sadness that my mother's parents had died when I was very young and that I didn't know my father's parents because they lived all the way in Hawaii. But, as we sat at Manzanar, holding onto each other in a stall, impossibly afraid of what was happening to us...I remember thinking that I was glad they weren't there, that they were spared what we were going through.

Pamela: Did you ever resent that your brothers weren't in the camps with you?

Aiko: God no. At the time I didn't know where they were and was scared for them every day we were at camp. Then, when I found out they had moved to Chicago, I knew that if they hadn't been sent there and gotten jobs and set up a life, made things ready for us, I don't know what we would have done after we finally left. They did their part while we were doing ours.

Pamela: Why didn't Japanese in Chicago have to go to camps?

Aiko: There weren't that many there. And it was a west coast thing. The order was to evacuate. Most Japanese stayed, not knowing what to do. A few, like my brothers, voluntarily moved.

Pamela: Did you ever go back to California again?

Aiko: No. There was nothing left for us there. Our house was emptied, our store was emptied, all our possessions given away or repossessed. All we had was what we brought with us. And we took that to Chicago. Chicago was one of the only places friendly to Japanese in the '40s.

(DEEP BREATH)

Aiko: Like I said. The camps were my beginning. Everything before no longer mattered.

Angela pressed pause on the tape, trying to imagine her grandmother, so young, clutching to her own mother and sisters, not knowing what would happen next. The fear she must've felt made Angela blanch at the faux fear she was experiencing now about her own baby. Her life of privilege had made living through the atrocities her grandparents experienced seem impossible.

She heard the front door open and Carl throw his keys into the bowl on the table. She leapt out of bed and ran downstairs. It was time. It was time to tell him she was pregnant.

6 Angela, Judith & Aiko

ANGELA RAN TOWARD CARL AND barreled into him, surprising him and knocking him off balance as he was taking off his running shoes. The smell of his sweat and the wetness of his shirt gave Angela no pause. She breathed him in and held him tight.

"Angela, honey, what is it?" he said as he hugged her back.

Angela stood back, her cheek slightly damp from pressing into his chest. She wiped her cheek off with her sleeve and looked up at Carl. "I have some good news." As the words came out of her mouth, she realized that she meant them, an uncontrollable smile crossing the entire width of her face.

Carl waited for her to continue, and for just a second, she closed her eyes to savor the moment. As she opened her eyes again, she took Carl's hands and squeezed. "I'm pregnant!"

Angela watched as the emotions rolled across Carl's face: surprise, joy, disbelief, comprehension. He let out a scream and picked her up and twirled her in the air. Angela laughed uncontrollably as he continued to twirl her around the foyer. As he put her down, he stood very still, held her face in both of his hands, and quietly, sweetly said, "I have never been happier about anything in my life, except, of course, from the day that I met you."

Angela kissed him and reveled in his sweaty taste and the joy that he always brought to her. Why she ever denied herself the warmth of his steadfastness due to her own insecurities was beyond her.

Carl took her hand and bounded up the stairs. "Come on. I'm gonna shower and then we're going out to celebrate." Angela eagerly followed, momentarily forgetting any feeling at all except for the elation emanating off the both of them. As they rounded out the top of the stairs and made their way into their bedroom, Carl paused. "What's all this?" he said, looking at all of the journals and tapes.

"Family heirlooms," Angela replied cautiously, "Auntie Pam gave them to me. Old journals of my mom's and tape recordings of Obachan telling her life story. They were in that wooden box you brought upstairs."

"For real?" Carl said as he picked up a few of the tapes. "Have you listened to any of them?"

"Only part of one. I just got them."

Carl stepped back toward Angela and brought her close to him for another hug. "I'm going to shower, and then I want to hear all about it."

As Carl jumped into the shower, Angela sat down on the bed and then stood up again as a rush of giddiness passed over her. Carl was so happy, and that happiness had infected her. She could do this. They could do this. Carl always made her feel better. When she went dark, he provided light.

Impatient to wait for Carl to finish in the bathroom so they could celebrate, she needed a distraction. She picked up another one of her mother's journals and began to read.

July 10, 1972

Today I met Edward. He is tall and blonde and as American as apple pie. I was at the library and saw him from across the way and couldn't help but stare. He was fucking beautiful. There wasn't even a real reason for me to be at the library, except for the fact that it was hot, and I just wanted a place to sit and get away. I brought a bunch of old books from college with me, just planned on flipping through them as a distraction. You know me. It's where I go when I have a hard day at work. The worst part about being a nurse is seeing your patients suffer. Anyway, eventually Edward (isn't that a great name?) caught me staring at him, and seriously,

I couldn't help myself, I just flashed him a huge smile. It was like one of those moments you see in a movie. "Their eyes meet, they smile, and the world changes." He walked right over to me with his stack of books, sat down next to me and said, "Hi, I'm Edward." (His books were all about computing code. He told me later he was trying to teach himself code, something called Pascal—how cool is that?)

So yeah, he just sat down and continued looking at his books. Like he was meant to sit there. Like it was completely normal that we were sharing a table. And honestly, it was. It was like we knew each other. I can't explain it. We just kept looking at each other, smiling, trying to do our work, laughing every time our eyes met. Eventually he just stood up, put his books in his bag, picked up mine in one hand, and then held out his other hand for me to take. And, damn straight I took it. I took it and it felt like my hand was meant to be there, together with his. We left the library and walked right out into the world like it was ours for the taking.

○○○

Angela put her mother's journal down and listened as Carl turned off the shower and started shaving. When she met Carl, she fought it every step of the way. To her, marrying a blonde-haired, blue-eyed American felt like a betrayal of her heritage, the last straw in her cultural white washing. But apparently her mother never felt that way. Her mother saw only her father. She saw love first, just the way Carl had. Angela started to wonder if there was something wrong with her. She also started to wish she had known this passionate version of her mother. All she ever got was judgment and distance.

As she heard Carl humming from the bathroom, the joy of the news of their baby radiating through every note he sang, she said a silent prayer that their baby could see the world the way Carl did. She picked up her mother's journal again.

○○○

September 25, 1972

What a terrible day. Edward and I had the biggest fight. We were walking down the street, minding our own business, holding hands, when this nasty woman came right up to us and spat on us. Of course, it was upsetting, but shit like this happens to me all the time. So, I do what I always do. I took a deep breath, held my head up high, and kept walking. Edward...didn't handle it the same way. He couldn't believe it and flew into a rage and I had to stop him from chasing after the woman. Part of me appreciated that he could want to defend my honor (or some shit like that). The other part of me realized just how oblivious he is. So, I called him on it, and he screamed at me. Basically, told me I was a jerk for thinking he didn't understand what racism is. I tried to tell him that it wasn't that he doesn't understand it, just that he had never experienced it so he couldn't really know. It was like we weren't even hearing each other. So, I do what I always do. I took a deep breath, held my head up high, and walked away.

○○○

Carl came out of the bathroom, towel wrapped around his waist, and pulled on some clothes. He joined Angela on the bed, kissed her stomach, and pulled her into a soft spoon. She felt his warmth consume her and flopped her mother's journal down on the bed next to her.

"It's been a long week, and now I know why you've been extra tired. Maybe we should just stay in. We have plenty of food," Carl said as he kissed her shoulder. "The only person in the world I want to be with right now is you."

"That sounds good to me," Angela said as she sunk more deeply into Carl's embrace. Had Obachan's funeral really only been yesterday?

After a few moments, curiosity getting the better of him, Carl sat up and started looking at the tapes. He picked one, seemingly at random, swapped out the one that was in the tape recorder, and pushed play.

○ ○ ○

(CLICK)

Pamela: So, you got transferred to Amache. Did you know where you were going?

Aiko: Yes. No. I knew we were going to Colorado. They told me the name, but there were a bunch of different names, so it was hard to keep track. And of course, I'd never been out of California before.

Pamela: What was it like?

Aiko: It was hot. And dusty. And there was nothing around for miles.

Pamela: Were there guards?

Aiko: Oh yes, guards, and guard towers.

Pamela: Were they armed?

Aiko: Of course, they were armed. And we were told that if we tried to leave, we'd be shot. The fence around the camps was high and covered in barbed wire.

Pamela: Where did you sleep?

Aiko: There were bunk beds. Everything was in one room. Our space was a kitchen, a dining room, a bedroom, everything in one small room.

Pamela: That must've been cramped.

Aiko: We were practically on top of each other. So, I spent as much time in the common areas and outside as possible. I learned to sew. Sometimes we played volleyball. Rats in a cage playing volleyball.

○○○

Angela pressed stop on the tape recorder, her eyes welling up with tears. It was enough to hear her Obachan's voice and feel her chest tightening with missing her. It was another to imagine her in a place like that. Carl pulled her close to him again and put his hand on her stomach. Angela closed her eyes and tried to get the image of her Obachan in the camps out of her mind. Instead she focused on Carl's breathing. On his heartbeat. On his quiet comfort. She was grateful their baby would never know the pain that some of her family knew. Maybe that was the blessing from the choices she and her mother had made. Her baby's life would be easier.

She turned to Carl, "Do you remember what you thought of me when we first met?"

Carl smiled. "I remember it like it was yesterday."

She flipped to her mother's journal and showed him the entry on how her parents met. He read it and handed it back to her. "That's romantic, but it's got nothing on us."

"How do you figure?" she asked

"C'mon, Angela, our story is classic!" he said with a look of genuine incredulity.

"Tell me, tell me our story from your perspective," Angela said, sitting up, hugging a pillow to her chest.

"Alright," Carl started.

"No, wait!" Angela stopped him. She looked through the box and found a blank tape cassette. She checked it to make sure it was blank and then rewound it back to the beginning.

"Okay, now go." She pressed record and waited for Carl to begin.

7
Angela & Carl

(CLICK)

Angela: Tape 1. The early years.

Carl: Ooh, so official.

Angela: Okay, so tell me, how did we meet?

Carl: We met at RPM. I was there with Bobby, getting a drink after work.

Angela: And you noticed me from across the room?

Carl: You say that like you're joking, but yes. You walked in with Claudia, although honestly, I didn't even notice she was standing next to you. The hostess motioned you over to the bar and you sat down. You were wearing a black-and-white-striped dress with a flowered jacket...

Angela: You remember what I was wearing?

Carl: Do you want me to tell this story or not?

Angela: Sorry, sorry.

Carl: You were wearing a black-and-white-striped dress with a flowered jacket and your hair was down. I've always been a sucker for long brown hair. I couldn't stop staring at you. Bobby was trying to talk to me, and I didn't hear anything he said. So, I walked over.

Angela: Yes, you walked over and what did you say?

Carl: Well, this is part of why I think our story is classic. Because I was in love and you...you were not.

Angela: (laughing)

Carl: So yeah, I walked over to you and after some basic introductions I asked, "So where are you from?"

Angela: To which I replied...

Carl: To which you replied something to the effect of "You're an asshole for asking me that."

Angela: (laughing)

Carl: And I remember standing there thinking, "What exactly did I just ask her?" And you just sat there staring at me, waiting for me to say something and I believe I said, "Okay, well, I'm from Milwaukee, if that makes you feel any better." Then you put your drink down and turned squarely toward me and said, "Where do you think I'm from?" and you put so much emphasis on the word "from," I started wondering if that word meant something different to you than it did to me.

Angela: Which I guess it kind of did.

Carl: Yes, it definitely did. And so, I said, "Chicago?" and your friend Claudia nearly spit out her drink laughing, and I finally got you to break a smile. And you said, "Sorry, I'm just used to people asking that question in a different way." And I said, "Is there more than one way to ask that question?"

Angela: Which, for the record, I thought was a cute answer

Carl: Well, you gave no sign of that! But your nose crunched up with this little signal of stubbornness and it took everything in my power not to run my finger down your nose to uncrinkle it.

Angela: Is that why you run your finger down my nose?

Carl: And after I kept asking you questions, I could tell there was a thaw, so I kept going, and kept talking to you, and I talked to you until your table got called and watched as you walked away.

Angela: And what were you thinking?

Carl: Honestly, I was dumbfounded. This beautiful woman had completely flummoxed me. And even as I stood there, I still didn't understand what I'd said wrong with the "Where are you from?" question. I went back and asked Bobby. He didn't get it either.

Angela: It honestly didn't dawn on you that asking someone "Where are you from?" can be seen as racist?

Carl: No. Even now, I still don't quite get it.

Angela: Because it implies that there's some other place. That people of color can't be from here.

Carl: I know that intellectually, and you've since explained it to me, but for me, that's still way too meta. I honestly just wanted to know more about you. Seemed an innocuous question.

Angela: Do you still ask people that question?

Carl: (laughing) After your response that night? No, no I do not.

Angela: That could have been the end of our story.

Carl: That's true. But I knew in my gut it wouldn't be. And before I left the bar, I walked over to your table, gave you my card and asked you for your phone number.

Angela: Which I did not give to you.

Carl: No, you did not give it to me. But Claudia kept the card. And Claudia emailed me your number. And I called you. And the rest is history.

Angela: So, why do you think that's such a classic story? That doesn't seem any more romantic than my parents.

Carl: Because I had to fight for it. And because Claudia had to go behind your back. And because you had to change your whole ridiculous viewpoint on who you would and wouldn't date to be with me. Your parents' story is just fine. Instant attraction and all. But our story is classic because we had to make it happen. You and me.

Angela: And Claudia.

Carl: Yes, and Claudia.

OOO

Angela turned off the tape recorder and looked at Carl and tried to think about what her life would have been like if Claudia hadn't emailed Carl for her. At the time she was furious, but now she couldn't imagine her life without Carl in it.

She turned back to the tapes, rummaging through them. "I think there's one in here about how my grandparents met. Should we listen?"

"Sure, why not," Carl said as he leaned back on the bed. "Let's keep the walk down memory lane going."

"I think this is it. It says Chicago 1946," Angela said as she swapped out tapes.

"Sounds good to me," Carl responded. "Fire it up."

Aiko & Angela

(CLICK)

Pamela: Okay, Mom. We've been doing this for a while, how are you holding up?

Aiko: Holding up? We've been talking with tea and cookies. I think I'll be okay.

Pamela: (laughing) Fair enough. I want you to tell me about your first days after you were released from the camps.

Aiko: Well, much of my family was already in Chicago, so I went there.

Pamela: How did you get there?

Aiko: We were given five dollars for a train ticket.

Pamela: Five dollars. After being detained for four years? Did they give you anything else?

Aiko: No. We had managed to ship some things in advance, small packages, nothing big, so we just had our suitcases.

Pamela: Just like when you came to the camps.

Aiko: Yes, and no. Well, really no. How it felt was entirely different. Going to a new city with nothing is scary. But not as scary as being sent to the camps in the first place.

Pamela: So, skipping the mechanics of it all, you get on a train, you go to Chicago, and then what?

Aiko: Then we moved into a new apartment.

Pamela: That your family already had set up?

Aiko: Yes, one of my brothers had been there for quite some time.

Pamela: And what was the apartment like?

Aiko: In retrospect it was small, but after the camps it felt like a palace. We still had to share beds, but we had a bathroom with a door and a shower, and we had a dining room and a kitchen.

Pamela: The little things.

Aiko: Yes, the little things.

Pamela: And did you go to work right away?

Aiko: Relatively. It took a couple months, but eventually I found a job as a seamstress at a factory that made work jumpsuits.

Pamela: And how long were you there?

Aiko: Right up until I started having children. My water broke while I was on the factory floor.

Pamela: Really? How have I never heard that before?

Aiko: You never asked.

○○○

ANGELA STOPPED THE TAPE AND looked over at Carl. It wasn't what they were expecting. They were swooning over love stories and instead they were confronted with how matter of fact Obachan was about her life after the camps. A life that could not have been anything but difficult.

"They must have pinched every penny," Carl said, "if she worked until she was literally giving birth."

"Makes our generation seem pretty soft, doesn't it?" Angela asked.

"No shit," Carl replied. "I get upset if the cable goes out. Did you know she worked at a factory like that?"

"I think I did. It sounds familiar. When her kids were all in school, she started working full time at the little grocery shop my Ojichan had opened. Although, knowing her, she was probably the one running the place all along even when her kids were little."

"I never got to see that shop," Carl said.

"I barely remember it myself. They closed it when Ojichan retired." Angela felt the sadness creep back, remembering that she would never see either of them again.

"Should we keep listening, see if Pamela finally asks how they met?"

"I don't think it's going to be on this tape. Now that I'm thinking about it. They didn't meet right away." Angela rummaged through the box. "Here, this one says 'Club Waikiki' on it. I'm pretty sure that's where he was bartending."

"No shit. She bagged the bartender? That's pretty awesome. Does the place still exist?"

"I don't think so," Angela said, still smirking at Carl's "bag the bartender" remark.

"I need to learn more about Club Waikiki," Carl said enthusiastically. "Pop it in"

"Okay, here we go," Angela said as she slid in the new tape. "Club Waikiki, 1948."

○○○

(CLICK)

Pamela: (laughing) Mom, you've got to be kidding me.

Aiko: (laughing) No, I'm dead serious. That's what he was wearing!

Pamela: I cannot picture Dad in that.

Aiko: What can I tell you? He was an idiot, even then.

OOO

Angela stopped the tape. "We must've missed something," she said as she tried to rewind it. She had never heard her Obachan call her Ojichan an idiot before. The playfulness of it made her ache as images of her Ojichan filled her mind. She couldn't picture him in anything much more than in one of his typical Hawaiian shirts. When she saw the name Club Waikiki, she just imagined him fitting right in. What could he possibly be wearing that was different?

She tried the tape recorder again, but it started in the same place. "Damnit," she said, frustrated.

"Mystery," Carl said, gently rubbing her back. "Maybe we can pick up more of the story if we keep listening."

"I hope so," Angela said as she pressed play again.

OOO

(CLICK)

Pamela: (laughing) Mom, you've got to be kidding me.

Aiko: (laughing) No, I'm dead serious. That's what he was wearing!

Pamela: I cannot picture Dad in that.

Aiko: What can I tell you? He was an idiot, even then.

Pamela: So, you just walked right behind the bar to take it off his head?

Aiko: Yes. And it was heavy. He had lined the hat with real fruit. So, I put it on the bar, picked up an apple and took a bite.

Pamela: Mom, that's kind of saucy!

Aiko: (laughing) I take it you have never pictured me young.

Pamela: Of course, I have. I guess I always just think of the store and our childhoods and the camps.

Aiko: That's not how babies are born.

Pamela: MOM, GROSS!

Aiko: (laughing) Your Dad loved working at Club Waikiki.

Pamela: How often did you go?

Aiko: Not often. Back then, I was still nervous about being around too many other Japanese people. We were trying to assimilate. To blend in. To show we were Americans. Club Waikiki was a good place to do that, a lot of white people went there, but I never stayed for long, even though I wanted to.

Pamela: What were you worried about?

Aiko: People, they would look at us, and automatically assume we were plotting something. Everyone was suspicious of us. Only certain areas of the city would even rent homes to Japanese. As safe as a place as Chicago could be, it was also hard. The day-to-day was hard.

Pamela: When did you start to feel like you belonged here?

Aiko: I'm still waiting...

(LONG PAUSE)

Pamela: So, back to Club Waikiki. You met Dad there. How long did he work there?

Aiko: Not too much longer. Once we started dating, he decided he wanted a job with better hours, a day job so we could hang out at night. That made me feel safer. He was really thoughtful like that. So, he started working at a restaurant and eventually he leased the shop before he bought it.

Pamela: Did you ever go back after he left that job?

Aiko: Sometimes.

Pamela: Do you ever wish he'd kept working there?

Aiko: (pause) Looking back, maybe. I wish I could have told myself that it would all be okay. That it would be hard (pause) but that we would never be rounded up again. (pause) I lived in fear of going back to the camps for a long time. And I think that did stop me from having some of the fun I could have had. But it is what it is. The times we did go there, it was like an escape. Live music, tropical drinks. I couldn't afford them, the drinks, but your Dad would pass them to me on the side. Looking back at that, at our flirting. At how little it took to make the world seem magical...

○○○

Angela's phone rang, startling her out of the story. She stopped the tape, looked down at her phone, and saw the word "Dad." A rock formed at the pit of her stomach. Suddenly she knew exactly why he was calling.

Word of her pregnancy must've gotten back to him by now. And she hadn't told him. She hadn't even thought to call him, which was strange, since she usually talked to him first. She had always found her Dad easy to talk to, approachable. As the guilt of her transgression washed over her, she braced herself, ready for him to be upset with her, disappointed, excited, everything all at once just like she had been. For better or worse, she and her father were a lot alike. Hopefully, he'd be forgiving. She wondered if she would be. She took a deep breath and answered the phone.

"Hi, Dad."

9
Angela & Judith

"HI, SWEETHEART. HOW YA DOIN'?"

"I'm doing okay, Dad. How are you?" Angela wondered if she sounded as nervous as she felt.

"Oh, I'm hanging in there. But I'd be lying if I said it hadn't been a rough few days."

"Yeah," Angela said, pausing for a second, not knowing what to say next. "Listen, Dad, I'm not sure if you've talked to Auntie Pam or talked to Mom but..."

"I'm going to stop you right there," Edward said, cutting her off. "I know we have a lot to talk about, but right now I need to tell you...I need to tell you that your mom's not doing so good."

"What do you mean *not doing so good*?" Angela asked, panic elevating. "I just saw her last night."

"I know, I know. But after you left, she just kind of curled up on the couch and didn't move. The word catatonic sounds wrong, but it's the only word that comes to mind. I finally got her to the bed, changed her clothes, but she still hasn't moved. She's just curled up. Barely blinking. Staring into space. If she were crying, I may be less worried. But she's just..."

"Oh Daddy, what can I do?"

"I think you should come over again. Maybe if you talked to her. Even just get her to take a sip of water."

"Okay, I'll be right there."

Angela turned to Carl. While her dad was talking, she had put the phone on speaker so he had heard most of the conversation. They both raced downstairs and out the door. Car sickness set in almost as soon as the car started moving. Being pregnant and panicked at the same time was not a good combination.

When they got to her parents' house, Edward was sitting out on the front doorstep. He looked tired and older than Angela had ever seen him. She practically jumped out of the car to hug him. "Thanks for coming over again, sweetie. I know you must be tired."

Edward held Angela for a long time and then stepped back and moved to shake Carl's hand. "Carl, why don't you stay outside here with me."

"Absolutely, Ed," Carl responded, giving Angela's hand a squeeze and then sitting down on the step. It was amazing to Angela how at ease Carl could seem in any situation, but she knew he was tired too. And worried.

Angela went upstairs and found her mother just as her father had described, curled up on the bed, staring at the wall. The room felt devoid of air, like a hospital bed where the patient had just died. Her father had pulled a chair over to the side of the bed already, and as Angela sat down in it, she tentatively placed her hand on her mother's arm. "Mama," she said. "Mama, it's Angela."

Judith stirred and tilted her head ever so slightly to look up at her daughter.

"Mama, please, what's going on? What is this?" Angela said, voice trembling.

Judith didn't move. Angela touched Judith's hand. It was freezing. "Mama, you're so cold. Here, let me get you a blanket." After Angela covered her mother up, she kneeled down next to the bed.

"Mama, I'm not sure what's going on, but it's normal to be sad after your mom dies. I'm really sad too."

Judith did not move.

"But I just told Carl that I'm pregnant and he was so happy, it was like the sun was out again." Angela waited for her mom to say something, but again, nothing.

"I haven't told Dad yet. I'm afraid I've made a debacle out of the announcement of the baby. It was just all so much with Obachan dying and getting the news at the same time. But it's happy news, right?"

A few, agonizingly long moments passed. "You know," Judith said, her voice cracking, "If I hadn't had children. If you hadn't been born. I'm not sure my mother would have ever spoken to me again." She paused, a stir of life coming back into her eyes while exhaustion still permeated the room. "And I always resented you for that. That I wasn't enough to bring my mother's love, but you were."

Angela sat shocked. She had never heard her mother say anything like that before. "Mama…I…I'm…"

"All my mom did was try to provide for us and take care of us and I hated her for it. I hated her for being so strict and for not trying to understand me. I hated her for letting me go. I hated her for never disowning Pamela the way she did me. Just because Pamela was better at pretending to be the exact daughter Mom wanted her to be. I couldn't pretend, Angela. Do you get that? I couldn't pretend." Judith's whole body shuddered, and her eyes met Angela's. "I think that's why, in some ways, we were never as close as you were to your father. Mom loved you so much. And she showed it. Maybe not in a way you recognize, but in a way that I never experienced myself. In ways Pamela never did either. And I took it out on you. And now you come to me, stirring up the past. Expecting me to be happy to dig all that back up again, right when I'm trying to remember the good times, when I'm trying to honor my mom if I can." Judith let out a bellow of pain.

"Mama, I don't know what to say. I'm sorry I didn't know these stories. I'm so sorry I didn't know."

"It's not your fault, Angela. It's mine. I didn't tell them to you. I did the same thing my mother did to me. It's the same thing all the women in our family do. I kept my stories for myself. But it's almost like I can see into the future. See you resenting me for finding such joy in a grandchild when I may not have allowed myself the same joy in you. And I see these things. And I think about my own mother, and I think that maybe we are all doomed to walk in each other's footsteps."

Angela got on her knees in front of her mother. "Mama, you were not the mother your mother was. And your life experience and hers and mine could not have been more different. I will not resent you for taking joy from this baby. Come on, Mama. Please, sit up."

Judith made eye contact with her daughter. With the cold vacant look, her dad had described earlier, Judith simply said, "Not yet," and resumed staring at the wall. Angela picked up the glass of water her father had left on the bedside table. It had a bendy straw in it. Angela's hand trembled as she held it to her mother's mouth. "I'm not leaving this room until you take a sip of water."

At first Angela didn't know if Judith had even heard her, but after a few moments, Judith obeyed, and then continued her siloed stare.

Angela put the glass down and stood up. She turned around to go find Carl, only to be startled by her dad standing in the doorway. He held his hand out for her and she took it. They walked silently together down the stairs.

"How much did you hear?" she asked.

"Enough," Edward answered.

"I'm sorry I didn't tell you about the baby in person. It's just all been so crazy. I only found out a couple weeks ago, right after I found out Obachan died. Daddy, please…"

"Don't worry, Angela. I'm not upset. It's okay. In fact, the idea that you are bringing new life into this world has been a lifeline of happiness for me since mom told me yesterday. This is truly a blessing."

Angela hugged her dad tightly. Tears began to stream down her face, and just like she had so many times as a child, she rubbed her face into her father's chest to wipe them away. He was always such a comfort to her, a safe place. As she pulled back, she asked, "Dad, was it really that bad, before you started having kids?"

"Yes. It was that bad."

"I don't understand how I never knew this before," Angela said.

"There was no reason to burden you with these old stories."

"Well, I want to hear them. I want to know them. I don't want to repeat the same mistakes."

Angela went and sat on the couch. The same couch she had recently been on, looking through photo albums. Suddenly that felt like a lifetime ago.

Edward sat on a chair opposite the couch as Carl came in from outside and took his place on the couch next to Angela.

"Okay, Ang, what do you want to know?"

"Tell me…" she said. "Tell me everything."

10 Angela & Edward

ANGELA, CARL, AND EDWARD GOT settled onto the couches in the living room. Edward had made tea and Angela felt simultaneously tired to the bone and electrified by family drama. She sipped her tea and waited for her father to start talking. Patience was key with her dad. He did everything in his own time.

"When your mom and I got together, it was a different time. You have to understand, interracial marriage was still controversial. It was only made legal countrywide in 1967."

"I can't imagine Ojichan and Obachan were following Supreme Court decisions," Angela said. Her grandparents' opinions were strong, but she never remembered them being overtly political.

"You'd be surprised," Edward answered. "Of course, I never talked to them about it, but I don't think they missed that ruling or its significance. But it wasn't about the ruling. It was about the ethos of the time. There was a large part of the country that, no matter what, was going to view our marriage as illegal and unnatural."

"You were a teenager when the laws changed, Ed," Carl said. "Did it matter to you?"

"To me? No, not really. Not when it happened. I hadn't met Judith yet or really given much thought to the topic. I can't even say I knew it happened when it happened. I was insulated, as Judith would later teach me. I mean, once I knew more about it, I thought it was the right thing to do. It seemed ridiculous to me that it was illegal in the first place. But I can't say it was one of the top issues I was paying attention to."

"Was it even a thought it your mind when you met Judith?" Carl asked.

"The legality of it? No. And honestly, not really the day-to-day of it either. I just saw Judith." Edward paused and ran his hand through his hair.

"What did you think then? When you met Mom?" Angela asked.

"As we started dating, and people would make comments, either to my face or behind my back, about dating a Japanese woman, I began thinking that everyone in the world was certifiably nuts—and to be honest—that the world was made of total assholes." He paused. "It was a hard time for me. I was young. I was an ideolog. I wanted to see the best in people. So, their reactions were enraging and heartbreaking. And honestly, people telling me there was something wrong with dating your mother probably only made me dig my heels in deeper. It probably deepened my feelings for her in a way that only a really stressful situation could."

"So, it wasn't just from Ojichan and Obachan? It was from everyone?"

"Not everyone. My parents and family never said a word. They loved Judith from day one. The whole Garrington side of the family did. But friends, colleagues. It obviously made a lot of people…uncomfortable."

"So, you felt like your whole relationship was a political statement?" Carl asked.

"Yes and no. Eventually I did feel like I was taking a stand. That I was above the assholes around us." Edward paused and gave Angela a soft smile. "I used to think I was naive to think that people would see our relationship and change their beliefs. But, but now I think small things, everyday acts, add up. I think about how different things are now and think…maybe Judith and I did make a difference, in our own way."

Angela smiled back at her dad and his quiet strength. "But you said things were bad with Ojichan and Obachan. And they didn't even come to your wedding. What happened?" Angela asked, nervous to hear the answer.

"Well, I showed up to their house to ask for their permission to marry Angela, and they said no."

"Wait," Angela interrupted. "In Mom's journal she wrote that they said yes!"

"I know," Edward answered. "I lied."

"You lied? Why?"

"Because I wanted to marry your mom. And if I told her they said no, we would have missed the joy of the proposal. We would have gone straight to rage. I wanted us to have our moment. For her to think things were okay. For her to say yes and for her to be happy. In retrospect, it was probably a stupid move, but we did have a few hours, that day, of being happy."

"Did you ever tell her the truth?" Carl asked.

"No."

Angela was stunned. It was like the tapes and journals her Auntie Pam had given her had opened a Pandora's box of family secrets. She took a minute to recover. "So, Mom thought she had her parents blessing. And when they found out you were engaged…"

"They were upset. Mostly with me. Her dad took me aside. Told me he thought he'd made his feelings clear. And I stood up to him. In the way only a headstrong young person can. He barely said anything back, he just walked back to where Judith was standing and gave her an ultimatum. He told her that she could either marry me or keep her family. She could have me or have them, but not both."

"What did Mom do?" Angela asked anxiously.

"She looked her dad straight in the face and said, 'I choose him,' and took my hand and we walked right out the front door."

"Oh my god," Angela gasped.

"And how long was it before you all talked again?" Carl asked.

"It took years, Carl."

"What broke the ice?" Carl inquired, his voice slightly softer than normal.

Edward turned to Angela. "Well, of course, sweetie. It was you."

"That's basically what Mom just told me. She also said she's resented me for it all these years. No wonder I'm a hot mess."

"Don't be too hard on your mom, Angela," Edward replied. "There may have been some resentment there, but if there was, it was so small, so dwarfed compared to how much she loved you. How much we all did. Love can move mountains. And when you were born, it brought us back together. That healed more wounds than resentment created. Love always wins."

"Is that why you never told me any of this? Because Mom resented me so much?"

"Angie, she didn't resent you. But things were tenuous. And, I guess, for the sake of a new beginning, of moving on, we opted for closing that chapter and kind of ignoring it. Why tell you about everything that came before? The only thing that mattered was that we were a family again."

"I don't know, Dad. Mom seems pretty pissed upstairs."

"Grief brings out strange emotions. And odd decisions. You of all people have seen this the last weeks as you've dealt with news of your pregnancy."

"Last weeks?" Carl asked, "What are you talking about?"

"Shit," Angela said out loud, but screamed it in her head. "I found out a couple weeks ago. Right after we got the call about Obachan. I was so stunned; I didn't know how to tell you. Or anyone. But Auntie Pamela figured it out. And so did Mom."

Carl didn't say anything. He just stared at his hands. The silence filled the room like San Francisco fog.

"Listen," Edward started, "I know you have a lot of questions. And I'm all for answering them. But we all need to recover. Thank you for coming over. And for talking to your Mom. I'm glad you got her to drink some water. That was a good step."

Angela stood up. "I'm not sure it helped. She seemed to just want to say horrible things to me."

Edward took his daughter in his arms. "Tomorrow, after you've had a good night's sleep, try to replay the conversation in your head. Try to hear what your mom was trying to say. She was trying to say that she loves you. And that she already loves your baby. And that she wants things to be different."

Angela bristled at his interpretation. All she could hear was the word "resented" chiming over and over again in her head.

Carl stood up and shook Edward's hand. As they walked toward the door, she saw that his whole body composure had changed, but for some reason she couldn't read him. As they stepped outside, she stopped him. "Carl, listen, I'm sorry…"

"I don't want to talk about it right now, Angela. I'm tired. Exhausted. Today started off with a lot of emotions and has just gotten more dramatic from there. Let's just go home, eat some food, watch some TV, and get some sleep."

Angela didn't dare say anything. She followed him to the car. The rest of the day and evening she tried to stay out of his way. So much for celebrating. She had ruined everything by not telling him sooner. It was killing her not knowing what he was thinking, but she didn't dare press it. She stayed quiet, and smiled at him whenever possible, and tried not to cry as he fell asleep without saying goodnight.

11 Carl

CARL FELT THE IMPACT OF the pavement reverberate through his knees every time his feet hit the ground. He had already run five miles, but his mind was racing with too many thoughts for him to stop now.

Right, left, right, left, right, left.

Normally he'd have a podcast or music on, taking full enjoyment of his daily runs, but today his mind was too full for that.

Right, left, right, left, right, left.

The past few days had been truly difficult. Coming off of Aiko's death and funeral and all the revelations that unfolded afterwards, including learning he was going to be a father—he was emotionally spent. So was Angela. But it was more than that. His current anxiety was more personal, more internal. He wasn't an angry person by nature. In fact, he was rarely angry at anyone. But he was royally pissed that Angela hadn't told him she was pregnant. That she waited weeks and that apparently multiple people knew before he did. What did it say about their relationship that he wasn't her first call? That she kept something so huge to herself?

Right, left, right, left, right, left.

He tried to write it off as the grief of Aiko's passing, but it was gnawing at him and felt like something more.

He reached a fork in his normal running route. If he headed north, it would be another two miles until he looped home. If he headed south, he'd be home within fifteen minutes. He hesitated and then headed north. Even if his knees were screaming, he wasn't ready to go back to the house, not yet.

Right, left, right, left, right, left.

His thoughts dwelled on what Ed told them about Angela's birth. About how a baby coming into the world was a bridge to reconciliation. About how Judith finally caved and told her parents she was pregnant and how the ice thawed and they welcomed her home. It had been a long, hard-fought reunion, but when Angela arrived it was a new beginning for all of them.

Right, left, right, left, right, left.

Carl thought about Angela as he ran up a particularly steep hill. He couldn't help but think that there was some part of her that agreed with her grandparents. That she felt that their own child wouldn't be an extension of their family. That who he was as a person, as a white man, was in some way bad, was in some way wrong for her. And maybe that's why she didn't tell him.

Right, left, right, left, right, left.

He picked up the pace and tried to reconcile what he knew of the Angela he loved—the feisty, smart, funny, affectionate, beautiful woman that he fell for the second he laid eyes on her—and the woman who would forever blame him for not being Japanese. What exactly was he supposed to do about that?

Right, left, right, left, right, left.

As he turned the corner that would lead him back south, back toward home, he stopped dead in his tracks, hunched over breathing heavily, an agonizing pain gripping his stomach as he had the thought: What if Angela makes our baby feel bad for being white?

He knew she would never do it on purpose, but what if she did it passively? Without realizing it?

He started walking back home, trying to figure out if there were ways that he could reinforce some of his own heritage, the things he loved about his family traditions and ways they could fuse them with hers. He had let his own cultural heritage take a backseat after marrying her, and he loved all of the enrichments that her family had brought to his understanding of the world. But, had he let up too much of his own identity in the process?

He started jogging again and wondered if he was overthinking it. They were going to have a baby. And they were both thrilled. And he would love that baby more than he had ever loved anyone in his whole life. Maybe even more than Angela. And he would do everything in his power to make that baby see how lucky it was to be born into a loving family. This wasn't about race. This was about openness and honesty. This was about their marriage and how he didn't talk to her or tell her. This was about him wondering…what else she might be keeping from him.

Right, left, right, left, right, left.

He picked up the pace again as he got closer to the house. So many thoughts were streaming through his mind. There were so many ways the conversation could go. He had to get home and talk to her as soon as possible, to let her know how much he loved her, and to not let his doubts fester within him.

Right, left, right, left, right, left.

12 Judith, Angela & Carl

June 3, 1975

Eddie and I are getting married today. It should be the happiest day of my life. I mean, of course, it is. But, there's such a shadow over today. I've been trying to pretend like everything's okay. And Eddie and I haven't talked about it. But it's like we don't even have to. We both know what's wrong. He just sees the look on my face when I start thinking about it and holds me. Just holds me. He's good like that. I still can't believe my parents aren't coming. THEY AREN'T COMING! It's all Pammy's fault. I was perfectly content to not even tell them I was getting married, but she had to go ahead and try and broker peace. And get my hopes up. And then tell me in her stupid Pammy way that they said no. Well first they said yes and then they said no. UGH. Why did I let Pammy even try and talk to them? If they can't understand that we're in the 20th century now, then it's not my job to teach them. I never imagined having a big wedding anyway, like they would ever pay for that. But I always thought my dad would walk me down the aisle. And now he's not. He's not even coming. Fine. Screw him. Eddie's dad is going to do it and that will be just fine. Time to put on my wedding dress and go be happy. It's my wedding day. Whether my parents are here or not.

○○○

THE SOUND OF CARL COMING in from his run startled Angela enough for her to reflexively look up from one of her mother's journals. Reading about her mother's life was gripping. It was like the most addictive novel she could ever pick up, with characters she thought she was familiar with but turns out she didn't really know at all.

Angela waited for Carl to come into the living room. He was gone on his run a long time, longer than usual. She always loved the way he looked after coming back from a run. She lounged on the couch in the living room, listening as she heard him jump into the shower. She was slightly disappointed that she didn't get to see him right away, but was still trying to give him his space. She returned to flipping through her mom's journal some more, thinking about how long her parents and her grandparents were apart. She was born in 1984. Ten years of separation. How did they come back from that?

She started looking for a journal from around the time she was born when Carl came into the room. He was uncharacteristically stoic, a large horizontal crease lining his brow. She put the journals down immediately.

Carl looked hesitant and sat down on the coffee table in front of her. "I love you, Ang, you know how much I love you."

"I know. I love you, too."

Carl's mouth made a small, involuntary smile, but it lasted only a moment. He looked down at the floor for a long beat before he looked straight at her. "I need to know why you didn't tell me about the baby right away."

Angela felt her stomach drop. Nausea washed over her, and not the morning sickness kind. She stared at the floor.

"Ang, come on, look at me. I need to know. Why didn't you tell me?"

Angela took a deep breath in and looked up at her husband. "Because I wasn't sure I wanted to keep the baby."

"Why?" Carl asked quietly. "Because of race?"

"No, not because of race. Well, not consciously because of race at least. Because I didn't know if I was ready. Because I love my job and our life. Because I haven't ever really wanted to be a mom." Angela looked back down at the floor again. "Because I don't know if I'm a good enough person to be a mom."

"What? Ang, that's ridiculous."

Angela sat up straighter. "It's not ridiculous. I've always felt like half a person. Not in one world or another. Incomplete. I have never had a good relationship with my own mother. And you know how these things trickle down," she paused. "And yes, regarding race, you know I feel like it's my fault that we aren't Japanese anymore. Most people can't even tell I'm Japanese when they look at me. I'm it. The straw that broke the camel's back. I guess I don't want to perpetuate that any more than I already have."

Angela paused again. "But it wasn't about that. When I found out, and found out about Obachan, it just felt like the world had closed in on me. I couldn't breathe. I couldn't function. It seemed like everything was ending. I didn't feel happy. It felt…dark."

Carl rubbed his hands on his face and through his fingers muttered, "That's exactly when you're supposed to come to me, Angela."

"I know. I know. I don't know why I didn't. But now it almost seems destined. Like, we have even more information now. Like how my existence changed everything. Maybe some part of me knew that. I don't want that for this baby. If history repeats itself, then we're in for some crazy family change and I don't want that. I just can't shake the feeling. That maybe…maybe I'm not supposed to be a mom."

Carl kneeled down in front of her. "First. You coming into this world brought your family back together. It didn't tear them apart. And second, you are going to be an amazing mom. I know it. I feel it. I have no doubt about it. But…" Carl took in a deep breath and looked down at the floor, "I need you to tell me the truth. I need to know. If I were Japanese, would you be feeling this way?"

Angela had to pause and think. She had never imagined him as Japanese. She had imagined marrying a Japanese person, but never imagined Carl as anything but what he was. The thought exercise alone was impossible. He was exactly who he was supposed to be. But she had to admit, there was something to what Carl said. She took one of his hands. "I think, that if I had married a Japanese man, it would have started out as a sense of obligation. As a sense of 'righting the ship.' That I was somehow restoring my family line. But now, after learning more about my family. After reading my mother's journals, I'm starting to realize how wrong that thinking would be."

Angela took both of Carl's hands into hers. "I know now, for all the problems that my mom and I have, and for how much I will never understand the things she says to me or the way she treats me, it's quite possible that I am my mother's daughter. She married for love and nothing less. Just like I did."

Carl softened a bit, but she could tell he still had more to say, so she waited. Finally, Carl looked her straight in the eyes and asked, "So, do you still feel like you don't know if you want to keep the baby?"

Angela stared straight back at him. "No. I don't feel that way. I have my insecurities, obviously, but I want this baby. I really do."

"How do you know?"

"Because when we were at Obachan's funeral, I started talking to it. And tending to myself because of it. And I realized that it was important to me to take care of it."

"Then Angela, why didn't you tell me then? We got home from the funeral and you still didn't tell me. You didn't tell me until the next day!"

"Honestly, I can't explain it. Except that the sequence made sense in my head at the time."

They sat in silence for a few moments, moments that resonated loudly like the long sounding pluck of a cello string.

"I'm sorry if I made you feel bad," Angela said. "I love you so much. And I can't wait to see you become a father. Because I think you'll be such a great one. And I'm scared, but I know you'll take care of me. Take care of us. And I'm so grateful for that already."

Carl practically leapt up on top of Angela on the couch, kissing her passionately. Both of their insecurities were wrapped up in that kiss, reassuring each other, comforting each other, both feeling a small sense of relief wash over them. As their kiss turned to more, Angela couldn't help but think to herself, *I will never keep anything from him again.*

13 Aiko & Carl

(CLICK)

Pamela: Tell me about school in the camps.

Aiko: School was pretty basic. Sometimes it gave the feeling of normal. Other times the classroom was so hot we'd have to sit outside. But even then, we couldn't spread out. We'd have to sit close together alongside the building to stay in the shade. The dust would get up our skirts.

Pamela: You were in middle school, right?

Aiko: Yes.

Pamela: Was there a separate building for the high school?

Aiko: Yes and no. At first, school was taught in several buildings around the camp. Mainly block 8H. Then, after a couple years, they constructed a new high school. It was very controversial at the time. The middle schoolers shared the space.

Pamela: Why was the high school controversial?

Aiko: Because the white people did not want their dollars to go toward educating "the enemy."

Pamela: "The enemy"...geesh.

Pamela: Was it integrated?

Aiko: No.

Pamela: What about the teachers? Were they all from the camps?

Aiko: No. Some were from the camps. Many were white.

Pamela: Did you get along with the teachers?

Aiko: As much as any kid does. They did a lot of trying to educate us on how to assimilate into the culture. They didn't care that we had already assimilated. Most of us were US born. But they were told they had to teach us how to be American. So, they did.

Pamela: People graduated in the camps, right?

Aiko: Yes.

Pamela: What were your graduations like?

Aiko: They tried to make it as normal as possible, but it was not. I remember them lining kids up against the barbed-wire fence for graduation photos.

OOO

CARL TURNED OFF THE TAPE recorder. It was getting late. He needed to get to sleep. Angela had gone to bed hours ago. But, over the last few weeks Angela had become obsessed with the tapes and the journals, devouring them like an ice cream on a hot day, and he was just trying to keep up. The worlds of Aiko and Judith were so foreign to him, and the complexity of their relationship was so raw, he marveled that all of them weren't complete basket cases. That being said, some of Angela's neuroticisms—over not fitting in—or assuming people were judging her—began to make sense.

He thought about turning the tape back on but wasn't in the mood. He honestly didn't know how Angela could put herself through the ringer by listening to Aiko's voice all the time. He worried she was swimming in grief, but her attitude portrayed the opposite. She seemed invigorated by her new family history project, throwing herself in with the same zeal she usually reserved for work. She had bought so many books on the Japanese incarceration camps and on race relations in the 1960s and 1970s that their living room looked like she was cramming for an intense final exam or was about to start writing a Ph.D. dissertation on American History.

It'd be one thing if that's all she was doing, but she was working constantly too. She'd been back at work about three weeks, diving in with as much gusto as before. There was always a story to cover. Always a new tweet or shooting or god knows what else. People thought banking was stressful, but watching someone try to cover the news made his job look like a walk in the park.

He tried to get her to slow down at least until the morning sickness had passed, but she claimed her work made things better, that she got so distracted by her projects that she didn't have time to throw up. He called bullshit, but since he wasn't with her all day, he had no real evidence to the contrary. She had always worked this much; it was one of the things he loved most about her. It had never really impacted him all that much. He had a demanding job too and they usually spent what free time they did have together. But now, he was starting to miss her, even though she was right there in front of him. She was retreating into the past, and he felt like he couldn't fully go there with her. Still, he wanted to try. So, here he was, listening to tapes in the middle of the night, even if it kind of broke his heart to do so.

He felt his chest tighten a bit and quietly went into their bedroom to watch her sleep for a few moments. She was just starting to really show and her baby bump was nothing short of miraculous. He constantly felt like touching her stomach, wishing he could be more a part of the growth of their baby. He bought every pregnancy and child-rearing book he could find, pouring over reviews on Amazon on every baby product he could think of, and trying to figure out what he wanted his parenting style to be. He couldn't help but notice that she hadn't picked up any of the baby books yet. He'd share nuggets of information with her, but she was mostly disengaged, breaking his heart just a little bit more.

Despite how tired he was, Carl knew he wouldn't be able to sleep, so he went back into the living room and picked up a small book that was written from the perspective of a young child in the camps, stylized in journal format. As he flipped through the pages, he wondered why Angela's family had never told their own story more widely. Their quiet acceptance of their past, in light of the things they overcame, was to him, the definition of humility.

And yet, he seemed to remember Aiko being staunchly arrogant, an attitude further identified by Judith in her journals. How could someone who was literally incarcerated based on her race go on to disown her daughter because she married a white man? The only conclusion was that the cognitive dissidence of matching racism with racism was not logical. It was visceral.

Carl continued to flip through the small fictionalized journal. The idea that a kid would be forced to live through such an experience as incarceration gave him the chills. He couldn't help but shiver at the thought that something like that could happen to their unborn child. He thought of current news reports describing attempts to ban people from the country based on religion or stories of children stranded in refugee camps unable to find care. This was not the world he wanted his progeny to live in.

And yet, what kind of person was he? If the incarceration camps were happening today, would he be doing anything about them? He knew he'd be against them, but would he protest? Would he march on the streets? Would he be calling his congressperson? Or would he just hold a general objection to the practice and go about his day-to-day life with little effect, as most white men are able to do? What was he doing about the current state of the world and country now? Anything?

He laid down on the couch and closed his eyes. Yesterday they had gone to their doctor and heard the heartbeat. The miracle of life boomed through a static-filled speaker. The ultrasound technician seemed to be in pleasant awe of the sound as well, which Carl found comforting. She must do dozens of ultrasounds a day, and yet the sound of each baby still made her smile. That was his kind of person.

He thought about what it was like to see their peanut-shaped baby appear on the screen. He felt like his heart was bursting out of his body, like he could weep tears of joy. He clutched Angela's hand so tightly that her fingertips turned a little red. He noticed and started to laugh, but then looked at Angela's face. She hadn't noticed at all. She didn't seem to notice anything. She was studious. Distant. Like she was looking at an art slide in a high school history class. "Angela, babe, what do you think?" he asked her.

"It's great," she said quietly. "I'm glad the baby is healthy."

And that was all he got. He came home and proudly placed the ultrasound photo on the fridge and she went almost immediately back into her books. Her history books. Not the baby books. She didn't call or text any of her friends and family to tell them about hearing the baby's heartbeat. She didn't even ask where he put the extra copies of the ultrasound photo they brought home with them. She just curled up on the couch and started reading again. That one action alone made Carl feel incredibly lonely. So, he did what he always did when he didn't know what else to do. He went for a run. And for the second time in the last month, he had an emotional breakdown along the way. And for the second time in the last month, Angela had no idea.

She had told him she wanted the baby. That she wanted to be a mom. She was doing everything she was supposed to. She was taking all the vitamins. Going to all the appointments. Cutting out all the foods she needed too. Why wouldn't she read the damn books too? He realized he was squeezing the fictionalized journal he was holding to the point where the binding on the side might split. There was some puzzle about her past she was trying to solve. If it meant that solving it would finally allow her to be in the present, to enjoy this moment with him, then he was going to help her figure it out. He put down the journal and picked up the tape recorder again.

14 Judith

JUDITH LOOKED AT HERSELF IN the mirror. She looked old. At least she felt like she did. The bags under her eyes seemed darker than they had ever been, puffy half circles reminding her of her own mortality. The past few weeks had been difficult to say the least. Ever since her "catatonic episode" (as she and Eddie now called it) Eddie had been fawning over her, smothering her in his attempts to help. She was simultaneously grateful for his love and care and frustrated that he wouldn't just let her be. Her mother had just died. She was supposed to be an emotional wreck, wasn't she?

She splashed some water on her face. Each time she closed her eyes another facet of her relationship with her mother would flash across her consciousness. The look on her mother's face when she told her she was going to marry Eddie. The scolding she got when she broke her arm when she was seven: "Why weren't you more careful Judy?!" The tension she felt when handing baby Angela over to her mother to hold for the first time. The jealousy she felt every time her mother was kind to Angela in ways she never received herself. Only occasionally would something happy flit into her mind—like when she got her acceptance letter into nursing school, or when she told her mom she was going to be part of her high school honor roll—but those moments were so ephemeral, so fleeting, that she barely registered them amidst her other memories. Wisps of sunlight within a hurricane-sized rainstorm.

These constant flashes of her mother's presence, her mother's impact on her life, made it next to impossible to rest, the backs of her eyelids like mini television screens constantly broadcasting her past. All she wanted to do was sleep. But no, as one last kick in the ass, her mother wasn't letting her. From heaven, or hell, or wherever she might be, her mother was giving her a hard time. Hell then, probably.

Judith leaned over the sink. She was also increasingly mad at Pamela. Shouldn't it have been her choice to give Angela the tapes and journals? *I suppose Pammy did make the tapes*, she thought to herself. But still, the journals were hers. Judith felt a surge of anxiety as she thought about her daughter reading her innermost thoughts and secrets like they were summer paperbacks. *God, I'm sure I wrote about my sex life with Eddie in those things*. She reminded herself that she gave Angela the go ahead to read them. But that had been a snap decision. If she had thought about it longer, when she was in a more rational state, she would have almost certainly said no. Now it was too late. She couldn't take them back. She had spent her entire life keeping secrets for Pamela. Biting her tongue when her parents went on rants about why Pamela wasn't married. Pretending like she knew less about Pamela's life than she did. And here Pamela was, just giving her journals out to people like it was nothing. It made her so angry.

She stood up straight and pulled her hair into a ponytail. Another splash of cold water on her face wouldn't do much else to help her. She had to go to work. She took a deep breath in and turned away from the mirror. She had been picking herself up, dusting herself off, and putting her best foot forward at work every day. Today would be no different. No matter what she was feeling, there were people at the hospital who needed her.

As she got into her car, she pulled her hospital ID out of the glove compartment and pinned it to her scrubs. As she buckled herself in, her seat belt strap pushed the clip of her ID into her chest, causing a slight cut. She let out a surprised, "Ow," as she looked down and saw a small amount of blood bleed through her shirt. She sighed. She always put her ID on when she got to work, not when she was leaving, for this very reason. She couldn't go to the hospital in these scrubs now. She unbuckled herself and walked back into the house. It felt like she was wading through a dense swamp.

Without being totally conscious of how she got there, she was back in the bathroom, getting a Band-Aid out of the medicine cabinet. She took off her shirt and started it soaking in the sink. After she was patched up and had a new shirt, she was back in the car again. She gave one moment's pause, wondering if she was too tired to drive, but decided she was fine. This was no more tired than she had been when she was in nursing school. Or when Angela was a baby. Or when Angela had to have her appendix out and she couldn't sleep until Angela was back home in her bed. She drove then. She worked then. She could do it now.

As she pulled out of the garage and backed down the driveway, she checked her rear-view mirror and immediately slammed on the breaks, lurching the car into a screeching halt. Breath heavy, sweat immediately pouring down the back of her neck, she turned around to see what was behind her. To her surprise, nothing was there, although that couldn't be. She could have sworn she saw something, no actually, someone. She pressed her eyes closed, as tightly as she could, and replayed the last few moments in her mind. What had she seen? It was a person. A woman. A small, old woman. She let out a gasp when she realized what she had seen. She had seen her mother in the rear-view mirror. Her dead mother. Heart still racing, she put the car in park and checked all of her mirrors again. Nothing.

She turned off the car, got out, and scanned the street up and down for someone, anyone, who she could have mistaken for her mother. The street was dead silent.

C'mon, Judy, she said to herself. *Pull yourself together.*

Then it dawned on her. She must've closed her eyes. She must've closed her eyes and seen her mother on the back of her eyelids, the spot where her mother now apparently lived.

Judith slowly got back in the car and pulled it back into the garage. As she was calling into the hospital to tell them she needed to take a sick day, she thought about how rare this was. When was the last time she took a sick day? She couldn't even remember. But here she was. Nearly debilitated from exhaustion because the ghost of mother past wouldn't leave her alone. She thought about calling Eddie, but it would only worry him. Angela had enough on her plate right now with work and the baby. And besides, the shame of what Angela might be reading about her in her old journals was enough to avoid Angela altogether. And she was too frustrated to call Pammy. When had she lost all of her friends? How did she not have anyone to call?

She went into her bedroom, changed into her pajamas, and laid on her living room couch. She pulled a throw blanket on top of herself and tried to cocoon her way into some type of comfort. She knew she wouldn't be able to sleep, but eventually figured she could at least watch some TV. Maybe the sounds of other people's lives would drown out the constant noise of her own. She pressed the power button and the first thing that came on to the screen was the movie *The Joy Luck Club*—probably the only modern-day movie about the relationships between Asian mothers and their daughters. "Fuck you," she said out loud as she turned the TV off again. She sat up and leaned her head back against the back of the couch, tilting her neck enough so that her head was ajar against the wall. She was a nurse. What would she tell a patient if she couldn't sleep?

As her neck started to strain from her awkward position and the ceiling started to look like it was getting closer and closer to her in some type of reverse vertigo, she heard a car door close in the garage. "Eddie?" she said as she sat up straight.

Soon, there he was in front of her. Just as handsome as the day they met. "Your friends called me, told me you called in sick. You never call in sick, so they knew something must be really wrong."

"Shouldn't you be at work?" Judith asked, wondering what friends he could possibly be referring to. Were her coworkers her friends?

"Work doesn't matter. What's going on with you?"

Judith curled up into him as he sat next to her on the couch.

"I just can't sleep."

Eddie pulled her close, his arms feeling like an additional blanket as they wrapped around her. He held her for a long time, not saying anything. Just holding her. Somehow, he knew it was exactly what she needed. After a few moments, maybe more than a few moments, she finally felt herself exhale.

"I think we need a change of scenery," he said.

"What do you mean?"

"You wait right here. I'm going to pack some bags and then we are going to go."

"Go where?" Judith was genuinely curious.

"To the one place I know you'll be relaxed enough to sleep."

"I don't want to go to the cabin," Judith said.

"No, not the cabin," Eddie answered. "I've got somewhere better in mind. You'll see."

Judith smiled, perhaps the first genuine smile she'd had in weeks. All these years and Eddie was still surprising her. Taking care of her. Knowing her better than she knew herself. He wasn't smothering. He was there. Always there. What would she ever do without him? But moreover, what had she ever done to truly deserve him?

When they got into the car, she still didn't know where they were going, and she was still in her pajamas, but she didn't care. With Eddie at the wheel and the hum of the engine, and the turn of the tires as they drove down the street, she felt safe and loved and was glad she didn't have to be in control of anything in that moment. She didn't tell Eddie about the ghost of her mother, but she knew she would eventually. For right now, she just focused on his face, hoping to burn it into her retinas so it would be his face, and not her mother's, that she saw when she closed her eyes. As the car warmed up her eyelids began to feel very heavy. Gravity took over but she thought her eyes were still open, staring at Eddie as he drove them on this mystery journey. Within moments, without even realizing it, Judith quietly fell asleep.

15 Edward

EDWARD LOOKED OVER AT HIS wife sleeping in the passenger seat. Even in the somewhat awkward position she fell asleep in, she was still the most beautiful woman he had ever seen. Somehow, she made a cramped neck look graceful. Her black hair was still pulled up into a high ponytail, puffed up on the top of her head, like she used to wear it when they first met. Her pajamas her slightly ajar. Edward's heart swelled and his eyes filled up with tears. It killed him to see her so upset and he could tell that she was still restless even if she was finally sleeping.

Part of him knew that Aiko's death would hit her hard, but he wasn't prepared for the depth of her sorrow. When her father had died, she went through a similar funk, but nothing compared to this. Plus, she had Angela and Carl's wedding to focus on. He was hoping that the thought of Angela's baby would be a similar incentive to stay engaged in day-to-day life. But he had his suspicions that the mother-daughter dynamics of her family were just too strong.

At first, he didn't know what to do when her friends at the hospital called. He was secretly hoping she had the flu. But, as he drove closer and closer to home, he knew it wasn't the flu. It was a broken heart. It had to be. And he knew his wife well enough to know that she had no idea what was going on. Her stubbornness would never let her see that she needed help. That she needed to heal.

He wasn't quite sure how to make it better, but he was determined to try. The idea of going away came to him just as he was pulling into the driveway. He thought about the happiest he had ever seen her, the most relaxed, and it was always when they were away from home. Disconnected. When she didn't feel the weight of responsibility pulling her down. It's not that she wasn't happy at home, but when they were on vacation, it was like she could inhale a full breath.

He wasn't surprised she thought of the cabin when he mentioned they were taking off. They usually went there after major life events. They went there after Angela went to college and Judith was grief stricken at having an empty home. They went there after one of Judith's favorite bosses retired and she couldn't bear the thought of working at the hospital without her. They went there after Pamela got diagnosed with breast cancer and Judith needed to collect herself before completely devoting her life to helping Pamela beat it. It was their spot to recuperate and get away.

But, when Edward was thinking of where to take her, the cabin didn't even come to mind. Instead he pictured her silhouette against the great expanse of the Mississippi River. And a warmth consumed him. A few years ago, they took one of their random drives. They liked to do that sometimes and always ended up somewhere interesting. One of Judith's mantras was, "You can always find something to do anywhere you go." It was one of Edward's favorite things about her. That day they had wound up at sleepy town on the Illinois-Iowa border. They pulled into a gas station and got a hiking trail map and some beef jerky and made their way to the closest trailhead. They hiked for hours. Toward the end of the day they were up along the ridge of a bluff just as the sun was setting. It was windy and getting cold. But she wanted to keep going. The random map they picked up claimed there was one spot at the top that was particularly beautiful, and her doggedness kicked into overdrive. She was determined to reach it and there was nothing he could do but follow.

When they finally reached the lookout point, he saw that the vista was indeed beautiful, but he was mostly thinking about how they would get back after dark, wondering how long it would take them to get to their car, thinking about whether they should stay overnight along the border or just drive back to Chicago. He almost missed the moment, caught up in his own thoughts, but then he felt her take his hand. The softness of her hand could still wow him. She turned to him, hair blowing across her face, and she smiled. It was a smile of pure joy, pride, and satisfaction. A smile that meant she was exactly where she wanted to be. And she had never looked so beautiful. Ever since then, it was the smile he saw in his heart every time he closed his eyes. It had become one of his most cherished memories.

They were going to go back. To find that sleepy town again. To find the small bed and breakfast they stumbled into that night, dirty from hiking back to their car in the dark. They were going to check in and find that trailhead and go back to that bluff. And he was going to turn her toward the great river and make her take five deep breaths. One for her. One for him. One for Aiko. One for Angela and Carl. And one for the baby. She was going to fully inhale. Breathe in. Breathe out. And then he was going to lead her back to a bed and hold her until she fell into a long, peaceful sleep.

16 Pamela

PAMELA HUNG UP HER COAT in her front hall closet and checked her answering machine. No light. No messages. Mostly she just got spam calls on her landline these days, but she still couldn't help but check. She pulled out her cell phone from her purse and looked to see if she had any messages she missed on her drive home from work. A big fat nothing.

She barely noticed when Sheila came into the room. "No word from Judy or Angela?"

"No, not since the funeral. Except for the logistics around mom's house, I literally haven't talked to them since."

"You know, you could call them."

"Yes, I could. But what would I say? Hey, I'm sad, are you sad too? Hey, I gave you a bunch of tapes and journals, why haven't you said thank you? Hey, I am part of this family too. Now that we have no parents, are we just dead to each other too?"

"For starters," Sheila replied.

Pamela walked toward Sheila and fell into an embrace. Sheila. Her rock. Her everything. Her life partner. Her secret life partner.

"I'm sorry. I know you're still pissed at me. You shouldn't have to be comforting me."

"I'm not pissed at you," Sheila said, placing her cheek on top of Pamela's head. Sheila was about seven inches taller than Pamela and liked how petite Pamela always felt to her. "I just don't understand why I couldn't come to the funeral. Everyone knows we are together."

Pamela didn't respond. She didn't have the energy to have this argument again. She never told her parents she was gay. And when she met Sheila, nearly twenty years ago, she never really incorporated her into the family. Sheila was incredibly gracious and forgiving about it. But it was there. Always. When Pamela's father died, she tried to tell her mother about Sheila. Instead of referring to her as her roommate, she used the word partner. "Mom, I'm bring my partner to the wake tonight and the funeral tomorrow." Her mother gave her a stare so withering, so fierce, that she knew it would kill their relationship if she did. So, she didn't. And in all the years since, she hadn't brought it up again. Sheila was not at Angela and Carl's wedding. On major holidays when they went to Sheila's family's house, Pamela was welcomed with open arms. When it was Pamela's family's turn, Sheila either stayed home or went to her own family's celebrations without Pamela. Pamela still marveled that Sheila hadn't left her yet. She could only chalk it up to their age. They grew up being afraid of being who they were. The secret of it felt familiar.

Sheila saw the look on Pamela's face. "You think too much sometimes. Come on, let's go for a walk."

"But I just got home."

"Now, let's go."

Pamela put her coat back on and they headed out. They lived on the north end of Albany Park, so they were only a few blocks away from a path that wound its way along the river. They had a loop that they loved to do that was just about two miles. It led them past playgrounds, dog parks, and so many beautiful trees. Any time of year the walk was full of the day-to-day life of a city that they both loved.

Pamela waited until they were on the path and then took Pamela's hand. "I know we haven't talked about this enough yet. At least not to the point where I've really justified it. But, having you at Mom's funeral, when she was so against our relationship, just felt wrong. Like I'd be saying, 'You're dead now, fuck you, I can be out to the whole family because you're gone.'"

Sheila squeezed Pamela's hand tightly. "Pam, baby. We have come through so much. We have fought so hard to be together. We have stuck with each other through thick and thin. I don't want to say 'fuck you' to your mom. I just want us to finally be who we are. It's not like when we met, or when we were kids. It's different now."

"I know, I know. I don't know why this is so hard for me." Pamela felt the urge to pull her hand away. To wrap her arms around herself. But she held fast to Sheila's hand. "I'm not ashamed of you, or of us."

Pamela stopped and turned and looked her lovely Sheila directly in the eyes. "Let me say that again. I'm not ashamed of you. Or of us. I'm still just so scared of my mother. She's dead and I still think she's going to come around the corner and yell at me."

"And what would she yell?"

"What do you mean?"

"What would she yell? If she found out that we met twenty years ago, fell in love, and have been together ever since. What would she yell?"

"I don't know. But watching Judy and Eddie be ostracized from the family all those years. Ten years of begging my parents to talk to them again. All the years of me being in the middle. I can only imagine what she would've done if she found out I was gay."

"You really don't think she knew?"

"We've had this conversation so many times before."

"I know we have, but we haven't had it since she's been gone. Since the consequences of you being yourself have now changed. She's not here to disown you anymore. She's not here to tell you that you can't be a part of the family anymore."

Pamela looked up at the trees. "I know. She's not here." Before she knew it, she was crying. Sheila wrapped her arms around Pamela. They stood there for a long time. Just holding. Just breathing.

"I'm sorry, love. I pushed. I pushed too hard. I just want you to be as proud of who you are as I am."

"It's just. It's just everything is different. I spent all these years trying to do everything I could to keep the family together. To document our history, to broker peace. And now, Mom's gone and it's like the family has fallen apart anyway. Judy hasn't called. Angela's going to have a baby and a new family of her own, and I…"

"And you have me. And you always will. But, babe, I think you're making a lot of assumptions about what Judy and Angela are feeling. Just swallow your pride and call them."

"I thought you were just telling me I need to have more pride in myself."

"That's not what I meant, and you know it. Call them. If you won't do it for them, then do it for me."

"I'll think about it," Pamela said, as she kissed Sheila on the forehead and then fell back into her arms.

"I hope you won't just think about it."

"Man, you are pushy tonight."

"Only because I love you."

"I love you, too," Pamela replied, and kissed Sheila on the lips.

Sheila stepped back and held her hand out to Pamela. "Come on, let's finish the loop before we head back for dinner."

17 Angela

ANGELA LOOKED AT THE CLOCK. It was getting close to 7:00 p.m. She hadn't been home before seven in a few weeks and she promised Carl that tonight she'd be there in time for dinner. Once she had pushed through the exhaustion of her first trimester, her second trimester had given her an unexpected burst of energy and she was planning on riding the wave as long as she could. She felt she owed it to her viewers and her producing team to work as hard as possible until she was off for maternity leave. It didn't help that the life of a TV news producer had never been so fast paced. Every day, every minute, she had to make choices about what to cover and what to air. There wasn't a news cycle anymore. Every second there was a news sharknado.

Unfortunately, this ebb of productivity was not necessarily conducive to being home on time. Nor did it mean she was focused. As she moved through her day, the stories of her mother and grandmother floated around her like ghosts. Active ghosts. Loud ghosts.

"I recognize those signs of oppression. Those are exactly the types of things the newspapers would say before they came for my family."

"I recognize those signs of racism. Those are exactly the kinds of things people used to say to me as I walked around holding my seemingly white baby, looking at me like I might have kidnapped her, or just assuming I was a nanny."

"Are you already moving on from that story? There's more there. If you don't dig deeper, you will be complicit."

"Why aren't they calling that an incarceration camp? That's what it is. I recognize those cages. I recognize those armed guards."

Even though she was passionately pitching ideas from new angles, at least new for her, these ghosts were never satisfied. She'd always been politically aware and had fought for diversity on TV, but now she found herself pushing even harder. What was the historical and legal precedent behind each story? How did what happened today fit into the larger context? Had something like this happened before? How does any story reflect the past and current state of race in America?

"Okay, okay, Ang," her producing assistant Teresa would say to her. "I get it. Go deeper."

"Angela, this isn't *60 Minutes*. We aren't making a documentary. We have to report the top lines and move on, there's too much to cover. You are not an investigative reporter," her boss Malcolm would say. She may not be an investigative reporter, but she was a news producer.

"This is exactly what I'm supposed to be doing, Malcom."

"No, it's not. You are supposed to be working with your team to report out what our audience needs to know today. Supporting materials are fine. But you're not in the field, Angela."

"I can assign my questions out. For the most part, that's what I've been doing."

"Yeah, but we are not Maddow. We don't go deep 70 years back in history. And you're not producing a special. Get back to the news. Now."

But Angela knew this was the news and she was determined to put it all into perspective. More importantly, to make sure that history didn't repeat itself.

Another way she was determined to change the climate of the news was to produce positive news segments. Not fluff. Not the news version of cat videos. But actual, productive ways people were making a difference, fighting back. She wanted to talk about the José Andrés's of the world, the lawyers who went to the airports to advocate for travelers after the first attempt at a Muslim ban, the teachers that could barely make rent but were still buying their students food. Maybe one out of ten of her good news stories made it to air, but she wasn't going to stop trying. She had an intrinsic need to show that this world, this world that she was about to bring a new life into, was populated by good people. By focusing on the good things people were doing for each other *despite* what was happening in the news, she felt their station was providing a service for what their community needed to hear. And quite frankly, what she needed to hear too. Informed and positive. That was her mandate.

The ghost of her Obachan was quietly persistent with her new mandate as well. "Angela, someone had to fight to get us out of those camps," the voice would say. Or her mother's voice, "Angela, someone had to fight to change the marriage laws. Who were those people?"

She looked at the clock again. Mandate or no mandate, she had to get going. She wasn't close to being done for the night but she closed her laptop and willed herself out the door so she could attempt to be home before he served up the food. Plus, Carl had said he had a surprise for her and she had no idea what it could be. He had become obsessed with figuring out the nursery, so she was guessing that maybe it was a new crib. She was having decision anxiety about which crib would be best, because honestly, what did she know about cribs? Carl didn't seem to be picking up on the fact that everything about become a mother completely terrified her. He was still gleefully reading baby books and she felt paralyzed by mortal terror every time she read something about giving birth or, god forbid, what it'd be like to have a colicky baby.

But maybe it wasn't a crib at all. Carl was good at surprises. Maybe it was something completely unrelated to the baby. That would be a welcome and refreshing change of pace.

When she got home, the dining room table was set and candles were lit. A wave of relief washed over her followed by the thought, *Damn, he's good.* She walked over to the table and heard Carl humming in the kitchen. She was about to sit down at her seat when she noticed that on her plate wasn't a salad or soup or even a napkin, but rather a large manila envelope. "Should I open this or wait for you?" she yelled into the kitchen. Her fingers were already fiddling with the seal, resisting the urge to tear it open.

Carl came into the dining room. He was so handsome. Even after all these years together, he still made her heart flutter a bit. "Go ahead, open it," he said as he wiped his hands on his apron. "Dinner's almost ready."

Angela carefully, but quickly, tore the envelope open and poured out two plane tickets. She looked at the destination. They said "Denver." And the dates were for a couple weeks away. She just stared at them, confused. Had they ever even talked about going to Denver?

Carl laughed. "You should see the look on your face," he said as he chuckled again.

"I mean, thank you. You know I love traveling, but..."

"But you don't get it," he said, completing her thought.

"I'm sorry, no, I don't."

"Well," Carl answered. "Denver is the closest major airport to Granada."

"Granada?" Angela asked, the realization of what he was saying washing over her. "We're going to Amache?"

"That's right!" Carl answered enthusiastically. "I know how much your family's history means to you. And I've been trying to figure out a way to be more involved. So, I figured, before this baby comes, we can go on one last trip together."

The words "one last trip together" echoed through Angela's brain like a pebble plummeting to the bottom of the Grand Canyon. She realized she wasn't paying attention.

"...going to fly into Denver, drive the three and a half hours to Granada, and we're going to see the old incarceration campgrounds."

Angela was genuinely taken aback. Was she smiling? She hoped she was smiling. This was so thoughtful and so well planned, but she had so many thoughts running through her head. She wondered if she could possibly take time off work right before going on maternity leave. But she also wondered how she couldn't, given the destination. She immediately started wondering if she could turn their trip into a segment for the news, or if she should keep the experience just to themselves. She wondered if she should invite her parents to come along, or if a trip like this would even be something her mom would want to do. She hadn't talked to her mom in weeks. She wondered so many things, she almost couldn't breathe.

She looked at Carl's face, eagerly awaiting a response. He was so thoughtful. And this was such an amazing gesture. Before she knew it, a swell of gratitude filled her chest. Gratitude and love. Because Carl had done this for her. For them. For her grandmother. Her eyes began to well up with tears.

"Thank you," she said. It was all she could muster in that moment.

"Of course," he replied as he kissed her forehead and squeezed her hand. "I'll be right back; I just have to make sure I don't burn dinner."

As he walked back into the kitchen she said down at the table and stared at the plane tickets. She was going to Amache. She got out a notepad from her purse and started taking notes for what to bring and supplies she may need. Her thoughts were still forming, but there was one thing she knew for sure: she was going to document her trip as well as possible. Her Auntie Pamela had gifted her so much already. She wanted to add to the family's story.

18 Aiko

(CLICK)

Pamela: Okay, Mom, we're going to do something a little different today. I'm going to ask you questions and you just tell me the first thing that pops into your head.

Aiko: Oookaayy...

Pamela: Don't worry, it'll be easy. First question: What's your favorite childhood memory?

Aiko: That is not easy!

Pamela: Don't think about it. Just say the first thing that pops into your head. Even if it's not your favorite of all time, it's just like rapid answer.

Aiko: Rapid answer. That sounds iffy. What was the question again?

Pamela: What's your favorite childhood memory?

Aiko: Okay. I guess it would be playing spies.

Pamela: Spies?

Aiko: Yes. All the girls on my block would gather and we would spy on the boys.

Pamela: Was this in the camps?

Aiko: Oh no. This was before. I was very young, maybe 9 or 10. But we did it every day. And we had fun.

Pamela: Was it only Japanese kids?

Aiko: No, of course, not. I didn't have very many Japanese friends when I was little. I don't think I even realized I was Japanese until they called us to go to the camps.

Pamela: Whoa.

Aiko: Yes, whoa.

Pamela: Okay, great! See, no problem. Second question...

Aiko: How many questions are there?

Pamela: Well, I have a bunch. How many are you willing to do?

Aiko: Six.

Pamela: Six? Why six?

Aiko: Six is my favorite number.

Pamela: Why?

Aiko: Because in Japanese culture, even numbers are bad luck. And I tend to like what I'm not supposed to.

Pamela: Wow. Okay. Six questions then. Question number two: Name something that you absolutely hate.

Aiko: Hate?

Pamela: Yes, something that makes you mad no matter what.

Aiko: That's quite the question.

Pamela: Come on, Mom. Just answer.

Aiko: Dust.

Pamela: Dust.

Aiko: Yes. Dust. Dust and sand. They both get everywhere. Are seemingly never ending. No matter how much you sweep, dust just comes back. And when dust storms, it ruins everything.

Pamela: We don't have too many dust storms here in Chicago.

Aiko: I did not always live in Chicago.

Pamela: Is that why you always made us clean the house every day? Even when it was clean? Because you hate dust?

Aiko: Nothing is ever clean. The war against dust is never ending.

Pamela: (laughter) Okay, question number three: Describe your perfect day.

Aiko: Technically that is not a question.

Pamela: MOM.

Aiko: Perfect day. I wake up. I read. I go for a long walk. I cook. I eat good food. I take a nap. I read some more. Maybe go to the movies at night.

Pamela: Are you with anyone?

Aiko: No. I am never alone. Between this family and my work, I am never alone. I think to be alone would be nice.

Pamela: I won't tell the rest of the family that one.

Aiko: (light laughter)

Pamela: Okay, question four: Do you have any big regrets?

Aiko: No.

Pamela: No? Nothing?

Aiko: No.

Pamela: Why not?

Aiko: What has happened, has happened. Regret has no point.

Pamela: Question five: What is your favorite food?

Aiko: These really are in no particular order, are they?

Pamela: That's the point, it's to keep your brain jumping around so you answer faster. It's supposed to make you more honest in your answers. Although, at this point, I don't think we are doing it right.

Aiko: I don't think we're doing it wrong.

Pamela: Okay, Mom, favorite food?

Aiko: Spaghetti and meatballs.

Pamela: I knew that was going to be your answer.

Aiko: What? Who doesn't love spaghetti and meatballs?

Pamela: Okay, question six: If you could change one thing about your life, what would it be?

Aiko: (pause) I don't know.

Pamela: Nope. You have to answer.

Aiko: Maybe I would change that it wouldn't snow so much in winter.

Pamela: Okay, that's something. But what about your life, you personally?

Aiko: You think I need to change?

Pamela: MOM. No, that's not what I'm saying. It's just supposed to be an interesting question.

Aiko: (light laughter) You are so easy to make frustrated.

Pamela: You are so frustrating!

Aiko: (light laughter) Okay. Change one thing. I guess. I guess I would want to travel more. I have not been to very many places.

Pamela: Would you go to Japan?

Aiko: Why? Because I'm Japanese?

Pamela: Well, yeah, I guess.

Aiko: Maybe. But I think my first choice would be Rome. I've always wanted to see Rome.

Pamela: Well maybe we will go one day.

Aiko: I bet they have good spaghetti there.

Pamela: Probably. Although, probably nothing like what we eat here.

Aiko: True enough.

Pamela: Okay, well, thanks for playing.

Aiko: Can I change one of my answers?

Pamela: Yeah, sure, I guess. Which one do you want to change?

Aiko: The one about regrets.

Pamela: Really? What do you want to change it to?

Aiko: All these talks we've been having. It has made so many memories surface. The other day, I got out an old box that I haven't looked at in many years. A wooden box that has been in my family for some time. When we got back from the camps, I kept many things in there, including a wooden bird pin. It was very popular to carve these birds in the camps. And a boy named Robert made me one. It is so beautiful, and he did such a lovely job painting it. And I took it from him in a playful way. I knew it was special enough because I have kept it all this time. But I didn't thank him enough in that moment. I regret that. I wish I had thanked him more. And I guess, that is also my change too. I wish I could tell him now that I still have that bird, all these years later. And that it means a lot to me that it came from him, in that place.

Pamela: Wow. Well. Maybe we can find Robert ourselves and tell him.

Aiko: Some things are better left thought and not done.

Pamela: Maybe, but, Mom, it's easier to find people now...

Aiko: No, we are just talking.

Pamela: Well, maybe you can show me the bird sometime.

Aiko: Yes. And one day, I will pass on that box too. And you can store your special memories in it.

Pamela: I'd like that.

Aiko: I'd like that too.

19 Carl

CARL'S MIND WAS DRIFTING. HE had so much to do he felt paralyzed about where to start. His day was jam-packed with meetings. He had two staff evaluations to finish writing up. He needed to send in three progress reports to his boss and he had to approve a project plan before the end of the day. But he also needed to get Angela to make up her mind about a crib. The baby needed somewhere to sleep. Their inability to decide on the small basics for their child became a metaphor to him that maybe they just weren't ready.

But he knew that they were. He just needed Angela to focus.

But then again, who was he to talk about focus? He had never felt so out of control. His relatively easy-going attitude was rapidly evaporating. There was just so much to do. Is this what parenthood was going to be like? Non-stop worrying and decision making and evaluation of life choices? Or was he just overthinking it?

On top of work and getting their place ready for the baby, he was still planning their trip to Colorado. There was a small museum located nearby called the Amache Museum that he was trying to book an appointment for. He really wanted to see it but was still negotiating the appointments-only timing of the small mom-and-pop exhibit. He was also trying to make sure there were places to stop along the way in case Angela needed to rest. He had never made a packing list before, but now that he was taking his pregnant wife on this pilgrimage, he wanted to make sure she had everything she could need.

It didn't help that he and Angela barely saw each other. Or that when they did, they would bicker. The night he had given her the tickets was such a great night, up to a point. She was with him again, present in the moment, but he could tell the wheels in her head had started turning and she was off in her own world again. He needed this trip, maybe more than she did. He wanted to spend some time with her.

Last night when she got home from work, they had a huge argument. She came in, hot and bothered. "Well, it happened again."

Carl looked up from his book. "What's that?"

"New girl at work today. Someone was telling her about the mandatory trainings throughout the year. Sexual harassment, appropriate language, whatnot. I mentioned that the one on racism was actually pretty good. She looked at me, I could tell she was judging me. I get it. She's Filipino. She thinks I'm white. She gave me that *'What do you know about it?'* look. So, I couldn't help myself. I said, 'You wouldn't believe the crap people have said to me about being half-Asian.' Without skipping a beat, without thinking about it at all, she says, 'You're half-Asian? You don't look half-Asian.' And I said, 'Yeah, crap just like that.'"

"Sounds about right. What did she say?"

"She didn't even get it. She just said, 'What kind of Asian are you?'"

"Really?"

"Yup."

"Did you answer her, or just punch her in the face?"

"I told her I was half-Japanese. She didn't really respond. It's just so frustrating."

"Well…" Carl started, before stopping himself.

"Well, what?"

"Well, you didn't have to tell her. You could have just moved on. You have to admit it. You have this need to prove that you're Asian. It's one of your things."

"It is not one of my things!"

"Okay…"

"I am Asian."

"I know you are. But sometimes it's like you want to bring the racism on."

"Tread very lightly, Campbell."

"I know you wish you looked more Asian. But you don't. You are so beautiful. I wish you could just love the way you are. Exactly how you are."

"Beauty and race are two different things. Maybe I do want to prove myself. Do you know how frustrating it is to identify as Asian and have NO ONE recognize you as that?"

"No, I don't."

"That's right. You have no hidden identity. You are a straight, white, cisgender, well-off, man."

"I can't help that," Carl said quietly. They'd had this conversation so many times. He wasn't sure he was up for it another time.

"Just like I can't help being Asian. And I have to declare it. Every time."

Carl wanted to say, "You don't have to," but thought better of it.

"You know what it reminds me of? I have a friend named Jen at work. And she and her wife Lauren have two kids. And one day she told me that when you are a lesbian couple with kids, you have to come out all the time. You have to constantly explain your family set up. That there are two moms. That you're married. She said she was always revealing herself to the world. It really struck a chord with me. I know it's not exactly the same, but it's the closest I've ever felt to someone explaining it. Every time I meet a new person, I have to say it again. Go through the whole dance. I'm Asian. You don't look Asian. Do you speak Japanese? Why not? It's exhausting."

Carl waited a beat. It was so hard to see her constantly churning like this. "Why do you care so much if people know you're Asian? I mean, honestly, what difference does it make if they think you're white?"

"Because I'm not."

"I know you're not, but who cares if people think that you are?"

Angela sat very still. Carl couldn't tell if she was going to scream at him or concede. He started to feel anxious. Conversations like this were always so difficult with her.

Angela stood up, slowly. She looked straight at him and held up her hand like a stop sign. "If you don't know the answer to that, then there's no way I can explain it to you." She turned and walked away, slamming the door to their bedroom.

This was the worst response. A slow burn anger. He was just sitting on the couch, minding his own business, and now they were in a fight. But he did last night what he had done a thousand times before. He went into the bedroom and did a whole recitation about everything he understood about white privilege and racial inequality and about what her family had gone through and how it had shaped her. He knew all of these things. He appreciated them. He honestly felt like he understood them. His only point was—why was this something people HAD to know about her? It was like she couldn't be happy unless people knew she was oppressed.

He glanced at his email. Seven more messages had come in just since he started spacing out on the Colorado tourism website again. He needed a cup of coffee. He reached into his jacket for his wallet. As he pulled it out, a small piece of paper came out with it, gently falling to the floor. He knew exactly what it was as he picked it up, momentarily panicked that he had ruined it. But it was fine. Unscathed. He turned it over and tears welled-up in his eyes as he looked at it. It was their latest ultrasound photo, one of many, most of which were being used as bookmarks in all of the parenting books he was still plowing his way through. But this one he kept for himself. He stared at the wavy black and white image; his daughter's head as clear as day.

They had just found out they were having a girl and he was completely unsurprised. Of course, they were having a girl. With the way Angela's family was dominated by strong female leads, it seemed impossible that they would have anything else. When the ultrasound technician announced it, he practically had to feign excitement, trying to remember in the moment that this was new information and not the forgone conclusion that he took it to be.

"It's a girl," the technician announced. "You can tell here by these three lines. Three lines means girl."

"Well, what if it were a boy?" Carl asked.

The technician looked at him quizzically. "Well, if it was a boy, there'd be a penis."

Carl felt his face turn bright red with embarrassment. He turned to Angela to see if she was laughing at him, but she was looking at her phone.

They were in the middle of their ultrasound and she was looking at her damn phone. He took the phone out of her hand and put it in his pocket.

"Sorry, work."

"Do you guys want printouts of the ultrasound?" The technician asked, already moving to print them. Carl assumed everyone always said yes. He waited for Angela to say something. But she didn't.

"Yes, of course, we'd love to have them." He turned to her, eyes begging, pleading for her to be engaged in the moment.

She smiled at him and squeezed his hand. "This is very exciting. I will have a lot of fun picking out little dresses."

It wasn't a huge thing, but it was something. And she did remain engaged the rest of the visit. Maybe he should take her phone away from her more often.

The verification of it led to one more thing they had to do: pick a name. Carl had suggested they name the baby Aiko, which sent Angela into a classic tailspin of existential angst. "But she'll be white with a Japanese name, do we really want her explaining herself every day?" "But if we don't name her that, will she ever remember her heritage?" "But if we do name her that, it will be the ultimate way to honor my grandmother, won't it?" "But what if my mom takes offense? I mean my grandmother wasn't always nice." "But, if my grandmother learned racial tolerance, then isn't that a sign of growth, maybe that's what we want in a name?"

Carl largely stayed out of Angela's circuitous conversation with herself and tried to think about what name he would like for their little girl. He erred on the side of simple, easy-to-pronounce, timeless. He liked names like Edna and Clara. Angela said those both sounded like old-people names. But, for the life of her, she couldn't think of anything else. She said they needed to keep "trying names on for size," calling the baby something for a whole day and seeing if it would stick. So far nothing had. Especially not Aiko. Once Carl saw the rabbit hole Angela was going down about Japanese first names, he ruled them out entirely. He didn't want Angela to spend the rest of their lives worrying about the societal implications of a name. Life was hard enough without Angela putting such weight on their daughter's day-to-day identity.

He tucked the ultrasound picture into his top desk drawer and headed out. He needed that coffee. And perhaps a walk around the block. Something, anything to de-fog his brain and get him back to focus. He needed to be the rock. For the people he worked with. For Angela. Being reliable was something he prided himself in. Being easy-going and finding the humor in situations was his signature. He didn't want to lose that part of himself in the haze of getting ready for the baby or in the trip planning or progress-reporting writing or crib-buying. He could do this all at once. He knew he could. He just needed to focus. Focus.

20 Angela

ANGELA'S BED WAS FULL OF clothes, books, and photography and videography equipment. It looked like she was trying to take the whole world with her on this trip. For some reason they had decided that they were only going to check one bag but based on the haul of items splayed out before her, she realized she'd have to convince Carl that they needed two. At least.

The trip was still a few days away, but she was so excited she couldn't help but start the packing process. She had decided to document the whole journey. She was going to pull together a package and try to shop it around with some of the producers that she knew. She had tried to plug it to Malcom, but he quickly scoffed.

"Angela, you are off the rails. We've talked about this. You are not working on *60 Minutes*. Breaking news. Developing stories. Local updates. Why have you forgotten what your job is?"

But she was determined. She didn't know what she'd have when she was done; however, human-interest stories worked in a lot of different formats, especially if she could sell it as a cautionary tale for some of the anti-Muslim / white supremacy movements that were now dominating the airwaves. She just didn't know what she was going to find when she got there. No matter how relevant the story would be, footage of a patch of grass wasn't going to convey her point.

There were a lot of stories popping up about Japanese incarceration lately, at least more than usual. It was like the remnants of what happened to Japanese Americans were still there, percolating under the surface, but never quite brought to the proper boil. Maybe she could change that. Maybe she could create a story that would finally break through. When photographs of Japanese Americans waiting at train stations to be hauled off to camps or being guarded by men with guns behind barbed wire fences materialized on her Facebook and Twitter feeds, she couldn't help but look for her grandmother, both relieved and disappointed she never saw the little twelve-year-old Aiko in any of the pictures. *But she was there*, Angela reminded herself. *She was there.*

"I need to tell this story," she countered to Malcom. "It's so important, and so relevant."

"Relevant to what? You're going to a place that hasn't been used since the 1940s."

"What if I interviewed living survivors?"

"Jesus, Angela, you're not a historian either."

"There are other organizations that have footage of survivor interviews, we could send permission requests."

"I'm going to say this one more time. If one of these old-timers gets hit by a bus, we will run that on the news. If a survivor of a Japanese incarceration camp marches up to the steps of Capitol Hill and stages a protest, we may run a quick hit. But we are not producing a goddamn documentary on your family history or the history of the Japanese American people. Now, take your vacation and then come back with your head in the game."

Angela knew on some level he was right. But she also knew that he just couldn't see her vision yet. She could barely see it herself. She couldn't even figure out how, or if, she fit into it all herself. She hadn't interviewed any survivors yet. She hadn't even reached out to any organization to attempt to.

George Takei was probably the most famous Japanese incarceration camp survivor. His musical, *Allegiance*, was recently on Broadway and Angela had seriously considered flying out to see it, but never made it. She hadn't reached out to him for an interview either. The movie, *Go for Broke*, about the 442nd battalion was also being remade but seemed to be facing promotion challenges and limited distribution. She never even donated to their effort.

Participating in telling the stories of Japanese Americans wasn't even on her radar before Auntie Pammy had given her the tapes and journals. None of the Japanese American events and causes really were. Being hapa was a core tenant of who she was and she let everyone know it. But she was starting to think that she was a fraud, just like the bullies in junior high and high school told her she was. There was this one time in high school when she wrote an article for their school paper about what the movie *Karate Kid II* meant to her—how seeing a white man fall for a Japanese woman somehow validated her existence. She thought it was a funny, quippy piece. The next day she had a note taped to her locker that said, "You will never be Asian." She never wrote about her Japanese identity again.

All this research proved was that she wasn't proud enough of her heritage to actually help preserve it. While her grandmother was still alive, Angela would talk about how her grandmother was in the camps like it was her own badge of honor, that it somehow proved something about her and her family. But she never talked to her grandmother about it.

Now was the time to put her money where her mouth was. Even though she hadn't interviewed anyone yet, she was starting to figure out who the main players were in the community. She had a list of potential contacts. Something though, was still holding her back from reaching out. She tried to explain it to Carl, but he didn't understand.

"You act like going on this trip is going to give you some sort of street cred," he said to her. "Like you'll get your Asian card punched or something."

It wasn't about her "Asian card." Or maybe it was. It was about her level of effort. It was about her walking the walk. She wanted to deserve to be part of the Japanese American community. Not just claim membership like she had been doing all her life.

A few weeks ago, she signed up to receive newsletters from the Japanese American Service Committee in Chicago and the national Japanese American Citizens League. She even made donations to both. But she still hadn't attended any events. Or gone to the JASC. She'd get the newsletters every week in her email and see the events going on and the workshops and the lectures and the seminars and think, *Shit, I don't do any of these things.* The most progress she made was earmarking a few events at the JASC that she wanted to attend, but she was so busy at work, she hadn't had any time.

She had figured out who had written books on Japanese incarceration and who had put together photography exhibits, but she hadn't reached out to anyone. She bought the Encyclopedia of Japanese American History and the

Japanese American National Museum in Los Angeles was next on her bucket list of travel destinations, but she hadn't made any plans to go there. She was coming at this from multiple angles—from her personal family story and from the lens of a TV producer—but she was still going it alone.

One day it hit her. Not only was she bad at being a Japanese American, apparently, she wasn't being a very good journalist either. Somehow this was all still too personal for her. And, if she was being honest with herself, there was a nagging feeling at the pit of her stomach that she didn't deserve to be a part of all of these things. It was the same nagging feeling that had been with her throughout her life. She wasn't actually Japanese. She was just an identity tourist.

She looked at her equipment. She thought it looked like too much to bring. But as she thought about the purpose of each piece, she couldn't find anything that was expendable. She needed all her lenses, her tripod, her Steadicam, her tertiary battery packs. All of it had to come.

As she started to piece together the jigsaw puzzle of fitting it all safely into her suitcase, the doorbell rang. The sound of it startled her completely. She thought about ignoring it, assuming it would be a random delivery person or a salesperson, but something told her to go. She trotted to the front door and opened it.

"Mom, hi. What are you doing here?" Angela said, surprised. "Aren't you supposed to be at work?"

"Hey. I switched my shifts because I knew you'd be home. I know you're going on your trip soon, but before you leave, we need to talk." Judith walked past Angela into the house. It took Angela a couple of seconds to pick her jaw up off the floor and close the front door to follow her Mom.

"Mom, what's up? What do we need to talk about?" Angela paused and thought about when she'd seen her mom last. Could it be that she hadn't seen her since she went over there right after the wake? She had called her mom and told her about the trip. She had thought about asking her to come, but just like with everything else, she chickened out. Convinced herself she had to do this on her own.

Judith sat down on the couch and patted her hand on the adjoining cushion for her daughter to join her.

Angela sat down and waited for her mom to start speaking. She had always felt slightly awkward around her mother, like she was never quite doing the right thing, but this took it to a whole new level. She started to flashback to what her mother looked like on her bed. The dead gaze in her eyes. Angela almost vomited with guilt at the thought that she hadn't seen her since then. Was her mother there to yell at her? To chastise her for being such a bad daughter? That would be uncharacteristic of her mother to do, but it wouldn't be unwarranted. The pain of waiting for Judith to speak seared into her chest.

Finally, Judith took a deep breath and gave her daughter a tentative smile. "Angela, honey, I know you think those tapes give you the whole story of what happened to your Obachan. But there is more. So much more to her story that she never told you. That she never told Pammy either. And, if you're going to go on this trip for her, I think it's about time someone laid out the truth."

21 Judith

JUDITH EYED HER DAUGHTER CAREFULLY. Angela was obviously nervous about what she was going to say next. Perhaps she had made it sound too melodramatic. But it was a bit dramatic. Of course, now that she was here, ready to tell her daughter what she knew, she was at a loss for where to start or what to say. She took a deep breath and began.

"Angela, I know that the tapes tell you about Mom's life in the camps. And I realize my journals give you a picture of what our relationship was like," Judith paused for a second, internally cringing again at the thought of her daughter reading her journals, "but what you may not know, and what my family never talks about, is that one of Mom's sisters died in the camp."

Angela let out an audible gasp. "What? What sister?"

"Mom had a younger sister. Much younger. She was only a toddler when they entered the camps. She was definitely a 'happy accident' baby. And Mom did a great deal to help take care of her. Sometimes I think Mom almost felt like she was her own child."

"What was her name?"

"Her name was Yukiye."

Neither of them said anything for what seemed like a long time. Judith felt a lump in her throat forming.

"You have to understand, for most of my life, I did not know about Yukiye either. Mom never spoke of her. But there was always a sadness to my mother that I never understood."

"How did you find out?"

"I found out because of you."

"Because of me? How's that possible? I feel like you and Dad keep telling me all these things are because of me. That's like, too much."

Judith smiled. Her daughter always had the most expressive facial movements. Right now, her entire face looked like a question mark.

"Never underestimate what a new life can do to change things," Judith said as she glanced at her daughter's growing pregnancy bump. "When I found out I was pregnant with you, I knew I wanted to give you a Japanese middle name. And I was looking some up at the library one day and came across one I really liked. As you know, at that time, my relationship with my mother was strained to say the least. But I still wanted to know what she thought of the name, so I called her and asked her if she liked it. If you haven't guessed already, the name was Yukiye."

"Oh. My. God. What are the odds? I mean, what did Obachan say?"

"She threw a fit. She thought I had somehow found out about her sister and was trying to hurt her by bringing it up. But of course, she didn't come right out and say that. She was basically just ranting and raving. It was fairly unintelligible. But I do remember she called me some awful names. And, quite honestly, I thought I might never speak to her again."

"Holy crap. Mom, how did you find out the truth?"

"Well, after she basically hung up on me, I didn't really know what to do next. I cried and cried and tried to figure out why she was so upset. But none of it made any sense."

"Whoa."

"Yes, whoa. And then, about a week later, she called me."

"That doesn't sound like Obachan."

"No. It was a rare moment indeed. Sometimes I wonder if it actually happened. But it did. I remember the day so clearly. Somehow just from the tone of the ring...remember this was before caller ID...I could tell it was her. I remember shaking as I picked up the phone. I was ready to be so mad at her but a part of me, this whisper inside of me, told me to shut up and listen. And, while she didn't apologize, she at least seemed to concede that there was no way I could have known who Yukiye was and proceeded to tell me the story of her little sister and why she got so upset."

"Do you remember what she said? I mean, I can't believe you didn't journal about this."

"Well, I don't think the journals you have go all the way up to the '80s, do they? Never mind, I don't want to know. And even if they did, I know I didn't write it down. It wasn't my story to tell. Even to myself. I knew I was meant to listen. And then to bury it just as she had. The only person I ever told was your father. Because, well, I tell him everything."

"You didn't even tell Auntie Pamela?"

"No, not even her. To this day I don't think she knows."

"She would want to know, Mom. I can't think of anyone who would want to know more."

"Maybe, but that's not our way."

"What do you mean?"

"If you hadn't noticed, our family isn't big on talking about things. Not important things at least. We keep them hidden. Locked away. Mom used to say that the only way to move forward was to leave the past behind. Or at least that was the sentiment. I think her actual words were more like 'the past is the past' and then a quick chastising look for even trying to talk to her. About anything."

"Why do you think she was like that?"

"I think she had to be. For peace of mind. For sanity. Sometimes I'd hear her crying in her bedroom and wonder what was going on. I never dared to ask."

"What do you think it was about?"

"Who knows? Could have been normal stuff. Maybe she just had a bad day. But the older I get, and the more I think about things, I think maybe she had nightmares. Or just plain regrets. She trained us to be stoic. She trained us to not make waves. It was her survival mechanism."

"But she talked to Auntie Pamela on those tapes, so she couldn't have been completely against talking about the past."

"I will never know how Pammy got her to do those tapes. But I'm glad that she did."

"Mom, you need to tell Auntie Pam about Yukiye, too."

"I know. And before you go on your trip, I plan to tell her. Have you talked to her in a while?"

Angela paused. "No, I guess not since the funeral. I've been so busy at work and with getting ready for the baby."

"You should call her, Angie."

"I know I should. I will. But, Mom. You're here telling me about this poor little girl. What did Obachan tell you? What happened?"

Judith smiled at her daughter. Well, internally smiled at least. She had learned over the years that not all of her smiles made it to her lips. Her daughter was just so curious. Always asking questions. Always wanting to know what was next. It was one of her favorite things about Angela. "It's a sad story really. Yukiye caught the flu when they were being transported from the holding grounds at the racetrack to the camps at Amache. Being surrounded by all those people and all that dust was just too much for her little body to take. Once they got to the camps, she never fully recovered. Then one day, she was playing outside and got some kind of rash. They still don't know what she rubbed up against, it may have even been a sun rash. And she scratched the rash so much it got infected. And the infection grew and before they knew it, it was too late. Mom told me she got an infection in her blood and there was nothing they could do."

"That's absolutely horrible."

"Yes. And it greatly affected Mom. Maybe even more than being in the camps did. A part of her died when her little sister did. After that phone call, a part of me understood my mother much better."

"Like why she would sometimes cry in her room?"

"Yes. And no. She always seemed sad to me. And never warm. Never loving. Like I said, maybe she was protecting herself. That she couldn't let herself love us as much as she loved Yukiye because she didn't want to be that hurt again. But…," and Judith paused, holding back real tears now, "…after being a mom for so long myself, I think it's more than that. I think she did love us as much as Yukiye, more even. And that we reminded her of Yukiye, too. And that pain and fear of losing us was almost too much for her to bear."

Angela put her hands on her abdomen for the briefest of moments, and then scooted closer to her mother. She wanted so badly to hug her mother in that moment, but that's just not something that they would normally do.

"Angie, I'm telling you this now, before you leave for your trip, because I have a favor to ask of you."

"Yes, Mom, of course, anything."

"When you are there, at Amache, thinking of Obachan, I want you to think of little Yukiye, too. Our family has never honored her the way that she deserved. And I want that to change with you."

"Okay…"

"I know this is out of the blue."

"No, I mean, yeah. But why did this even come to your mind?"

"When we were at Mom's funeral, and I saw all those people there to honor her. I thought about how little I knew her."

"I did the exact same thing."

"And it dawned on me that even though I didn't know her real life, or all her friends, there was this one thing I knew about her that no one else did. And I held on to that. Like it was something that somehow proved I was her daughter. For weeks I've thought about it."

"So, why are you telling me now?"

"Because I don't want us to end up like that. I don't want you to be standing at my funeral, holding onto stories from the past. Keeping secrets and wondering if things could have been different."

"Mom…"

Judith held up her hand. "I know we aren't close. And that I'm in large part to blame for that. But maybe we can't move on until we bury this secret. Add Yukiye to the family tree. And then say goodbye to her for all of us."

The enormity of what her mother was asking her to do hit her like a ton of bricks. She didn't even feel like she necessarily had the right to go on this pilgrimage and now she was being tasked with honoring someone she had never met, and someone the rest of her family knew nothing about. And in her memory, her mother had never asked her for anything like this before. Or asked anything personal of her at all really. Judith noticed Angela's stillness and thought maybe she had asked too much.

Angela tried to give her mother as reassuring of a smile as possible. "I promise, Mom. I promise I will find a way to honor Yukiye."

22 Aiko

(CLICK)

Pamela: What was the scariest thing that ever happened to you in the camps?

Aiko: Scariest?

Pamela: Yeah, like was there ever anything big that happened that scared you?

Aiko: You talk like it was some kind of action movie.

Pamela: Well, I mean, there were men with guns, right?

Aiko: Yes

Pamela: So...?

Aiko: So, no. I can't remember a big thing that scared me.

Pamela: That surprises me.

Aiko: Why?

Pamela: Because the whole thing is so scary!

Aiko: Yes. Well. Maybe in retrospect.

Pamela: No, Mom, like, in all respects.

Aiko: Well, in the moment, I was a child. I didn't think of things the same way I do now.

Pamela: And if you were an adult? Do you think you would have been scared then?

Aiko: I don't know.

Pamela: You really were never scared?

Aiko: I didn't say I was never scared. I just said nothing big and scary happened. (Pause) I suppose, when you live under a constant fear, you get used to it.

Pamela: Get used to what?

Aiko: Well, we were fenced in. There were guard posts that had men with guns. We were yelled at. And I suppose that was scary. (Long Pause) And even on the best days. When a boy would smile at me from across the room. Or we'd get to order something from a catalog. Or when my friends and I would laugh so hard our sides would hurt. There was still no escaping the fact that we were there. In the desert. With no home to go to.

Pamela: So, it was just kind of an everyday fear.

Aiko: Yes, I think you could put it that way.

Pamela: Do you ever feel that fear now?

Aiko: What do you mean?

Pamela: Like, do you worry you'll get rounded up again? Or do you have nightmares that you are back in the camps?

Aiko: No.

Pamela: No? Really? I think I'd worry about that all the time.

Aiko: I do not think it will happen again. But, if it did, and no one fought for us again. And we were rounded up with no protest again. Then I would know that I would survive it. Because I survived it once. I could do it again.

Pamela: But you weren't a mom before. Wouldn't you worry about us?

(LONG PAUSE)

Pamela: Nevermind. Forget I asked.

Pamela: So, if there was nothing big or scary, were there other moments that stood out? I mean, some people must've died in the camps. Were there funerals?

(LONG PAUSE)

Pamela: Did you know anyone that died?

(LONG PAUSE)

Pamela: Mom?

Aiko: Yes, I knew people that died.

(LONG PAUSE)

Pamela: I'm sorry, I shouldn't have asked.

Aiko: Death is a part of life. So are the good moments, mixed with the bad. The best we can hope for is to live peacefully in the moments in between.

Pamela: Not live for the good moments?

Aiko: In my experience, there are not enough of them.

Pamela: I'm going to try to not take that personally.

Aiko: Pamela, my hope for you is that one day you will understand that we have limited control over our lives or what happens to us. The best we can do is to follow the rules laid out for us and hope for the best.

Pamela: Do you really believe that?

Aiko: Yes.

Pamela: We are going to have to agree to disagree on that one.

Aiko: We have had very different lives.

Pamela: That's true, but I am trying to learn about yours.

Aiko: There isn't much to know.

Pamela: I don't think that's true. (Pause) So, if there wasn't a big scary moment in the camps, was there a big happy moment that you recall?

Aiko: No. There were no big moments. Happy or scary. (Long Pause) And, I think, I think, I don't know how to say this. I think you can't know the ins and outs of a big moment when you're stuck in the middle of one, even after you leave it.

Pamela: So, like, in some ways, you become the moment.

Aiko: Yes. Or at the very least, the moment becomes you.

23 Judith & Pamela

JUDITH LEFT ANGELA'S HOUSE KNOWING she had one more stop to make. She had to see Pamela and talk to her before Angela did. But maybe she had two stops to make. Almost on autopilot, she drove south, past Pam's house to her parents' bungalow. The house she grew up in. The house her father had died in. The house her mother had died in. The house that now sat empty. She hadn't been back since the wake and it was indelibly part of all the memories of her parents. After the wake, Judith and Pamela split the cost of having professional packers and cleaners come in to clear out the house and get it ready for staging to sell. All her parents' things went into a storage locker and the sisters agreed they would go through everything together when they felt more emotionally prepared. So, even though her parents were gone, there was still the huge task of going through their neatly packed and stored belongings. She wasn't sure if she'd ever be ready.

She pulled up in front of the house. Somehow there was always a parking space right in front. She turned the car off and stared at the "FOR SALE" sign in the yard. The sign had just been placed there last week and they had already gotten a few offers. It would have a new family in it before she knew it. It was going to sell for more than she thought it would too. She and Pamela would split the money evenly between the two of them, although they had never talked about it. Her mother's will was as simple as it could be. It said that everything she owned would go to her daughters. They barely had to coordinate.

Judith thought about how little she and her sister had spoken since the funeral. Pamela would probably use her half of the money to continue to take care of their mother, putting it toward her half of the storage locker fees or somehow finding another way to tie the money back to their parents. Was it terrible that she wanted to use at least part of it to go on a trip? She thought about how happy it would make Eddie if they took a true vacation. Somewhere with a beach, and umbrella drinks, and sun that just wouldn't quit.

A wave of guilt washed over her as she realized she was fantasizing about taking money from her dead mother's house to have a holiday. Could she be a more terrible person?

She started the car again and within a few minutes she was at Pamela's. Sometimes she forgot how close Pamela lived to her parents. How easy it made it for Pamela to take care of them and then proceed to tell Judith how much she wasn't doing. It's not like she lived that far. They were all Northsiders. But there was just something inside of Pamela that made her feel like keeping the family together was her responsibility. Like being more than a mile away was somehow a dereliction of duty.

As she closed the car door and started walking toward Pamela's front door, she realized she probably should have called first. It wasn't too late, but how often did people just drop by anymore? Did people ever just drop by? Or was that just a trope from the movies and TV shows of her youth? Angela had dropped by her house the other day. Maybe she was being hip and young.

She rang the doorbell and immediately heard footsteps. The door opened. "Judith," Sheila said, clearly taken aback. "Is everything okay?"

"Yes, thank you. Everything's fine. I just came…There's just something… Is Pammy here?"

"Yes, of course," Sheila said, welcoming Judith in with a further opening of the door and a waving in with her hand. "I'm glad you're here. She's been really missing you."

Judith did her best to smile at Sheila, but honestly didn't know what to say. Had she been missing Pamela?

"Pam, honey, your sister is here."

Pamela came out of the kitchen, wiping her hands with a dish towel. "What did you say? I was just finishing up the dishes…" Pamela's voice trailed off as she saw Judith in their foyer. "Judith, my goodness. What are you doing here? Is everything alright?"

"Yes. Hello. Everything is fine. How have you been?"

Pamela didn't answer, staring at her sister. "I'm going to give you two some time. Pam, I'll be in the bedroom if you need me." Sheila squeezed Pamela's forearm and walked out of view.

"I've been fine, thanks. I guess. How are you?"

"I'm okay. Well, I've been better."

"Been better, what do you mean?"

"Well, I've been seeing the ghost of our mother for one thing," Judith said, trying to ebb the awkwardness with a light laugh. But when she looked up, she saw a look of panic in Pamela's eyes. "Is there somewhere we can go and talk?"

"Yes, yes of course," Pamela said, wringing her hands with the dish towel she was still clutching. "Just let me grab my purse." Judith waited as her sister collected herself, then followed as Pamela walked out the door and led them about three blocks down her street to a small café. They both ordered green tea. Then sat across from each other at a small table in silence.

"So, Mom's ghost. What does that mean?"

"For a couple weeks, after she died, I kept having all these memories. Flashbacks. And I'd see her when I closed my eyes. And then one day I was trying to drive to work and I thought I saw her in my rearview mirror. I swear she was standing there."

"What did you do?"

"I got out of the car and started looking for her. Then I called in sick and Eddie took me to the river for a few days. I got some sleep. And I haven't seen her since. Not in ghost form at least. I still have dreams about her."

"I have dreams too," Pamela replied, quietly.

"You do?"

"Did you ever see Dad's ghost after he died?"

"No. I was too focused on Mom."

"We were all always too focused on Mom."

"Do you think that's because he was fighting in the war, and she was the victim of it?"

Pamela looked like she was really thinking about that. "Mom was no victim. She was just so closed off. I think we were just always trying to please her so she'd open up."

"I miss Dad. I miss his hugs. And his laugh."

"He kept us sane."

"He really did."

"Do you think there are any skeletons in his closet?"

"I don't know. Maybe. Probably. We will never know."

"Why didn't you ever make tapes of Dad like you did with Mom?"

"I don't know, Judy. Why didn't you? And, why didn't you tell me any of this? Seeing ghosts. What the hell is going on? Where have you been?"

"I don't know, Pam. Where have you been?" Judith's voice had more edge to it than she intended it to. She needed to bring the register of the conversation down. "I'm sorry. I didn't mean it like that."

"It's okay. Sheila keeps telling me I should call you. She says I'm pouting like a child."

"She's probably right."

"Sheila's always right," Pamela answered. They both let out a light laugh.

"Why didn't you bring her to the funeral?"

"Listen, Judy, no offense, but I really don't want to talk about that right now. What did you come to say?"

Judith looked at her sister's face. It was so much like their mother's. Stubborn and prideful. Yet wounded in some way. "You know that Angela is going to Amache."

"She's what?" Pamela said incredulously.

"In a couple of days. She's making some sort of pilgrimage."

"Are you going with her?"

"No. It's just her and Carl. I haven't talked to her much since the funeral either. I only know what I do through a few texts and calls I've gotten from her. And I gleaned a little more from seeing her tonight. I was just there, telling her the same thing I need to tell you."

"What's going on, Judith?"

"Did mom ever tell you about Yukiye?"

"Her sister Yukiye?"

Judith sat there stunned. She honestly thought she was the only one who knew. "Yes. Her sister Yukiye."

"Yes, she told me about her. But it wasn't until just a few years ago. When did she tell you?"

"When I was pregnant with Angela. I was thinking about giving her a Japanese name and called Mom out of the blue to ask her what she thought of the name Yukiye, and she lost it on me."

"You called Mom when you were pregnant? But you weren't talking then."

"No, we weren't. Not really. But, when I found out I was pregnant, I called to tell her and Dad. And then I called a few more times before Angie was born, too."

"I had no idea."

"Apparently the Oshiro's are good at keeping secrets," Judith replied.

"What's that supposed to mean?" Pamela said, almost standing up, but forcing herself to stay seated.

"Nothing. It means nothing."

"Is that why you came here? Because you thought I didn't know about Yukiye?"

"Yes. Because I asked Angela to honor her when she goes to Amache. Because I feel like we need to let some parts of our past go. I've been holding onto Yukiye's story for decades. I wanted to finally put it to rest." Judith felt her head hang down. She was so tired. She looked up at her sister. "Why did Mom decide to tell you?"

"I was working on the family tree one day. And I called her to ask her if she knew the middle names of some people—like some of her uncles or some of the people on Dad's side—and she told me to make sure Yukiye was on there. And I got confused because I didn't recall there being a Yukiye on either side of the family. And Mom got all flustered because she said she thought she had told me already. At the time I thought it was one of her memory slips. You know how she was toward the end. But now, I guess, she was just remembering telling it to you."

"Or maybe she just assumed she had told you, since you guys talked about a lot of things with those tapes."

"Maybe. Either way. It's a sad story."

"They are all sad stories," Judith answered.

"No, they aren't. Our family is full of really amazing stories."

"I guess I wouldn't know."

"All you have to do is ask."

"If only that were so. Why didn't you tell me about Yukiye then?"

"You've never really been interested in the family tree stuff. But that's a pot calling the kettle black. Apparently, you've known for decades. Why didn't you tell me?"

"It wasn't my story to tell."

"That's a lame excuse."

"Mom asked me not to tell anyone."

"I'm not just anyone."

Judith took a sip of her tea. It was starting to cool. She hated drinking lukewarm tea.

"So…Amache," Pamela continued, "Why aren't you going? You could have honored Yukiye yourself."

"Angela didn't ask me to go."

"Would you have if she did?"

"Probably not."

"Because that's not your story to tell either?"

"Angela's on some sort of mission. You can see it in her eyes."

"A mission to do what?"

"I'm not sure. But giving her those tapes and journals has changed her."

"So now this is all my fault?"

"Jesus, Pammy. I didn't say that."

"So, Angela is listening to the tapes?"

"Yes. And I told her she should call you. She said that she would."

"Well, she hasn't."

"I think she's waiting."

"Waiting for what?"

"Until she's figured it out."

"You're talking in riddles. Just spit it out. Figured what out?"

"Figured out what having this baby means. To her. To the family. She's freaking out about being a mom, so she's burying herself in work and looking for answers in all the wrong places."

"Sounds like you have some experience with that."

"Maybe we are all destined to live out our parents' lives over and over again."

"So, what part of Mom's life are we living out right now?"

"The part where we bottle up the pain so tightly it only comes out in fits and bursts."

"And in ghost sightings."

Judith laughed. "Yes, and in ghost sightings," she paused. "Do you think that's why Mom used to cry sometimes? Because ghosts were talking to her too?"

"I think Mom was a ghost."

"What do you mean?"

"There was the person she was born. From all accounts free-spirited. A little boy crazy. Fun. And then there was the person we knew. Guarded. Paranoid. Stoic. Those camps ghosted her. And ghosted us in return."

"Do you think I should stop Angela from going to Amache?'

"Sounds like nothing would stop her from that. And, you're probably right. If we say Yukiye's name out loud, maybe we can put one more secret to bed."

"Do you think secrets are what are holding us back?"

"Holding us back from what?"

"I'm not even sure."

Judith and Pamela sat there for a few minutes more before Judith finally stood up. "I need to get home. I've been gone longer than I thought. I'm sure Eddie is worried," she paused and looked at her sister. She knew she should say something profound, something big sister would say, but nothing came to her mind. "Thank you."

Judith walked her sister home. As she turned to leave Pamela at the front door, Sheila opened the door, clearly anticipating Pamela's return. Judith paused and soaked in that moment, Shelia and Pam standing together, arm in arm in the doorway. "Thank you for taking care of Pam, Sheila. I have always been happy that she found you." Pamela's face lit up in surprise. And then morphed into a smile.

"I'm happy she found me too," Sheila replied, holding Pamela a little tighter.

As Judith got into her car and drove away, Sheila closed the front door and looked at Pamela. "Well that was certainly an interesting visit."

"Judy got one thing right," Pamela said as she wrapped her arms around Sheila and rested her head on Sheila's chest.

"Oh yeah, what's that?" Sheila said as she kissed the top of Pamela's head. "I am happy I found you too."

24 Edward

EDWARD WAS TRYING NOT TO pace around his living room, but he couldn't help it. Every time he tried to sit down, read a book, or watch TV, his nervous energy would get the better of him and he'd be back on his feet.

Judith had left for Angela's hours ago. He normally wasn't such a hover when it came to her time and where she went, but these weren't normal times. She was just starting to seem like her old self again. He had put all his energy into taking care of her, into being there for her. Her recovery was his number one priority. And now she was walking into the emotional equivalent of a lion's den.

He looked at his watch again. When she left, Judith told him she didn't even think she'd be gone an hour. Now it was zeroing in on three. His imagination got the best of him. Was she sitting in her car somewhere, seeing images of her dead mother? Had that caused a car accident? Did she decide to just leave and never come back? Was Angela having to deal with her mother in a sorry state? Judith had said she never wanted her daughter to see her that way again.

He thought about his wife and all that she had been through. He calmed himself with the thought that she was healing. But, as with most healing, a few new wounds opened before she could fully recover. Judith started opening up to him about the grief around Aiko's death and, perhaps prompted by Angela's new family heritage obsessions, Judith started talking about the family history too. He was surprised when Judith brought up Yukiye, although part of him knew he shouldn't have been. And as the days passed, Judith kept saying how she didn't want to be the only one in the family to know that story, that Yukiye deserved to be part of the family history too.

Edward wondered why Judith didn't start with Pamela. After all, Pamela was the family historian. She knew more about them all than they could ever imagine. She kept the family tree. She made all those tapes Angela was obsessed with. But Judith didn't even seem to consider it. She was adamant that Angela would be her confidante.

Just as Edward was about to make another lap through the kitchen, he heard steps walking to the front door. He practically ran to greet her, his heart jumping into his throat as the eternity passed between the key entering the keyhole and the door opening toward him.

As soon as he saw her face, he started breathing again. She didn't look distraught. Quite the contrary. She looked lighter, maybe even relieved. As he approached her, she smiled. He grabbed her into a tight hug. "I take it it went well?"

"Yes," Judith said as she squeezed him back. As they reluctantly disconnected, she began taking off her coat and set it on their coat rack. "I am glad I told her."

"You were gone for so long; I was starting to get worried."

Judith looked at him with the same face she had for years. The face that told him she knew him better than he'd ever know himself. She placed one hand on the side of his face, "Starting to?"

He smiled. Of course, she knew.

"I'm sorry I didn't call or text. I should have. And I'm sorry that I worried you. I stopped by Pammy's too."

"You did?"

"Yes, I wanted to tell her about Yukiye as well, but she already knew."

"Of course, she did."

"Both conversations were so awkward. I wish I was better at…being a person."

Edward laughed. "You're the most amazing person I know."

"So amazing I made you worried sick."

"That's my own fault. And, don't worry about it. I understand. I'm sorry I assumed the worst."

"I don't blame you," she said as she walked to the kitchen and poured herself a glass of water. "I would've assumed the worst as well."

"So, Pamela already knew. How did Angela take the news of Yukiye?"

"About how you'd expect. Stunned. But in a wonder kind of way."

"Did you ask her?" He took a seat on one of the kitchen stools, knowing in his heart she was fine but still scanning her face for any signs of fatigue or distress.

"Yes. And she said she would honor Yukiye while she was there." Judith came around the kitchen island and leaned into Edward. He slid his arm around her waist as he had a million times before. It was where his hand belonged. "I almost wish I could go with her."

"I think this is something she needs to do on her own," Edward replied, half meaning it, half wanting Judith to stay right here where the whole reality of her mother's internment couldn't trigger her feelings of mother-daughter guilt.

"I agree. And she will document it well. She's so much like Pammy that way."

"This coming from the queen of journals."

"Ah yes, but those were entirely self-serving. Pammy and Angela make things that are meant to be shared." Judith took another sip of water and kissed Edward on the cheek. "Thank you for worrying about me."

Edward looked at her, hard. She was so strong. Stronger than he could have ever imagined. He remembered back to the days when Angela would come home after being bullied for being mixed race. The look of utter defiance in her face as she went straight to the parent contact list, found the address of the family's house, and drove straight there to talk to them about it. Or the day they dropped Angela off to college. She was a force of nature, getting Angela everything she needed, making sure every possible need of Angela's was met, and how she held him when they got home to the empty house and he wept at the departure of their daughter. She held him. It was about time he got the chance to return the favor. "You have always taken care of me. I will always take care of you."

They kissed. A good, long kiss. After all these years, it still excited him to kiss her. He could not imagine ever tiring of it.

As they pulled back, she smiled at him. "I know we aren't going to go with Angela to Amache, but I do think we should make a little trip of our own," she said.

"Oh yeah? To where?"

"I was thinking maybe Hawaii."

"Ooo, Hawaii. I like the sound of that," he said as he kissed her neck.

"I think it would be fun. We deserve a vacation."

"Yeah, we do," Edward said, beaming with delight. She really was turning the corner. They hadn't been on a good vacation in years.

"And, I know this isn't very vacation-y, but I want to see if I can find a way to find out a little bit about my father while we are there. My whole life, we've been so wrapped up in my mother's story, we never really took the time to focus on him. Even at his funeral, it was about how we were going to take care of my mom. I know he was a quiet force behind their marriage, but it never seemed like it. She was always the one in control."

"Hmm, a relationship where the woman dominates the landscape. I wouldn't know anything about that," Edward teased.

"Oh, shut up," Judith replied as she playfully pushed him. "I was nowhere near the diva my mother was."

"That's true," Edward conceded. "We can vacation and find a way to think of your dad."

"You know, Dad was on the island when Pearl Harbor was bombed."

"Yes, I have heard something about that," he teased. Her dad's stories from the day of the bombing were legendary tales, always told with a dramatic flair. "Somehow, all the Hawaiian words in his lexicon would come out when he would tell us."

"Ha. True."

"So, this is really happening? We are going to swim in the ocean, walk the beaches, see the sunset over the Pacific?" He kissed her after every question, and he could feel her body smile.

"Well, we'd do other things too."

"Yeah we will," he said as he nuzzled his face into her neck.

"I meant going to see the sights," she said with a small laugh.

He looked up at her again and kissed her forehead. "I only have one question," he smiled.

"What?"

"When do we leave?"

25 Pamela

Dear Diary,

It's been five months. Five months since my mother died. Five months since the funeral. Five months since I gave Angie the journals and tapes. Five months since I removed myself from the role of family documentarian. Family author. Family keeper. I knew Angie wouldn't take on the responsibility if I asked her to do it. But, she's so much like me, I knew she'd dive into it if it was presented to her through curiosity. As a puzzle to solve. A story to chase. She's SO much like me that way.

Sheila's always telling me to be more honest with the people close to me, but honestly, shouldn't they have to do some of the work too? I'm so disappointed Angie hasn't included me more. Okay, okay, more than disappointed. I'm hurt. There, I said it. Maybe not to her, but at least I'm saying it to myself now. I mean, all those tapes are there because I recorded them. All those journals are there because I saved them. I've heard that she's obsessed with them. But not from her. She hasn't called me to talk about them. She has not picked up the damn phone. Or emailed. Or texted. Or ANYTHING.

I thought she'd have a million questions for me. That it might bring us closer. I thought that I could dispel some of my grief over losing Mom by becoming a little bit closer to Angie.

But it hasn't happened that way.

I know I'm a big girl. I could just call her and ask her how it's going. But I want her to call me. I want her to thank me. Truth be told, I want her to praise me for all the work that went into preserving our family history like this. Gosh, isn't that terrible? I am expecting my niece to help me with my grief through some form of positive reinforcement. Come on, Pam, grow up!

But seriously, would it be too much to ask for her to just call me?

And now she's going to Amache. She hasn't asked me about that either. I know she's going with Carl, but I would love to go on that trip. And Judy just called me to say that she and Eddie are going to Hawaii. Both of them taking these family pilgrimages and neither of them inviting me. Me, who got this whole ball rolling.

Would that be too much to ask?

I just have to decide if I want to be the bigger person. If I should just call Angie and tell her how I feel. Or maybe I should call Judy and have her tell Angie to call me. Oh my gosh, I sound like a crazy person. I just wish I was a part of what was going on.

I miss my Mom.

XOXO,

Pam

26 Judith, Angela & Carl

October 23, 1975

Pammy's trying to broker peace again. She made a scrapbook from the wedding this summer and gave it to Mom and Dad for Mom's birthday. I can only imagine the look on Mom's face when she opened it. Mom does not care about sentimental crap like that. "The less you have, the less you carry." How many times has Mom said that to us in our lifetime? But Pammy thought it would show Mom how much she missed by not being there. Apparently, it didn't go over well. Mom started crying. Pammy tried to convince me she was crying because she was upset she missed the wedding, but I know what she was really crying about. She was crying because she thinks I'm betraying her and our family. She's so messed up. She's just so messed up.

○○○

ANGELA RUBBED HER BELLY AS she looked out the cab window. There wasn't any traffic on the way to the airport, which surprised her and oddly disappointed her. Part of her wanted it to take a long time so that she could ease her way into the trip, daydream a little longer before the chaos of checking bags and the security line.

Just recently the baby had started to kick, making her eminent arrival all the more real. What would she tell her daughter about this trip?

Carl must have seen the look of anxiety on her face because she felt him squeeze her hand. She gave him a small squeeze back, but never turned away from the window.

This was it. She was on her way to Colorado. She just wished she could tell Obachan what she was doing.

The cab driver broke into her thoughts to ask what airline they were taking. Carl answered as Angela heard the tires of the cab make start-and-stop halting sounds as they approached the airport, something they did to the roads to slow down drivers as they approached the departure gates. She had been to O'Hare so many times. That sound was ingrained into her brain. Would her daughter know it too?

As they approached the gate a quiet stillness came over Angela. She had never had an out-of-body experience before, but maybe this is what people were talking about whey they said they did. She barely registered the people around her as Carl checked their bag. She barely noticed the passage of time as they weaved their way around the black canvas crowd lines to get to the security gate. She didn't really snap to consciousness until they were sitting at their gate and Carl asked her to watch his backpack while he went to the bathroom. "What?" she asked. He smiled at her and simply said, "It's okay. Just stay here, I'll be right back."

Had he been talking to her the whole time? Or was he that good at giving her space?

She rubbed her belly again and started thinking about baby names again. She was coming around on Edna, but she hadn't told Carl that yet. She had gotten past the "old lady" sound of the name and was too caught up on it sounding too much like her Dad's name. Really, she just kept calling her daughter different things to see if something would stick. She found herself scrolling through baby name websites on her phone. Nothing popped out as appealing.

Carl made his way back to her and gently squeezed her hand again. "What's going on in that brain of yours?"

"I was just thinking about names again," she replied.

"I think we should pull a *How I Met Your Mother* and give the baby the middle name 'Wait for It,' and call it a day."

Angela smiled. "You would think that," she teased back.

"Anything in particular popping out for you today?"

"Honestly, I was thinking about Edna until I thought about how much it sounded like Edward."

"Dang, I hadn't thought about that," Carl replied.

"I don't know. I may be back onto Japanese names again."

"What? Really?"

"Yeah, I mean. I just want this baby to know where she came from. At least," Angela paused. "At least more than I did."

"She will, honey. I promise. Come on, it's time to board."

Carl smiled as he felt Angela's nose nestle into his arm. She fell asleep almost as soon as the plane took off, immediately scooping up his arm after the wheels left the runway for her own personal pillow. He loved the feeling of her holding him, any part of him. He lightly kissed the top of her head and was surprised as he felt a sob well up in his chest. He swallowed deeply to push it back down. Where did that come from?

He picked up his book to try to distract himself. He was reading *A Different Mirror: A History of Multicultural America* by Ronald Takaki. Someone at work had recommended it to him. He loved it, but it was also a bit jarring. He had never given the circumstance of his existence or his privilege much thought. The privilege to be anonymous. Unquestioned. Unchallenged. To be accepted in nearly every setting. To walk through life without any insecurity about whether or not he should be there. To never have a fear around who he was or what he looked like. He used to equate the awkward feeling he might get if he went into a different cultural setting, like the first time he went with his friend Ash to a Shabbat dinner or when he was his friend Indra's date to her cousin's wedding. He had never experienced a Hindu wedding before and it completely overwhelmed him, in the best way possible, a feast for the eyes and the senses. But even then, it was just the delight and awkwardness of something new. He never felt like violence, prejudice, or any other repercussions would occur from his presence. He never felt anything but entitled to his experiences.

The more he tried to focus on the page, the more his eyes wouldn't let him. They were too tired and his brain was too consumed by his emotions to focus. When would he get his focus back? He turned his head toward the window and looked out at the clouds. How strange a sensation to know that you were moving 500 miles per hour but felt like you were just sitting still.

He leaned his head back and closed his eyes. He thought about Angela and everything they were about to see and witness. "You will be her rock. You will be her pillar. You will be her strength." He kept repeating that mantra to himself over and over again. He wanted to be totally there for her, so that she could experience every emotion she needed to and lean on him whenever she wanted to. Another odd sensation…to know that you were about to experience one of the most emotional moments of your life and that you chose to put yourself through it. Would it be as overwhelming as he anticipated it would be? Would it be a near-religious experience? Or would he just be standing in a field in Colorado? There was literally no way to know.

He hadn't wanted to tell Angela, but their recent projects had gotten him thinking about his own family heritage, a mix of German and British. He even sent in for one of the genealogy tests only to get the results—surprise! You're white! Part of him was hoping there would be some hidden East Asian in him so that he could show her they were connected in that way, but when he got the results they seemed so silly that he never even told her he took the test.

He did text his mom though to see if they had any old family recipes or stories she could share. In all honesty, she didn't really. They were apparently as American as apple pie, their main culinary roots deriving from salads that had marshmallows in them and random fruits and vegetables that were inexplicably pickled. So, he decided to continue to ride on the coattails of Angela's journey.

It did not escape him that their baby's birth would officially mean that he had genetic roots to the Japanese American story, including the incarceration camps. That he was connected to this godforsaken chapter in American history—but also to the incredible decade's resilience that came after it. He was sure his family must have had a similar resilience at some point, but it was forgotten now.

He took another deep breath and did his best to look down at his wife. Is that what Angela feared? That eventually her family would be a whitewash of "nothing-roots" to a history that had no real meaning or relevance to today? He shuddered at the thought. Maybe he would have to revisit his family's history and learn more about the first of his ancestors to come to America, learn about what their lives had been like and what they had to do to survive in a new country.

He shook off his feelings of discontent and reminded himself that his job now was to take care of Angela. His chest swelled with a near sob again as he felt his arm sleeve wetting with just a bit of moisture from her mouth. Sometimes the reality of her…that she was there…that they found each other…that they chose each other…that he got to be the one that got to be with her…to touch her…to hold her…completely overwhelmed him. He knew he got the better end of the deal when he married her. She was out of his league and he would spend the rest of his life trying to be a better person for her. And now, trying to be a better person for their daughter. Even if they weren't in the best place now, they would be again.

He placed another kiss on the top of Angela's head and took a deep breath in. Whether it was love or pheromones or something as simple as how much he liked the smell of her shampoo, the essence that filled his lungs on his inhale finally broke him. Tears started silently streaming down his face. He was the luckiest man on the planet. Even when he didn't fully understand her. Even when things were entirely perfect. He loved her so much. And, no matter what, he was going to make sure that Angela and their daughter were taken care of. "You will be her rock. You will be her pillar. You will be her strength," he echoed before pausing and changing it forever: "You will be their rock. You will be their pillar. You will be their strength."

27 Judith

JUDITH CHECKED HER PHONE FOR the hundredth time that day. Angela should have landed in Colorado by now and Judith was sort of anticipating that she would get regular texts. She had to remind herself that there probably weren't any updates as of yet. Their plane was scheduled to land only a couple hours ago. Still, Judith did the mental math one more time. The airplane landed two hours ago. It takes 15-20 minutes to get to the gate. Then they have to walk to baggage claim and wait for their bags. Then they have to get the rental car. All of that could take a good hour. All in all, there was a very good chance they weren't even on the road from the airport yet. She looked at her watch again. Why was time moving so slowly?

"You know, a watched pot never boils," Edward said, startling her as he walked into the kitchen. "You're going to burn a hole in the kitchen floor if you keep up all this pacing."

"I know, I know. I just wish I knew what was happening."

Edward checked his watch. "They probably are just leaving the airport."

Judith tried hard not to roll her eyes. Why was he so calm anyway? Their pregnant daughter was on a family odyssey and he was acting like this was any other day.

Edward, as always, seemed to sense her every thought and mood and kissed her forehead. "It will all be okay. She's going to check in. She's going to tell us every detail. And she's at the perfect part of her pregnancy for this. Just try to relax."

Judith gave him a half smile and wondered if the words "just try to relax" had ever worked on anyone ever. By the time someone was saying, "just try to relax" wasn't it too late anyway? Plus, if the rest of the world was anything like her, the words themselves would cause a purely amygdala-based reaction that would provoke the exact opposite response.

She needed a distraction.

She picked up her phone and tried to call Pammy. She'd been trying to call Pammy for a few days but Pammy wasn't picking up. The last time they talked was when Judith had called to tell her about their plans to go to Hawaii. Judith thought stopping by Pammy's house would break the ice and get them back to normal. At least what was normal for them. Usually, they talked at least once a week, even if it wasn't about anything too important. Now that she was feeling better, she was indeed missing her sister.

The last time they talked, it went about as terribly as it could have.

"You're going where?"

"To Hawaii. And I thought while I was there, I could try to learn a little bit about Dad, like we talked about."

"You're going to learn about Dad?"

"Yeah and have a vacation. You know, clear my head. Maybe get rid of the ghosts."

Pamela didn't speak for a long time. "Great. Sounds great, Judy." And then dial tone. Pam hung up. Judith stared at the phone. What had happened?

She honestly thought telling Pammy about Hawaii would be a good thing. That Pammy would be happy for them. Pammy was always telling Judith to take more vacations. Part of her thought she should just drive over to Pammy's house and knock on her door again. But, after getting her voicemail for the umpteenth time, Judith thought that maybe today wasn't the day to do that. The last thing Pammy needed was to be brought into Judith's anxiety over Angela's trip. She probably shouldn't have even tried calling her in the first place. If Pammy wanted to talk to her, she'd call back.

She resumed her pacing around the kitchen, ultimately realizing the pacing was of no help. She washed the few dishes that were in the sink and even dried them and put them away. Then she started scrubbing the counters. And the cabinets looked dirty too. When was the last time she got the industrial grade stuff out and really scrubbed the sink? Soon enough her bucket was out and she was filling it with floor cleaner. But first she needed to take everything out of the fridge, clean the fridge shelves and put everything back in. Then she could clean the floors. She was just about to take it to the next level and put the mop up on the ceiling when her phone finally beeped. It was a text from Angela.

"Made it to Denver just fine. Got the car and are at the hotel for the night. Love you."

Edward walked into the room. Angela had sent him the same text. Judith felt his arms wrap around her waist.

"Do you know what I love most about your worries over our daughter?"

"Oh, please do tell me," Judith retorted.

"The house is SO clean."

Judith turned around and playfully hit him on the shoulder and gave him a small kiss on the chin.

"Oh yeah, are you saying this is a pattern?" Judith answered, knowing full well that it was.

"Didn't you notice that we had every cleaning supply you needed? I stocked up as soon as I heard Angela was taking this trip."

"You did not," Judith said, shocked at the forethought.

"Better to be prepared then re-live the catastrophe of her first week at college. Do you remember that? We had absolutely no cleaning supplies in the house, and you started screaming at me—'How could you let this happen?'—and I had no idea what you were talking about. It took me years to piece together!" he said with a laugh.

"You think you know me so well."

"I do. I do indeed. But do you know what else I know?"

"What's that?"

"That our daughter, who never cleaned up her room, who went through her 'I don't need to shower' phase in high school, that still to this day doesn't know that you have to change the air filter in the central air unit and just thinks it happens automagically instead of Carl doing it, will NOT be cleaning like this when we are in Hawaii."

"You don't know. Maybe she has a latent cleaning gene," Judith said as she rested her head on Edward's shoulder. "I just hope she finds what she's looking for out there."

"She will, hon. I am sure she will."

Judith smiled at her husband and honestly felt better. Still, there was a lot of trip left and her nervous energy was at an all-time high. "As long as I'm already in the zone," she said, "I'm going to go clean the bathroom."

As she darted in that direction, she heard Edward say, "There's a whole new bottle of tub and tile cleaner under the sink."

She couldn't help but smile. He really had thought of everything. Before she made it to the bathroom though, she circled back to the kitchen. Edward was sitting on one of their kitchen stools. She reached passed him and grabbed her phone. "You know, just in case." And with a sheepish smile, she was off to see what else she could keep herself busy with until her daughter texted again.

28 Angela

THE SUN WAS BRIGHT ENOUGH that Angela figured it was finally an acceptable hour to wake up. She had been tossing and turning all night, the anticipation of their drive to Amache and the discomfort of trying to sleep without her big pregnancy pillow duking it out for what could disrupt her sleep more. She sat up on the side of the bed and picked up her phone from the nightstand and let out an audible grunt.

"What…what is it?" Carl said sleepily, rolling over toward her and placing his hand on her lower back. Angela immediately felt better. He knew how much her lower back had started to hurt and he tried to rub it whenever he could. Even just his hand on it made her feel more relaxed.

"Nothing, just…" she let out a big sigh, "…just still no text from my mom."

Carl didn't say anything. He knew Angela would keep going.

"She comes over to my house to drop this bombshell of a story. Then she bugs me for days to tell her everything about the trip. And I text her that we arrive, and nothing. No response. My dad takes the time to respond. Remember? He said, 'We are glad you arrived safely. Drive safe and we love you!' But my mom—nothing. Apparently, she's too busy to acknowledge that we're even here. I should have known as much. Unless it involves her directly, she just doesn't care. She's always been like this—stuck in her own little world, half the time pretending like I don't exist."

Carl scooted up and sat behind her and began rubbing her lower back in earnest. "Angie, you know that's not true."

"I just thought that she'd have more interest in this trip than she has in other things. I mean, she really opened up when she came over and told me about

Yukiye. And I feel like I know her so much better after reading her journals. I'm just sad we're back to the same old mom—distant. Uncaring."

Carl gave Angela a tight hug. "Your mother is many things. Confusing is one of them. But she cares. You know, I bet your father was just responding for the both of them. He did say 'we.'"

"Argh, stop trying to defend her!" Angela said as she stormed into the hotel bathroom. She could hear Carl fall back into the bed. A part of her wanted Carl to be right. But she had her whole life's experience as proof otherwise. She angrily brushed her teeth and then stepped into the shower, hoping the longer she stood under the hot water, the more her feelings of disappointment would wash away. This wasn't the way she wanted to start the day. They were about to embark on one of the biggest adventures of her life. Something truly meaningful for the whole family. She needed to get her mind in the game.

She turned the water to cool for a moment before she got out and started doing another mental inventory of the equipment she'd brought with her that she'd want to use to film at Amache. Turning her brain to professional mode always helped calm her down.

When she got out of the bathroom, Carl was standing by the window, talking on the phone.

"Yes, yes. That's true. We won't forget." He turned toward Angela. "Ah, here she is out of the shower, you can tell her yourself. One sec." He held his hand out for Angela to take as he whispered, "It's your mom."

"She called?" Angela whispered back.

"No, I called her."

Angela stared at him with disbelief as she took the phone from Carl. Why was she nervous to talk to her own mother? Her wet hair was dripping down her back, soaking the hotel robe she had just put on. She took a deep breath and took the phone. "Hi, Mom."

"Good morning! I was just telling Carl that I was looking at the forecast and there might be some light rain in Colorado today, so you'll want to remember to bring some extra plastic bags for all your cameras just in case."

"You were looking at the weather in Colorado?"

"Yes, I wanted to be able to visualize your day as much as I could. Your dad introduced me to the satellite view on Google maps last night too. Doesn't look like there will be much to see when you get there but it's hard to tell. I'm sure being there will be different."

"You looked up images on Google maps?"

"Yes, Angela. Are you okay? Why do you keep repeating whatever I say into question form?"

Her mother's chastising tone snapped her out of it. "Yes, I'm fine. We will send you updates along the way."

"Yes, please do. And please send some to Pammy too. I'm sure she'll want them as well, although I don't know what she's really been up to lately. Maybe you'll get more of a response from her than I have."

"Yes, that's a good idea. I will do that. Things okay between you two?"

"Yes. I'm sure they are fine. You know Pammy. Okay…well…I will let you go. I know you have a long drive in front of you and it will be a big day for you."

"Thanks, Mom. Say bye to Dad for me."

"Of course. Bye."

"Bye." Angela stood dumbfounded, staring at the phone in her hand. She looked over to Carl. "She was looking up images on Google maps. She was looking up the weather."

"I heard," he said, trying hard not to have an "I-told-you-so" tone in his voice.

"What prompted you to call her anyway? How? Why?"

"It's actually kind of fun to see you this flummoxed," Carl said teasingly. "Your mom loves you, Angie. It's amazing to me that you can't see it sometimes, but she does. She doesn't communicate the way you want her to, but it's right there, plain as day."

Angela felt the tears coming fast and furious as he was speaking. She wanted to blame the pregnancy hormones, but the emotional disconnect between her and her mother was a dam that was always at the ready to break. "I thought this afternoon was supposed to be when I had the emotional breakdown," she managed to say.

She sat down on the bed and Carl sat down next to her. "There's no rule that says you can only have one emotional breakdown in a day." He kissed her on the cheek and gave her a little squeeze and said, "My turn to shower," and left Angela sitting on the bed. She looked at the phone in her hand again and thought about her mother. It was almost too much to process but she made herself a promise, right then and there, that she would try to see her mother in a new way. A different way. Then rubbed her belly with the other hand. "And I promise you, little one…you and I will be different. You will never, not once, doubt how much I love you."

29 Aiko

(CLICK)

Pamela: Let's talk again about how you got to the camps. You said you were taken to Manzanar, but was that your first stop?

Aiko: No. Yes. We might have briefly been taken to Santa Anita.

Pamela: What's Santa Anita?

Aiko: It was a racetrack. And they set it up as a place to go after the relocation order went into effect.

Pamela: How many people were there?

Aiko: I have no idea. Hundreds. Maybe thousands. Seemed like millions, although I know that couldn't be true. (pause) Honestly, I'm having trouble remembering the sequence of things. You'd think I'd know how long I was in each place, but I really don't.

Pamela: What do you remember about it?

Aiko: The hay. I was allergic to the hay.

Pamela: How allergic?

Aiko: Not deathly, but enough. It made my eyes water and my nose run and I itched all over. But there was no escaping it. They made us sleep in the horse stalls and we had to use the hay in our bedding.

Pamela: That sounds awful.

Aiko: It was awful. We went from our home to being treated like animals. (pause) But we were all certain it was temporary. And we were all stunned into silence.

Pamela: Did you get any medicine for your allergies?

Aiko: No. Although, I didn't ask. I'm not sure there was even a nurse there. There was one nurse at Amache, but I don't recall seeing one at Santa Anita.

Pamela: How long were you there before you went to Manzanar?

Aiko: I honestly don't remember.

Pamela: Longer or shorter than how long you were at Manzanar?

Aiko: Shorter, for us. But I know some families were at Santa Anita for a long time.

Pamela: So, you reported as ordered, were forced to live in horse stalls, were shipped to another relocation center, all before ending up at Amache.

Aiko: Yes, that is how I recall it.

Pamela: Do you think it may have happened differently?

Aiko: No, I think that's right. Sometimes it feels like that time in my life was a total blur. Sometimes I remember it with perfect clarity. There was one night, this piece of hay was just sticking into me. And no matter where I moved or how I turned, I could feel it. It was like the princess and the pea, only I was no princess. And I remember crying and was very near close to screaming and my mother yelled at me to not make a fuss. But the piece of hay just kept poking me. It took me a long time to realize it had gotten stuck in my underwear and after I pulled it out, there was a big red mark on my thigh which everyone in my family had to see, because we were all in that horse stall together.

Pamela: No privacy then.

Aiko: No, privacy was not a part of that time.

Pamela: What else do you remember, about arriving at Amache?

Aiko: I remember having hope it would be better than where we had come from. That we had some hope that our homes would be more than what we had in our horse stalls or the barracks. And maybe they were. But I still remember my mother's wet eyes when she saw where we were assigned. And how small it was. And how she used all of her power to not cry. She was determined to make the best of it. Even as a kid I could see that.

Pamela: Why was she determined to make the best of it?

Aiko: Because we had to prove to them that we were not a problem. That if we did what we were asked, they would see us as model Americans. Because, in some way, this was our contribution to the war effort. It was up to us to prove to them we weren't animals. And only animals would make a scene in a horse stall or a barrack or makeshift living quarters. And we were not animals. We were Americans.

30 Pamela

PAMELA LOOKED AT HER PHONE. Her sister was calling her again. She didn't pick up. At some point she knew she would have to, but she wasn't ready. Not yet. She felt kind of lightheaded. That had been happening to her a lot lately. She even went to the doctor, worried she might be in some kind of cancer relapse, but after running a few tests the doctor assured her she wasn't. She was just stressed. Exhausted. Her doctor recommended she consider seeing a therapist.

Pamela almost laughed out loud at the suggestion, imagining what her mother might have said if she found out therapy was even an option. She would have told Pamela that she was weak. That strength comes from within. If that was the case, then these days, Pamela was feeling pretty hollow.

She tried to sit up, willing herself into the day, but her head felt foggy and she was having trouble finding her balance. Why did exhaustion make her wobbly? There was some connection between her head and her legs that she would never truly understand.

But she hadn't been sleeping. Not much anyway. It was like Judy had inceptioned her into seeing visions of their mother and she kept having dreams about her, mostly about her mother yelling at her about not being good enough. "Why are you wearing that? You look like a boy. Wear a dress every once in a while," or, "You're always reading books, but never writing anything. But, if you're always reading, what would you even have to write about?" Those were classics. At least she hadn't lost it like Judy and wasn't seeing the ghost of her mother in her driveway. Still, Sheila was getting pretty fed up. She'd even taken to kicking Pamela onto the couch a couple nights ago.

She needed to figure out how to channel this exhaustion, this grief, this regret into something else, because it was pulling her down and she wasn't sure if she was ever going to get up again.

She did like that Angela had started sending her updates from her road trip. They hadn't really started their true journey yet, but at least there was a hint of her being included. All the last text said though was, "On the road to Amache. Will be a long drive." That wasn't an update. That wasn't even a traffic report. It made her wonder, after all these months, what finally prompted Angela to reach out. Had that been Angela's plan all along? Was it just because Judy told her to? Her heart still panged that she wasn't more involved, but at least she wasn't completely forgotten.

She worked from home and set her own hours, the beauty of freelance editing, so the motivation of getting up and going to the office wasn't available to her. But at a minimum knew she had to shower. Sheila would be pissed if she got home from work and she hadn't showered—again. She dragged herself into the bathroom and as the hot water poured onto her, she thought about the one thing she hadn't given to Angela. The one thing she kept for herself.

After she got dressed, she went to her living room and got out the scrapbook. One of her aunties had made it and it included page after page of newspaper clippings and photographs that had been salvaged across decades. What possessed her auntie to save newspaper clippings from when she was just a child through to when she was an adult was beyond her, but she had, and they were preserved in this one scrapbook. Pamela knew that at some point she should take it somewhere and digitize everything so that it wouldn't ever be lost, but she hadn't done that quite yet. For now, she just sat there, flipping through page by page.

She had thought about giving it to Angela, but told herself she didn't because all these articles could be looked up online. The research could be done so Angela didn't need it. But really it was because this had been gifted to her. It's the one thing she didn't have to create for herself or ask for. She had been chosen as its keeper.

After a few moments, she picked up her phone. Flipping through these clippings drove something home for her—there were too few Japanese American families left in the United States. She felt the weight of that on her shoulders. She always felt the weight of her family on her shoulders. She cared too much about their history. About where they came from. Her father always told her to live in the present more. Her parents, always telling her what her problem was. Ultimately, she let out a deep sigh, staring at old newspaper articles of families being torn apart by being placed in separate camps or killed in the war, and tried to put her life into perspective. She told herself what she always told herself: By comparison, she had it pretty easy.

When she really thought about why she was so upset, she had to finally admit to herself that *she* was the only reason she wasn't talking to her family right now. She could have called Angela to ask her more about her trip. She could have talked to her sister about how she was feeling, even asked to go along with them to Hawaii. The only person losing out was her and it was her fault. Damn, she hated it that Sheila was always right. Sheila and her Mom were actually a lot alike. Both had their own gravitational pull. Her Mom had always taught her that you have to make life what you want it, it won't do it for you. Pamela supposed this was one of those times.

She took another deep breath and picked up the phone to call her sister. She knew her sister's hospital shift schedule and was sure she was off this morning. If she was off, that meant Edward was likely home too. The older Edward got, the more he worked from home. His exact words were, "You can code from anywhere." Thinking of Edward and Judy home together made her miss Sheila. Sheila always left so early in the morning; the life of a high school history teacher.

As the other end of the line started ringing, she debated what she was going to say. She only had a moment, but she knew she'd need an excuse for why she hadn't been answering her phone. She knew better than anyone how easily her sister could channel the guilt and accusatory tone of their mother all too well. When Judith finally answered, she didn't even say hello.

"Where have you been?"

"Hello to you too, Judy."

"Seriously, Pammy, I've been trying you for days. Where have you been?"

"I haven't been feeling well." It was the truth. If only the partial truth.

"What do you mean, do you have a cold?"

Pamela suddenly realized that a recovering cancer patient had to be more specific about what she meant when she said she wasn't feeling well, especially with the sister that took care of her through every cancer treatment.

"Yes, just a cold. I went to the doctor, just to be safe, and she said it was nothing to worry about."

"Well that's good," Judith paused, "but I still don't understand why that means you can't answer your phone."

Knowing that no excuse would ever be good enough for Judith, she settled with, "I'm sorry, Judy. I'm sorry to make you worry. I'm fine. And I'm calling you back."

Judith paused for a moment before replying, "I'm glad you are okay."

After some idle chitchat, Pamela did a gut check and decided it was now or never.

"Judy, I know that you and Eddie deserve some couple time, and that a trip to Hawaii is an inherently romantic venture, but I was wondering…I was wondering if I could go with you. Actually, I was wondering if we could go with you. Both Sheila and me."

Pamela tried not to break into a sweat while she waited for Judith to answer, but panic settled in quickly nonetheless. Would her sister say yes out of guilt? Or say no out of honesty? The few seconds it took Judith to reply seemed like a lifetime.

"Pammy, of course, you can come. I'm sorry I didn't think of it earlier. You are both more than welcome."

Pamela let out an audible sigh of relief, and before she knew it, she was crying.

"My goodness, Pammy, why are you sobbing over there?" Judith asked with a mix of concern and annoyance.

"I don't know," Pamela answered. "I guess I've just been feeling left out lately. And I guess I just assumed you would say no. And, Sheila. She's going to be so happy."

"Oh, Pammy," Judith answered. "That's terrible. I bet you weren't sick at all were you? You've just been stewing over there?"

"It's more than just stewing," Pamela answered. "But I'm fine. I will be fine."

"Fine or not, I'm coming over."

"No," Pamela said, "you really don't have to."

"Forget it. I'm coming over. And we are going to start planning our trip."

31 Edward

THE HOUSE WAS EERILY QUIET after Judith left for Pamela's. It was a type of quiet Edward didn't even know existed until years ago when Angela left for college and the lack of noise in his own home chilled him down to his bones. It's incredible, the profound stillness that can happen via the absence of someone else.

This quiet was a little different though. Maybe the calm before the storm? He thought it would give him a chance to get some work done, but that was a lost cause. He'd have to make up for it later. He was used to pulling late nights to code. He had resisted management all these years so he could stay a developer. On days like today, that choice really paid off. As long as he got his work done at some point today, he'd be okay.

Any minute now Angela would arrive at the actual campgrounds. And soon enough, Judith would come home with new details about their Hawaii trip, no doubt taking any chance of a romantic getaway away from them. Soon his world would be bustling with information, synapses firing.

Such was the life of their family. The women ruled it all. He was just lucky to be along for the ride.

It had been that way since the day he met Judith. She entered his life like a whirlwind of possibility. She opened his eyes and introduced him to a whole new world, with new foods and customs (and drama) that he had never known before. She was his sun. And he was perfectly content orbiting around her. Then Angela arrived and his world had two suns and the horizon had never looked so bright.

He thought back to the very early days of his life with Judith, when she would try to pretend like her family disowning her didn't affect her. When she would stubbornly jut her chin up into the air and act like nothing could bother her. "Their loss," she would say, assuming she was succeeding at masking her pain, only to be broadcasting the exact opposite. Of course, she was strong. One foot in front of the other. And she was doggedly determined to build them a good life together. But he always wondered, at what cost? Was he really worth it? Did her own brightness blind her to the nuance of colors around her?

And then he'd remind himself, it wasn't about him. He was the man she was in love with, yes, but what was happening between her and her family then, and even now, was somehow separate from him. And now, their trip to Hawaii was a little separate from him too. He would be along for the ride instead of in the driver's seat. Something he should have expected. After all these years, he should've seen Pamela's addition to their trip coming.

He wasn't upset about it. He just needed to adjust. Life with Judith and Angela meant a thousand little adjustments every day. He was sometimes in awe of the wake either of them left in their stead. In some ways, he felt like he should be closer to Carl, for Carl may be the only other man on the planet to understand how he felt or where he was coming from. But he hadn't talked to Carl about any of this. At least not yet. There was a lifetime for that, he supposed. And he was confident the birth of his first granddaughter would bring the family even closer together.

When he and Judith first started dating, it was still so controversial and perhaps he was a little blinded by that as well. The sheer determination they both had to choose love over everything else was a force to be reckoned with. Their love had its own weight, much like Judith had her own magnetic pull.

His memories began to blossom like a flower in spring. It was the late 1970s. He and Judy were at a restaurant. He was so in love, lost in her eyes. They were holding hands across the table.

○○○

"I'm sorry, but we're going to have to ask you to leave," their waiter said, obviously nervous.

"What? Why?" he asked.

"I'm afraid you're making some of the other customers uncomfortable."

"Exactly how are we doing that?"

"Listen, sir. I'm just the messenger. We've gotten a couple complaints. Please don't make this harder than it has to be."

Edward looked around the restaurant, spotting the furtive glances of the other patrons, wondering which ones, if any, had complained.

"I'd like to speak to your manager."

"Edward, let's just go. It's their loss. We will just get up and not pay. Walk out. Screw this restaurant anyway."

As Judith was speaking, the manager came over. "Is there a problem?"

"Yes sir, I was just asking them…"

Edward cut the waiter off. "He was just forcing us to leave."

"Sir, if you would please understand, we have to think of the comfort of the majority of our patrons. Perhaps if you would like to eat in Chinatown…"

With that, Judy stood up. She stared right into the eyes of the manager. Edward waited, adrenaline coursing through his veins, wondering what she was going to do.

But, she did nothing. She picked up her jacket, held out her hand for Edward's, and they walked out of the restaurant. And they never talked about it again.

With experiences like that littering their marriage, the birth of his daughter was their proof that love creates love.

But then he thought back to when she was little, and how she used to always talk about how she was going to marry someone who was also half-Japanese.

○○○

"Daddy," she'd say. "When I grow up, I'm going to make a whole Japanese person."

"Angie baby, what do you mean?"

"I mean, half plus half equals one. If I marry another half-Japanese person, then I can make a whole Japanese person."

"Sweetie, that's not how it works. Besides, you are a whole person, just how you are."

"I used to think that, Daddy. I used to think that every year, I'd get a little more Japanese. So, when I was all grown up, I'd be just like Mommy. But now I know. I'm not getting any more Japanese. So, I will have to make a new Japanese person."

○○○

A part of him would smile and internally laugh because it was the perfect kid logic that in reality made no sense. But a bigger part of him would ache. Because she didn't see herself as whole. And maybe she never would. Sometimes he wondered why she didn't feel the pull the other way. Why it was her Japanese side that called to her. But that was a fleeting thought. It was obvious. It was because she wanted to be like her mother. Angela was orbiting around Judy's sun just like he was.

He thought of his precious, beautiful daughter and this journey she was on. He knew she was struggling with the fact that her baby would only be a quarter

Japanese, a "quappa" she would joke. But she also hated that joke; he could see it written all over her face. He knew that part of this journey was to give herself, and her baby, some kind of justification. But he never said anything to her. Because it was her journey to take. And it was her life lesson to learn. To learn that the color of one's skin is an important part of one's life story, but that love is more important. All of the women in his life, from Aiko, to Judith, to Angela, down to his unborn grandchild, were loved. And his own mother was loved too. So were his cousins and his grandmothers. All of them. Not too bad of a lot in life to be surrounded by women, beautiful and loved, inside and out.

He stood at the front window, looking out, soaking in the silence of his house. Waiting for what would happen next. And breathed a big sigh of gratitude that whatever it was, he would be blessed to be a part of it.

He took one more deep breath and turned toward his home office. Maybe he could get some work done. It was what he knew. It was comforting to him. He put his headphones on, pumped up his favorite Jimi Hendrix album, and dove in.

32 Amache

ANGELA AND CARL PULLED OVER to the side of the road. Carl had been driving, but for the final leg of their journey it was going to be Angela in the driver's seat. They got out of the car and opened the trunk. Angela started prepping equipment and handed Carl the camera.

"Any last-minute questions on how to use the handheld Steadicam?"

"Ang, I got it. Don't worry." Carl took her hand and tried to give Angela a reassuring squeeze.

"I know, I know. I'm just nervous I guess."

"Totally understandable. Take your time. We can get back in the car whenever you're ready."

There really was no rush. The phase "middle of nowhere" was invented to describe a highway just like this. As far as the eye could see there appeared to be nothing. Not even regular farmland. Just land. Barren land. No view of the mountains. No vegetation. Nothing lush or at all appealing. The further they got from the beautiful and outdoorsy nirvana of Denver, the closer they got to what seemed like a dystopian hellscape. They had been pulled over for a few minutes already and not a single car had passed them from either direction. Angela took a deep breath. She was ready.

She got into the driver's side and adjusted the seat. She took another deep breath and pulled back onto the highway.

"So, how are you feeling?" Carl had the camera pointed at her. She was used to being the one behind the camera, not the one on it. Thankfully, her mind was so focused on where they were going, she didn't really mind it.

"I'm feeling okay. I guess I expected there to be more around. I knew we were going to be in a remote location, but I wasn't expecting it to be so incredibly isolated. I can understand why they chose this location now."

"We are here when it's nice out too. Imagine if there was no green, no leaves on the trees."

"Yes. True. It would seem even worse." Angela slowed the car down a bit. "I think we are here."

At the intersection of RD 23.5 and US 50 there was a wooden sign that read "1942-1945 Amache Japanese American Relocation Center." The sign was made of wood and the top of the sign was an arrow pointing them down an access road.

"Blink and you might miss it," Angela said, almost to herself.

They pulled into a small parking lot and Angela got out. Carl panned the scenery for a moment and then zoomed in on Angela's face. She was staring straight ahead, expression inscrutable.

"First impressions?" Carl asked.

"There's literally nothing here," Angela said quietly, pensively. "I thought…I mean I knew there would be no real buildings left, but it's striking to really see it. Here in this country, we memorialize everything, and here, it's like…" she paused, clearly not knowing what to say next, "…the absence of anything is absolutely striking. I guess I should be glad the land was even saved. That there's even something at all."

They walked for a few moments over to a collection of small signs. Much like any other national park, the National Park Service had a series of signs and maps to help any visitor. The first one they stopped at was titled "Exploring Amache." Angela read the sign out loud, "At first glance, one may think that nothing remains of the Granada Relocation Center. But even though over 560 buildings were removed or demolished after the center closed in 1945, much can be seen of the facility. Can you see the road network and the concrete building foundations? They provide an unusually clear image of the size and layout of the compound, giving a strong sense of the strict military regimentation of the site."

Angela pause for a moment and held her hand up to the sign. She placed her fingers over the words "military regimentation" as she repeated them out loud. Next to the written words was a map depicting key areas of interest. It was well marked. The scale of the camp was also striking.

They walked around and read the other signs that were in the small welcome area. There was information on how Granada High School students were working to preserve the space, about the weather in the area, there was a sign called "Behind the Fence: Daily Life" that discussed the living situations for the detainees, and a sign simply labeled "Amache" that gave more history of the war and the circumstances that led to the incarceration. Angela dwelled on the "Daily Life" sign. She began reading out loud again. "A family of six would gather in a 20'x24' portion of the barracks building. These quarters had no running water, no toilet, poor insulation, and a single light bulb."

Angela placed her hand on her belly, knowing that some women were pregnant while they were here. That many had small children. That some people were alone, living with strangers. The photos underneath showed imagines of women gardening and children gathered together for what looked like school. She thought of her mother and her grandmother. She thought of Yukiye.

Carl kept the camera focused on Angela's face. They had both agreed ahead of time that they wanted to record Angela's initial and genuine reactions. She didn't know if she would break down crying, or be flooded with memories of her grandmother, or if she would be shocked by what she saw. Instead, she felt a dull, deep sadness, so much so that she wasn't even aware the camera was on her anymore. She was lost in thought, the dry wind hitting her face as she continued to read about life at Amache. "Evacuees remember the lack of privacy as one of the most oppressive aspects of camp life. The regimented, communal life of the camp diminished the older generation's traditional leadership role and disrupted the family unit, impacting Japanese American communities and families for years after the camp closed." Angela let out an involuntary snort. "You can say that again."

She stepped back and looked at the informational markers again. "This is it, these signs. How are there only these signs?"

"Well, we don't know that for sure," Carl responded. "This place is pretty big. We probably can't even really walk it. We will have to get into our car to drive down some of these old roads. There may be other signs in other places."

"You're right," Angela said. She turned to the camera looking determined. "As soon as I'm done taking photos of all of these signs, we're going to see what else there is."

Angela noticed two other signs that she wanted to photograph before they started driving. One was an old wooden sign labeled "Amache Japanese Relocation Camp." It displayed a map of the grounds, but the map was carved directly into the wood. Also carved into the wood, in cursive: "The drawing for this map was originally drawn by Eddie Kubota who was a high school student at Amache."

"Imagine," Angela said, "having so much time to literally walk the grounds of this whole place. To map it out."

"Maybe he did it as a school project," Carl offered.

"Maybe. Or maybe from memory. The years are on here. Do you think he did it after he left?"

The question hung in the air, both knowing there was no way to answer it.

The other marker was a large red stone. On it was a brown plaque with gold letters. The plaque was in both English and Japanese. "Granada Relocation Center (Amache) has been designated a National Historic Landmark." After a brief history of the relocation, it continued "This site possesses national significance in illustrating the history of the United States of America."

Angela let out an indecipherable noise after she read it, causing Carl to laugh out loud. "What was that?"

"I don't know," Angela paused. "So many thoughts are hitting me at once. Like, I'm so glad that someone fought to save this land. That it's here and that it's a landmark and that people will remember. But on the other hand, it's like this grandiose language for what appears to be the absolute bare minimum that could be done. If all you saw was this stone, this one marker, you'd practically need a decoder ring to understand what happened here. I guess I'm a little frustrated. I'm having trouble visualizing it. It's taking every ounce of my imagination to try to picture what was here."

They got into the car and started driving down the dirt roads that went the length and width of the site. Occasionally, they would stop and get out when there was a sign, or a series of signs, that denoted what was once there. The signs were wooden, painted in white, with green and black lettering. The signs themselves were surrounded in barbed wire.

"Imagine, having to protect a sign with barbed wire. You know that's there because someone, at some point, tried to take down these signs." Angela got out her camera and was taking photos of a sign that read "Site of Military Police Compound. The U.S. Army kept a detachment of their Military Police Unit to guard the internees, to prevent their leaving without official government approval. The internees were told that the MP's were there to protect the internees."

Carl snickered, "Yes, here to protect you, don't mind the guns pointed at you."

"Right?" Angela chuckled as she snapped more photographs. She was at a down angle, trying to make the barbed wire clearly crisscross the length of her photo. As she stood up, she said, "We need to find something that's worth sending my mom a photo."

As they drove around, taking photos of literal tumbleweed, desert plains, and slabs of foundational cement from long-gone buildings that were now being overtaken by shrubbery, they eventually came to a sign that read, "Site of Amache High School. Its construction cost $301,000.00, which created a national controversy."

"I can only imagine. They got the whole country to agree to lock these people up, and then they spent money to build them a school. Mixed messaging."

Carl did his best to move the Steadicam across the sign. "I think I'm getting good at this B-roll thing," he said. "You should send your mom and Auntie Pamela a photo of this sign."

"You're right, this is perfect."

Angela did her best to take a photo of the sign. She had to reach her phone above the barbed wire surrounding it to get a clear shot. She sent them three photos. One was a clear shot of the sign. One was the sign surrounded by barbed wire. One was panned out, showing just how sparse the landscape was around the spot. She got a response almost immediately.

"It's from Auntie Pam. She says, 'Mom once told me how uncomfortable the new high school made her. She felt like a target. And, after being demoralized for so long, that they didn't deserve it.'"

"That's heartbreaking," Carl said, dropping the camera for a moment, then quickly remembering his role.

Angela's phone pinged again. "This one is from Mom. 'Thanks for the photos.'"

"Classic text," Carl said.

"Yeah," Angela answered, "Completely devoid of emotion. It's like I sent her a photo of my shoe."

They both laughed. "She probably just doesn't know what to say," Carl offered.

"That makes two of us," Angela replied. "I mean, we've been driving around for over an hour now. The spattering of white signs. The few leftover pieces of foundation. What are we even looking for at this point?"

"It looks like there are some actual buildings that way," Carl pointed with the camera. "I think it's the cemetery."

"I guess that's our next stop," Angela offered. She took another photo for her family, a panoramic of where they were standing. It was the closest she could get to a 360 degree view of their location. Before she sent it, she looked around. How could she convey the utter desolation of this place to anyone who couldn't experience it for themselves? What image would best demonstrate that for her family? For her eventual viewers? She hadn't figured it out yet, but she was on the lookout.

They got back into the car and made their way to the far corner of the site. The cemetery was surrounded by a chain link fence. A sign on the outside of the fence read "Medal of Honor Recipient Kiyoshi Muranaga A private in the 442nd, was killed in action near Suvereto, Italy (1944). He posthumously received the medal of honor in June of 2000."

"Imagine," Angela said after she read it for the camera. "Being here, wanting to prove you were American, signing up to serve in the Army, dying for your country, and not being recognized for it until 56 years after you died."

"At least it finally happened, I guess." Carl knew his words sounded hollow, but there was some truth to it. This entire chapter of American history could have been completely swept under the rug.

"Yes, it's true. At least. I know the reparations in the '80s and the Congressional Medal of Honor in 2010 meant a lot to the people that were still alive. I guess, at this point, you have to focus on the survivors, and not dwell on the thousands of people who died before they knew their country appreciated them."

Angela stepped into the cemetery. In the center was a large concrete stone pillar that read "Dedicated to the 31 patriotic Japanese Americans who volunteered from Amache and dutifully gave their lives in World War II to the approximately 7,000 persons who were relocated at Amache and to the 120 who died there during this period of relocation August 27 1942 – October 15 1945."

"That's a lot to squeeze onto one pillar," Angela said as she walked around it. Around the other three sides of the pillar were names, presumably of the fallen soldiers. Still, she had her eyes out for Yukiye's name. She knew it wouldn't be there, but there was a part of her that still wanted to look.

There was a large grassy area beyond the pillar that was obviously kept up, unlike the rest of the grounds. There were several small headstones scattered across the grass. One of them was lower to the ground, almost flat against the earth's surface. It read "Evacuees Unknown. Rest in Peace." Once she saw it, she simply said, "Here. Here is where we honor you." She dropped to her knees in front of the headstone.

Angela spun the backpack she was wearing around to her front and unzipped it. She paused for a moment before pulling out a small bag and pouring the contents out across the headstone, covering the ground in dozens of multi-colored origami paper cranes. She had folded them herself, so there weren't as many as she would have liked. Only then, as she was scattering them, did she think about how nice it would have been if she, her Mom, and Auntie Pamela had made them together, as they had before most other major life events.

She then pulled out a series of flat paper ovals, which she expanded into puffy paper lanterns. She placed an electric candle in the center of each one. Even though the candles were turned on, the light from the glaring sun overtook any light they emitted. The candles did serve to anchor the lanterns though. She placed the lanterns around the headstone as an homage to Obon, the Japanese Festival of the Dead. She hated to admit that she had first heard of the festival through the movie *Karate Kid Part II*, but as they were researching for the trip, she started to learn about its true significance. One more sign to her that she was, perhaps, just pretending to be Japanese. Was this ceremony all for show too?

Angela did her best to push away her insecurities and shifted to sit down crisscross style in front of the headstone, cranes and lanterns, and pulled out a small book of poetry. It was a macabre book, one she found at the library that contained poems to read in times of bereavement. She turned to the page she had bookmarked and read a poem out loud in its entirety before concluding and closing the book and placing it on her lap. She took a deep breath. "Yukiye. My mother asked me to honor you. I wish I had known more about you. I wish I could have asked Obachan about you. I wish I knew what you looked like or what games you liked to play. But as I sit here, I know that you are with us. That you have never left us. And that even though we might never meet, your presence has been alongside us all these years. I wish you nothing but peace. And I thank you for being a part of our family."

Angela closed her eyes and sat there for a while longer. Slowly breathing in and out, occasionally hearing the paper lanterns rustling in the wind, heart and head full of her mother, her auntie, her father, her husband, her grandparents. She thought of each and every person whose lives had been touched by Amache, whether they realized it or not. And she felt gratitude that she was able to be there. To see it for herself. And that, when she was ready to leave, she knew she could stand up and drive out of there, without the threat of an armed guard or the shunning of an entire society. She felt the weight of the past and the freedom of the present consume her all at once, and then fought for her last thought to be of Yukiye before she finally stood up and slowly opened her eyes.

33 Judith & Edward

"I JUST DON'T THINK I have it in me."

"Have what in you? What are you talking about?"

"I just don't think I can be the kind of mom Angela needs me to be right now." Judith placed her hands over her face. She wasn't crying, but it looked like she might start any second.

"Seriously, what are you talking about?" Edward moved from the chair he was sitting in to the couch next to Judith and put his arm around her back.

"It's just. She's sending me these photos from Amache. And I don't even know what to say. I feel like I should have some kind of words of wisdom to share with her. Or some kind of emotions to convey to her. And I just don't. I don't feel anything."

"Well, clearly that's not true. You've managed to work yourself up into a perfectly reasonable panic attack," Edward said, only partly teasing. "Talk to me. What do you mean you don't feel anything?"

"I'm just. I'm looking at these photos. And I thought I'd feel something. Like a connection to my mom. Like a vision of her there. Or a memory of some story she told me would come rushing back. Or I'd remember some long-lost tale she told me when I was a kid that seeing the photos would trigger. But nothing. Nothing's there. These photos don't look like anything. They look like a field. Or a desert prairie. They look like nothing. And they don't remind me of my mom. At all."

"Well, that's understandable. There are no buildings or anything to trigger the kind of stories you're talking about."

"But, that's just it. She never told me any stories. She never talked about the camps, not really at least. My mother was the master of the guilt trip, but she never threw the camps in our faces. She never played the martyr. In a lot of ways, it was like it never happened."

"It was probably too painful for her to talk about."

"I know. And I know so much of how she treated us was because of the pain she experienced. But I mean, the whole experience manifested itself in her in this cold, distant way. And she made me that way too."

"You aren't cold or distant," Edward said, pulling her close into his chest.

"Not with you. But I have been with Angie. I know I keep her at arm's length. Because that's what my mother did to me. And I don't know any better."

"If you didn't know any better, you wouldn't be worried now, about how you are treating our grown, adult daughter. And, Judy, I was there with you, side by side raising Angie. You gave her so much love. She's this amazing person now because of how much you loved her."

"You have always had blinders when it comes to me. I didn't give her half of what she deserved."

"Judy, I hate it when you talk like this. You are a good person. The best person I know. Trust me on this one. Angie felt love."

Judith looked at Edward, tears brimming along the bottom of her eyes. He could tell she was using all of her power not to cry. "Just let it out, Judy. Let it out."

Judith began sobbing in earnest after he said that, head buried into his chest. "I just wish. I just wish…"

"What do you wish, Judy? Tell me, sweetie. Just tell me."

"I wish I had asked my mom about the camps. Like Pammy did. I wish I had talked to her about them. Tried to understand her. I mean, look at these photos. Look at where they put her. For years, locked up in this dust barrel of a place. I keep saying she never told me about the camps. But I never really asked her either. I never asked her." Judith continued sobbing until her tears nearly ran dry, Edward patiently holding her and occasionally kissing the top of her head.

When her breathing had almost returned to normal, he quietly said, "I thought you said the pictures weren't making you feel anything." With that, they both burst out laughing. It was one of those laughs that felt like it almost wouldn't stop. Almost painful in how aggressive it was.

As they recovered from their momentary hysterics, they collapsed back into each other onto the couch. Edward pulled out his phone. "Come on, let's look at the photos together. Talk to me about how you feel. Tell me your story."

They started flipping through all of the photos that Angela had sent and Judith did as Edward asked. She talked about what she imagined might have been there. She talked about things she remembered from Pammy's tapes of her mom. She talked about things she had learned from school or books she read. She talked about how hard it had been to tell Angela about Yukiye.

"We never really talked to Angela about the camps when she was growing up, did we?"

"I don't know," Edward said. "We must have. We certainly didn't ignore the topic."

"Yeah, but we didn't make it foundational either. We didn't become activists or relate it to things going on around us. When civil rights abuses were going on in the news, we didn't relate it back to what happened to my own family. We didn't personalize it."

"I guess not. But look. Angie's there right now. It's personal to her. And it will be to our grandchild too."

"I wonder though. What if Pammy hadn't given her those tapes? Would she even care?"

"Of course, she would care. She would've made this pilgrimage eventually."

"Why? I never did."

"You and Angie are on different paths. You had to deal with the aftermath of the camps. Angie is the one that needs to discover them."

"I wonder…" Judith said, thoughts trailing off. They continued to look and re-look at the pictures for a while more, before they both got tired and decided it was time for bed. "I hope she sends more," Judith said as they were entering their bedroom.

"I do too. Even if they don't make us feel anything."

Judith threw a pillow at him and smiled.

34 Pamela

PAMELA CURLED UP IN HER favorite chair with a cup of hot cocoa and a book, her favorite pastime. She so enjoyed the sound and smell of opening a brand-new novel, the crinkle of the book spine as it sprang to life. But as she started reading the words on the page, none of them really entered her brain. She thought reading would stop her thoughts from spinning. But the spinning thoughts were winning.

Reluctantly, she put down her book and picked up her phone and began scrolling through the pictures Angela had sent for the hundredth time. She stopped on the one video they texted, Carl texted actually, a few seconds of Angela, sitting in front of a grave marker, eyes closed, praying. The only sound was the rustling of the wind. Pamela wondered if Carl even told Angela he had sent it. Seemed like something Angela would have wanted sent in a different way. More production value maybe? Pamela swelled with regret that she hadn't insisted on going along too. She wanted so badly to have been there. She thought about going herself, but who would want to make that kind of trip alone?

Pamela tilted her head back and closed her eyes, letting her memories take over her.

○○○

"Mama, come on. It's just a few questions!"

"No, Pamela. I said no."

"But, Mama, this is perfect for my class. The professor loved the idea too. He said no one from his class has ever interviewed a camp survivor before."

"Survivor. I'm not a survivor. I was just a girl. Pick someone else."

"Fine. Whatever word you want to use. Don't you get it? I'd be the first one to interview someone on this. It'd be so good!"

"So, this is about you, not about me. If it's about you, then just make it up."

"Aiko, you can't actually expect her to make it up." Pamela's dad weighed in. He almost never chimed into one of their arguments.

"Why not? She's an English major. She can write."

"Aiko," he said as he walked into the kitchen. "Answer the girl's questions."

Aiko stared at him for a few seconds longer than was comfortable and then turned around and started doing the dishes. Pamela and her father exchanged a look and he nudged her forward with a small upward movement of his chin.

Pamela stood next to her mother. "Mama, this isn't just about me. This is about you too. Your story deserves to be told. We only learn from history if history is out in the open. People need to hear what happened to you."

"So, this is about other people then."

"Argh! Mama!"

Aiko stopped washing the dishes. "How long will this take?"

"Quick. It will be quick, I swear."

"I will think about it." Aiko turned back to doing the dishes and Pamela slowly walked away and did a silent victory dance as she approached her father. She knew an 'I will think about it' meant yes. It was always what her mother said right before she was about to agree. Her dad gave her a big smile. He knew it too.

○○○

Pamela opened her eyes and reached for the drawer in her end table. In it she kept only one thing, the report that she had written for her class. It was the only thing she had ever received an "A+" on. At the time, her professor encouraged her to keep writing. Time after time he told her there was a book there. She had seriously thought about it, after all, writing a book had always been her dream. But her dream was to write fiction, not nonfiction. She didn't know how to go about being a nonfiction writer, the rules, the footnotes, the research. Her professor, Professor Bellgreene, said he would help her, but she turned him down. The hubris of youth to simultaneously think her words were less important and her time more important than they were.

Something inside of her was stirring. She began re-reading the paper. There was so much there. It was well annotated with references to each tape that she made. She had told her mother the interview would be quick, but once they got going, she had days' worth of conversations. Part of her thought she should write the book now, but so many people had already done that.

She glanced over at one of the many bookshelves that lined her living room wall. On the bookshelf almost directly in front of her was an entire shelf dedicated to books on Japanese Americans and their times in the incarceration camps. From memoirs to children's books to photojournalism, the topic had been covered. What could she possibly add?

She watched the video of Angela praying again and did her best to suppress her own ambition. "No," she thought. "It's Angela who has the story now. It's no longer my story to tell."

35 Carl

CARL LOVED THE FEELING OF coming home after a long trip. The second he stepped through their front door he let out an audible sigh of relief and his home hugged him like a warm blanket. There was something about the smell, about the feel of his own place that started recharging his battery.

Their trip had been great, exactly what they intended it to be, but he was absolutely exhausted. It had definitely not been a vacation. He spent so much time worrying about Angela…about her emotional state, about following all of her routines with prenatal vitamins and drinking enough water, about filming their experience exactly the way they discussed, about getting the B-roll footage and the right camera angles, about sidelining his own emotions so that Angela could have this experience, that he barely even realized how the trip was affecting him.

He deviated from their plan only once, sending Judith and Pamela a small video of Angela praying for Yukiye. The video was only a few seconds long, but was the most stressful few seconds of the trip. He had to ensure that the Steadicam was perfectly situated on Angela while using his phone at the same time, and he was petrified he would mess up the most important moment of their experience. The only reason he risked it was because he had the Steadicam on a tripod, so he wasn't holding it, but he was sweating bullets that in the few seconds he had his hands off of it and on his phone, she would decide to turn or stand up or move and he wouldn't have the camera moving along with her. They had decided to save that footage as an emotional bang for the viewer, whatever viewer it was she was creating the package for, but Carl didn't want Judith and Pamela to have to wait to see something like that. He wanted them to know she had followed through and how beautiful a moment it was. He took the risk for them and for himself. He wanted that moment on his phone too. At some point he would have to tell Angela about his sent "spoiler" footage.

When they arrived home, Angela went straight for the shower, which gave him some time to sit quietly on his own. He poured himself a drink of water and threw himself on the couch, pulling a pillow over his head. Before he knew it, he was crying. All of the emotions of the past few days came pouring out of him, a dam that had just been waiting to break.

He wasn't even sure what the tears were over. If he was crying because he was happy they had accomplished their goal, or if it was just exhaustion, or if it was because he was finally letting himself feel everything he had been trying not to feel. The weight of it all. That in the country he lived in, the country he loved, people were shipped off to live in that desolate place, someone he knew included. He thought about how parched he had been. How dusty it was. How isolated he felt. How odd it was to be in a place and not see anyone or anything for miles. He thought about the guard tower. And he thought about what he would've done. Both as a white man knowing this was happening. And as if he was a Japanese man and his family was forced to live there. He thought about what it would feel like if he and Angela were forced to give up everything they had and if their baby had been born in a place like that.

He was still crying when Angela came out from the shower. "My goodness, Carl, what's wrong?" She moved over to the couch and he lifted his head so she could sit down and he could rest his cheek on her leg. He rubbed his face into her and inadvertently wiped his nose on her robe. She began stroking his hair.

"I'm just so sorry your family had to live through something like that."

"Oh, sweetie, I know. I know you are."

"What if something like that is happening now, and we're just not doing anything about it?"

"Carl, what do you mean?"

"I mean, there's so much shit going on right now. And whatever you create from this trip will be important. But what are we actually doing? I mean, what am I actually doing to help?"

Angela leaned over and kissed his forehead. "Well, I think you do more than you realize. How many donations have you made in the last year to the

ACLU or to nonprofits helping provide legal services or to Everytown? Any time there's a chance to donate, you do it. I don't think you should discount that. And, as for this project, don't you know I wouldn't be able to do any of the things I'm doing without you?"

Carl sat up and gave her a faint smile. "I appreciate that, and I love that, but I feel like I need to do more. I need to figure out my own angle on this. I don't want to be complicit."

"Okay, I think that's good. I think that's really good. But you don't have to figure that out right now. Or even today or tomorrow. Right now, why don't you go shower and get into some sweats and let's order a ton of food and just enjoy being home."

"That sounds pretty great." Carl got up and started making his way toward the bathroom. He turned back to Angela who was still sitting contemplatively on the couch. "Thank you."

"For what?"

"For saying that you need me. I really need to hear that. You've been so independent lately."

"Oh, baby, of course I need you." Carl looked at Angela's face. He could tell she really meant it. "And thank you for one other thing. For never making me feel too guilty."

"Guilty about what?"

"Guilty about not knowing what it's like."

"What it's like…?"

"What it's like to be different."

"We are all different," Angela said, walking toward him. She gave him a giant hug and he sunk his nose into her neck. "If it helps, you're the weirdest person I know."

Carl burst out laughing. "So, you finally admit it. You think I'm weird."

"I don't think you're weird, I know you're weird. But you're my kind of weird. And I love you for it." She kissed his cheek, and turned him around. "Now go. Shower. Now."

"I'm going, I'm going," he said as he made his way.

36 Angela

A COUPLE WEEKS AFTER THE big Amache trip, Angela was busier than ever. She had been pouring over the footage from their trip every free moment that she had. She almost wished her fingers were bleeding so she could say, "See, I worked until my fingers were red!" but it wasn't quite that dramatic. She had pleaded with Malcolm to let her use the editing programs at work for the footage she brought back, promising him it wouldn't get in the way of her work.

"We are a 24-hour shop," Malcom bellowed. "How in the world are you going to stay out of the way of everyone else?"

"It's software, Malcom. It's not like we use it one at a time."

"I know that!"

"Trust me. If my regular work slips at all, I will drop it. You saw the footage I got. I showed you the photos and the B-roll. There's something here."

"All I saw was a bunch of grass." He paused. "If it gets in the way of your work in any way…"

"Thank you!" She bounded out of his office, feeling the victory. Somehow, she roped Teresa into helping her. Teresa was young and eager enough to want to work on something on spec. It just meant they had to do more work off their normal hours when their production cycles were slower. Which also meant less time at home. Actually, that meant barely any time at home. She was now in a funky sleeping pattern, and the closer she got to the third trimester, the more exhausted she was. The double whammy of being pregnant and having a passion project was about to take her down.

"I've reached new levels of exhaustion that I didn't know were possible," she said out loud to no one in particular as she plunked her head down on her desk.

She just had to keep going. For some reason, she had decided that the package must be complete before her third trimester. In her logic, if she finished it before then, she could push it through for approvals and it might just air before the baby came. In her head, the baby's arrival was a before and after benchmark like no other. Everything had to get done before her daughter was born. Everything.

Angela still hadn't managed to raise her head off her desk when her phone rang. She could see the display screen through the cracks of her fingers, but knew without even looking that it was Carl. He had been so worried about her, telling her to slow down, telling her to take care of herself and the baby. She heard him, and she knew he was right, but she was also inexplicably driven to complete what she had started.

She finally lifted her head back up and saw that it was close to midnight. Her goal was to stay until 1:00 a.m. but she knew that would be impossible. In fact, she wasn't even sure if she was alert enough to drive home. Carl would absolutely kill her if he had to come and pick her up and she hated calling for a car service when she was alone this late at night. She looked at her phone. Carl had left a message.

"Ang, honey. Are you okay? It's so late. Please come home."

"On my way," she said to herself. She stood up and did a few squats to get her blood flowing. Squats used to be her go-to wake-up method, but now that she was getting bigger, it was getting harder and harder to stand back up. Not impossible yet, but noticeably uncomfortable. She went to the bathroom and splashed some water on her face, but she still felt drowsy. She took a deep breath and knew what she had to do.

"Hey, babe."

"Ang, why didn't you pick up when I called you earlier? Are you okay?"

"Yes, I'm fine. Just tired. So tired I couldn't even pick up my phone. I think I'm going to need you to come and pick me up."

There was a long pause at the other end of the line. "These late nights. They have to stop. I'm not kidding."

"We can talk about it in the morning."

"Yes. In the morning. And until you hear me. I know this project is important to you, Ang. It's important to me too. But it's not worth risking your health. It's not worth being so tired you can't even drive yourself home."

"Just come and get me, okay?"

"Fine. I'll be there in 20 minutes."

They barely spoke on the way home. Angela wasn't sure if she was even awake for most of the drive. The motion of the car seemed to be merging with dreams of camera footage slowly panning over the desolate Amache fields.

Things had gotten really crazy when she had finally figured out her angle for the piece. She was using her Obachan's tapes and overlaying them with the footage she had taken at Amache and was interspersing the video/audio with archival photos from the days of the camps. But she was also adding in rhetoric from the news of today with sound clips from her own team reporting on ICE deporting Latinos and calls for the Muslim ban and the potential for DACA recipients to be sent home. She was painting the picture that we were repeating our own mistakes. But she had to make sure that it included her trademark positivity. And, at best, a solution.

It had required hours of searching for just the right parts of each medium to use and begging for favors from all of the sound editors and mixers and production editor colleagues to make it happen. As she started asking around and more people got wind of what she was doing, more people volunteered to help. Suddenly she was shadow managing a whole crew, which was thrilling, but also scary. She just couldn't figure out how it was going to end. What would make the most impact? What would make it a must-see segment that viewers could never forget?

The sound of Carl's door slamming shut woke Angela up out of her working dream. He walked over to her side of the car and opened the door and helped her out. As soon as they were both in the house and the front door was closed, he turned to her. "This has to stop."

"I know, I heard you. I'm almost done."

"You are not almost done. You are nowhere near done. And you're not going to finish like this."

"I am almost done. I'm trying to get it done faster so these long hours can stop. I don't want to be this exhausted either."

"I thought this would end after our trip," he said quietly.

"You thought what would end after the trip? I wasn't even working on this then."

"I thought you'd come back to me. That I'd get you back."

"I have no idea what you're talking about," Angela said, frustrated. She tried to make her way past him, but he stopped her by taking her arm. Not forcefully, but with enough intent that it startled her.

"Ever since the funeral. Ever since we got those damn tapes. It's like you've been gone. Like you aren't here. You're obsessed, Angela. Absolutely obsessed. I just," he stopped and took a deep breath. "I just want my wife back."

"You want your wife back? I'm right here. I thought we were doing this together. You said you wanted to contribute, that you were moved by what we saw at Amache, and you didn't want to be complicit."

"Together? Before the trip, you retreated into those books and those tapes. You have barely paid attention to life around you. I've been sharing baby stuff with you and you act like you don't care. We haven't gone on a date in months. We never see each other. How can we be doing this together? You're not even home to tell me how it's going. Or what you're working on. I was moved by our Amache trip, but have we even talked about it since?"

"Carl, we took that vacation together. Of course, you're a part of this."

"A vacation? That wasn't a vacation. That was work. And it was exhausting. And you still haven't thanked me for it."

"I thanked you for it. What the f are you talking about? Of course, I thanked you for it."

"You thanked me for the tickets. That's it. Not for anything I did for you on the trip. Or anything I've done for you since. But, how could you? You are never home."

"Carl, if you don't understand how important this is to me…"

"I do understand it, Angela. I really do. But it's not everything. It's just not. And I miss my wife. Can't you hear me? I'm telling you; I miss my wife."

Angela didn't know what to say. She thought Carl understood what she was going through and what she was trying to do. He had come with her on the trip and he had been so supportive. She thought they were on the same page. "I'm too tired to talk about this right now. We are both going to say things we regret." She walked past him into the bedroom and changed her clothes as quickly as possible. She felt tears start to stream down her face. Carl didn't follow her in and she wondered if he was ever going to. But she was so exhausted, once she turned off the bedroom light, she was asleep almost before her head hit her pillow.

When she woke up the next morning it was late. Really late. She almost started to panic when she saw a note on her nightstand. "I called in sick for you today. Rest. Sleep. Don't work."

Carl was forcing her hand, but she was so exhausted, she didn't care. She got up to use the bathroom and then crawled right back into bed. She didn't know how long she had been asleep again when she sat almost straight up and realized she had it. She knew how the segment needed to end. She opened her nightstand and grabbed a small pad of paper and a pen and frantically started scribbling down her ideas before they flew out of her head. Before she knew it, she was storyboarding the ending, her bed covered in crude sketches laying out the last few minutes frame by frame. Eventually she had to get out of bed to use the whole thing like a massive storyboard wall. When she was done, she just looked down and knew in her gut she was right. This was going to do it. She got her phone and took photos of her work just in case something happened to the pages. She then carefully numbered each piece of paper and placed them, sequentially, in an envelope.

Now that she knew what to do, a huge wave of relief washed over her. She was going to reach her goal. She thought about texting Carl the good news but decided not to. She was supposed to be resting and he'd be so angry if he knew she wasn't. Instead, she went to the kitchen and treated herself to a bowl of chocolate ice cream. Then she once again crawled back into bed and fell asleep. She had so much to do. This might be the last sleep she got for a while.

37 Angela

ANGELA'S PHONE BEEPED AGAIN. ANOTHER text message from her mother. "Good god, what could she possibly want now?"

The message read "You are coming over tonight to hear about our Hawaii trip. No more excuses. We will see you at 7 p.m. Love, your MOTHER."

Of course, she would put "mother" in all caps. Who knew guilt-trip by text message would become such a ubiquitous thing?

Her mother had been pinging her about the Hawaii trip for days.

"We booked a hotel right on the water!" Angela sighed. It was Hawaii. Every hotel was right on the water.

"We got a really nice rental car. It has a convertible top!" Just say it's a convertible!

"Spam sushi!" Obachan used to make Spam sushi, but Angela could never bring herself to eat it.

At a different stage of life, Angela would have craved and relished in this kind of information from her mother, like the walls between them had finally come tumbling down. But now, she was so busy, each text seemed like it was explicitly meant to irritate her. She also couldn't get past the feeling that her mother was trying to prove some kind of point—like this was how informative she should have been on her Colorado trip. It's like each message was saying, "See, it isn't that hard to text every…little…detail."

Angela had more important things to worry about anyway. She had formalized her storyboards and had to pitch it to her boss. If he liked it, he could either green-light a special edition of the nightly news or he could kick it over to a different production lane so the piece could end up on a longer format show. She was fine with either. She just wanted it to air. She also knew she could just post it online and hope it went viral. But having a platform would be better.

She took a deep breath and walked into Malcolm's office. "You have three minutes," he grunted, not even looking up from his laptop.

"Two segments. One six minutes. One five minutes for a total of eleven. Multimedia incorporating footage from my trip, with footage from current events, connected by the audio of my own grandmother telling the stories of her incarceration."

"Sounds like a high school project."

Angela tried not to let that bother her and continued. "We shift away from the crash and burn of it all and move to focus on the people making a difference. We bounce back and forth between the people who fought to end incarceration and the people fighting back now. We tie the past with the present, not through how bad it is, but through resilience."

"You've graduated to a college project. What's the overall point. What story are you breaking? Why is this news?"

"It's news because we are the only ones doing it. In this dumpster fire of a TV climate, we will stand out. We will be unapologetically optimistic."

"I don't like it."

Angela waited, already forming back-up plans in her head. Where she could post it if she was to go completely off-book, what her social media plan would be.

"I don't like it, but I'll run it up the chain."

"Do you need anything from me to send up?"

"I need you to get out of my office."

Angela smiled, said thank you, and ran back to her office. Teresa was waiting there for her and they jumped up and down at the news. It wasn't a no. It was a definite maybe.

Within 24 hours, she got her final answer—it was a go. The network was already toying with the idea of some type of re-cap special, and this fit right in. They gave her two weeks to pull it together, which was next to nothing, but now that it was officially greenlit, her shadow team weren't the only people working on it. She had her whole team back, and then some, which was great. Everyone was excited about what they were doing.

She looked at the clock. It was only 4:00 p.m. but she still had hours of work to do. There was no way she was going to make her mother's timeline. She was about to text her mother just that when another text came through. "Ang, just come to dinner." It was from her father. They were tag teaming her.

Before she could even put her phone back down, her phone pinged again. It was Carl. "We're going to your parents' house for dinner. End of story." The triple team. Geez. Did someone need a kidney or something?

She set an alarm on her phone for 6:00 p.m., knowing that if she didn't, she'd work straight through the evening. When the blaring sound of a fire truck siren came shooting out of her phone a couple hours later, she could barely believe it. It was like no time had passed at all. She reluctantly sent a Slack message to her team, letting them know she was going offline, and headed out the door muttering, "Tripled teamed me," as she walked.

When she arrived at home, right on time, Carl almost looked impressed. But as Angela looked at Carl, she realized he also looked tired. It had only been two days since their big fight, and he was still sleeping on the couch. Every morning she wanted to yell at him, "If you miss me so much, why are you sleeping in a different room!" but she didn't. She ignored it. Their relationship had turned into the polite niceties of two strangers sharing a meal at a B&B.

Carl gave her a quick hello and they were back out the door. They barely spoke on the car ride to her parents' house. She didn't want to be the one to break first. Her gut told her she needed to apologize, but until she figured out exactly what she was supposed to be apologizing for, she wasn't going to say anything. She started to feel like she couldn't breathe. When she was younger, she used to have panic attacks, but she hadn't had one in years. Not since she met Carl. He was this calming force in her life. Two days without him in her bed and she felt like the world was closing in on her. But she still felt like she had done nothing wrong. Why couldn't he see how much she needed to work on this segment?

Throughout the whole dinner, Angela's mother just talked and talked about the upcoming trip. It was like she had already been on it. She knew exactly what they were going to do and when. Angela tried to listen, but was more looking at Carl, who was silently shoving the food back and forth on his plate. Didn't anyone else notice he was barely eating?

"Angela, will you show me how to work it?"

It took a small kick from her father under the table for her to process that her mother had just asked her a question. "I'm sorry, Mama, what did you ask?"

"The camera I bought—will you show me how to work it?"

Judith passed Angela a fairly high-quality hand-held digital video camera. Angela had to admit, her mother had good taste. "Sure, Mama, I can show you."

Angela was a little touched. Her mother had never really asked her for help like this before. She was suddenly flush with another wave of guilt, this time for real. This trip was obviously important to her mother. Why was she blowing it off like it was no big deal?

Another wave hit Angela. Maybe she could use footage from her mother's trip in her segment too. But before she could formulate the thought into words, Carl finally spoke. "Not everything is about your segment, Angela."

Angela was totally taken aback. The look on Carl's face was one of anger. A face that she rarely, if ever saw. Especially not directed at her. He had not only managed to read her mind about what she was thinking, but he was chastising her for it too. Angrily so.

"Judith, let's clear the table," Edward said quietly.

Judith and Edward picked up their own plates and walked out of the room.

"What was that?" Angela asked defensively.

Carl continued to silently push the food around on his plate. His anger had faded, and he just looked tired again.

"Carl, what's going on?"

Carl threw his fork down on his plate. "What's going on? What's going on? Isn't that the point, Ang? You don't even know! Tell me five things your mother told you tonight at dinner. Or, better yet, tell me five things I've told you about me in the last week. I bet you can't do it."

Angela wanted to prove him wrong. She felt a red heat well up in her chest. But as she prepared to throw example after example back in his face, she realized she had nothing to say.

"I knew it," Carl muttered.

"Carl, I'm sorry, but you know how important this segment is to me. How it might change people's minds. What it will mean for my career. What it will mean to my family…"

"Your family?" Carl bellowed back. "Your family is right here, and you don't even care." Carl took a deep breath and then looked Angela directly in the eye. "You know, we went on that trip together. I was there with you. Every step of the way. Supporting you. Filming you. Being a good husband to you. And the second we got back you reclaimed the whole trip like it was your experience and yours alone. And you threw yourself into work. And you stopped caring about anything or anyone else. Have you even noticed I finished putting together the baby's room? Did you even hear your mother talk about her father's experiences growing up in Hawaii? Or register that Sheila is coming with them on a family trip for the first time ever and what a big deal that is to Pamela? Did you know your dad had an MRI last week because he's been having pain in his hip? Or that my mother is going back to work? You don't know anything of these things. Because for weeks you've been obsessed with nothing but yourself. Don't tell me what means what to this family."

Angela, rendered completely speechless, began to cry. Suddenly she truly couldn't breathe. Her effort to bring air into her lungs failed her at every attempt. Her face turned hot. Her palms started to sweat. It was a familiar feeling, a full-blown panic attack. As she started to slightly convulse, Carl was soon right by her side. Her parents came running in from the kitchen. All of them worked to get her to the couch where she could lay down and try to catch her breath. She could barely see, and she knew soon that her body would shut down just enough that she'd either black out or fall asleep. It was amazing how normal a furious panic attack could feel. But all she could really think about were Carl's words—"Don't tell me what means what to this family"—as she looked at his face. His face that had changed from anger to worry. His face that she had not seen enough of these past few weeks. His face that she loved more than any other, that just a few moments ago had been so angry at her. His face that was telling her she was a bad person, but yet was right next to her, obviously worried. His face. She saw Carl's face.

And just as she was about to say she was sorry, the panic overtook her, and all she saw was black.

38 Edward

EDWARD LISTENED FROM THE KITCHEN as Judith and Angela talked in the other room. Angela was doing her best to be patient while she showed Judith how the camera worked, but Edward could tell she was getting frustrated. Sometimes he marveled at how similar—and how different—the two loves of his life were. It was their dichotomies that defined them. Judith was adventurous and giving and led with her heart first but was also emotionally closed off. Angela was impulsive and passionate and creative but was also too wrapped up in her own thoughts and the way she thought things should be done. He understood both of them so well, but a lot of times he felt like they spoke different languages from each other. He had dutifully served his role as family translator all these years and was actively resisting the urge to run into the other room and help moderate this little tutorial. But he knew they needed their time together. That this was Angela's way of saying she was sorry for not paying enough attention to her mother.

Edward felt tired. No wonder. It had been an eventful dinner. One capped off by a panic attack from Angela that he hadn't seen in years. She used to get them all the time in high school and in college. He had no idea she was still having them. After Angela had recovered, Carl had wanted them to go home, but Angela insisted on showing her mother how to use the camera first. Edward laughed to himself as he watched Carl cave and sink into the living room chair with a book. *I know that move, kid*, he thought to himself.

I wonder how the baby will fit into all of this? he mused as he finished up drying the dishes. If the three generational dynamic was anything like what Aiko, Judith, and Angela had, this new little girl would get along with Judith just fine. Somehow the grandmother-granddaughter bond was always strong. It was the mother-daughter bond that drove people crazy.

Edward decided the only way he was going to prevent himself from stepping in and "translating" was to stop eavesdropping. So, he went into their bedroom to start packing. Their trip was still a few days away, but he needed to do something. He almost asked Carl if he'd like to join, but then realized what a weird thing that would be ask; packing with his son-in-law seemed like a hard no. But frankly, he didn't have the energy to think of something more appropriate, so poor Carl was still left to his book. The book he probably wasn't even reading as he fumed that Angela was still not home resting. Edward understood Carl too. And knew that all of Carl's anger derived from worry that Angela wasn't taking care of herself. He saw how much Carl loved Angela. And it gave him no end of comfort that Angela had found someone to love her as much as he loved Judith.

As he pulled his suitcase out of the closet, he realized he had no idea what to pack. There was the normal stuff like shorts and T-shirts, but was that it? Toiletries. Basics. He felt like something was missing. Angela had brought so many things on the Colorado trip it must have clogged his judgement. For him, this was just a regular vacation. He could probably fit it all into one overhead duffle.

As he was switching out his suitcase for a duffle bag, a photo album on the top shelf of his closet caught his eye. It was the only one that wasn't out in the front room with all the others. It was more of a scrapbook than a photo album. A few pieces from his own father's life story that had been cobbled together over the years. He had almost forgotten it was there. He pulled it down and walked to the doorway of the front room. He caught Carl's eye and made a head motion for him to follow him to the kitchen.

As Carl entered the kitchen, Edward opened up the scrapbook delicately on the counter. The pages were almost falling apart.

"So, what's this?" Carl asked. He seemed tired, but perhaps glad to be thinking about something other than Angela for a moment.

"A few things of my dad's."

"Oh yeah? Not enough family drama for you tonight?"

Edward laughed out loud. "Very little drama on my side of the family. We were all pretty quiet people."

"Makes sense, I guess. The yin and yang of it all. My family is pretty laid back too."

Edward felt an active kinship with Carl. He wondered if Carl felt the same way.

"Look at that," Carl said, pointing to a picture of Edward's father in uniform. "Did he fight in World War II too?"

"Well, he was in the war, and often in dangerous situations, but he wasn't fighting. He was in one of the combat engineers' battalions. His specialty was bridges."

"Bridges? Really? Like what kind of bridges?"

"Oh, all sorts. When soldiers had to get from one place to another, either over rocky terrain or over a river or creek, and they couldn't just walk because of the equipment they were hauling or the size of the gaps between land, engineers would build bridges right there on site, often with the materials at hand."

"Holy crap. What did he do when he got back?"

"He was a math teacher," Edward said quietly as he continued to flip the pages.

"Math teacher. I guess that makes sense. You'd have to be pretty good at math on the fly to pull off a bridge on the go."

"Yes. Although, he didn't talk about it that often."

"Seems like a lot of folks from that generation just decided not to talk about the war."

"Or anything in general really," Edward quipped, almost to himself.

"You should honor him when you go to Hawaii," Carl said as he took over flipping the pages.

"What do you mean?"

"I mean, there are a ton of World War II memorials there. And that's part of why Judith and Pam are going. You should get in on the action."

Edward suddenly found himself emotional and was staring hard at the kitchen table. The idea hadn't even occurred to him. Judith took up all the oxygen sometimes. But Carl was right. Maybe there could be a way this trip could be a little bit about his side of the family too. "Carl, I think you may be onto something." Now Edward just needed to figure out exactly what he was going to do.

39 Hawaii

THE WARM AIR HIT THEIR faces like a heat bomb before they had even exited the plane. As soon as they stepped off onto the jetway, they started stripping off the layers they had worn for the flight. It was a long journey, longer than they expected. It felt like they had been traveling for days.

"The first thing I want to do is take a shower," Pamela quipped as she tied her cardigan around her waist. "I feel like I have plane all over me."

"What does that even mean?" Judith responded. "I thought we were going to go to see the ocean first."

"When did we decide that?"

"We said it when we were boarding our first flight. You said it'd be better to get dirty in the ocean and then shower than have to shower twice."

"Well, what did I know? That plan won't work for me anymore."

Edward and Sheila exchanged knowing glances. "Guys, we will have time for everything. I promise," Edward offered. "I think going back to the hotel to drop off our bags and change into more weather appropriate clothes would be great. I know I'd be more comfortable at the ocean if I wasn't in jeans."

"I told you not to wear jeans," Judith replied. "I hope you don't take her side the whole trip."

Edward let out an audible sigh. He was hoping they would laugh. Neither sister did.

The ride to the hotel, hotel check-in, and subsequent showers and getting ready time were mostly met with silence. Edward was pretty sure that Judith and Pamela were both just dealing with the emotions of the trip—and the exhaustion of travel—and hoped that their whole vacation wouldn't be this tense. While he waited for them both to be ready to go, he stepped out onto the hotel balcony and marveled at their view. The pool below them extended to the end of hotel deck, which gave the illusion that the water flowed right into the never-ending ocean. He had never seen an infinity pool in person before and he had to admit it was breathtaking. He stood there and forced himself to take three deep breaths in and out. In and out. In and out. It was his job to be the calm one. The neutral one. The peacekeeper. If he could keep finding vistas as peaceful as this one, he was up to the task.

When they were finally ready to go, Edward decided to make a bold gesture and laid out his plan for the day. "We only have a few hours before bed, so I say no family stuff today. Let's enjoy the fact that we're in Hawaii first. I say we go to the ocean. Stick our feet in. Then sit in some beach chairs and get some drinks. The big ones. With fruit and flowers pouring out of them. Then I saw that later tonight at the hotel restaurant there's an outdoor luau at dinner. I say we go there, eat as much as we can, take in the performances, and then get a good night's sleep."

He could see from their faces that Sheila was all for his plan, but that Judith and Pamela had different ideas for the day and each was calculating whether or not they could adjust their own expectations. He marveled as he looked back and forth at the two of them. Their thinking faces were almost exactly the same. Genetics was a crazy business.

Sheila grabbed Pamela's hand and gave her a smile. It was such a loving smile, it made Edward blush. "I think that sounds like a good plan," Pamela said, softening as she saw how happy that made Sheila.

"I think so too," Judith concurred.

Edward stood in dumbfounded silence for perhaps a second too long, amazed that his gambit had worked. Before they could change their minds, he grabbed his travel backpack and they were out the door.

As they navigated their way out of the hotel and down to the beach, he took the lead, willing his plan to work. As they all stuck their feet in the ocean, he could see their tension thaw. After the first few sips of the giant drinks they had on their beach chairs, the laughter started. By the time they were gawking at the fire breathers and the belly dancers, they were genuinely enjoying themselves. This is the vacation he wanted. Nothing but being in the moment. Enjoying something new. Living for now. The weight of the real intent of their trip was nowhere to be found. And the sisters had never looked more beautiful as they smiled and laughed together. He couldn't help but pat himself on the back a little bit. Maybe he should take the lead more often.

When they got back upstairs to their rooms, they made a plan to meet Pamela and Sheila at the breakfast buffet at 8:00 a.m. Edward and Judith entered their room and before Judith was barely in the door, he scooped her up and kissed her. She playfully scooted her way into the room, mimicking the belly dancing they had just seen. She had never been sexier. He kissed her passionately again and kept them in vacation mode as long as possible. For decades, any time he touched Judith, it made him feel like a teenager in love. Now it was time to make sure that this vacation was everything it could be.

In Pamela and Sheila's room, the mood was not much different.

"Have I told you how much it means to me to be on this trip with you and Eddie and Judith?" Sheila said as she began kissing the back of Pamela's neck.

"You may have mentioned something about that," Pamela answered as she turned around to face her life partner.

"When you first asked me," Sheila replied, "I was so surprised. At how normal the request was. And how abnormal at the same time."

"I'm sorry that you have had to put up with this for so long. Twenty years of not being included. I don't know how to ever really apologize for it."

"You don't have to apologize for it. But you can try and make up for it."

"Oh really," Pamela said with a smile. "And just how am I going to do that?"

"Well, I have some ideas," Sheila said, as she pulled Pamela down onto the bed.

○○○

The next morning at breakfast, Edward tried to take the lead on planning again. "I think we should start by going to the Pearl Harbor War Memorial. The website says tickets can be hard to get and are first come first serve. If we get tickets, I say we spend the morning there."

"There are a lot of different things you can do there, I really don't want to do all of them," Judith chimed in, "but we can do the main one—USS *Arizona*."

"I guess that's fine," Pamela responded, "but I'd rather spend time walking around the neighborhood that dad used to live in."

"We can do that in the afternoon," Edward added. "I've already mapped out how to get from the Pearl Harbor site to his neighborhood."

"I don't know," Judith said. "It'll be hot in the afternoon, is that really when we want to be walking around? Maybe we should just do walking stuff in the morning and evenings and do inside stuff in the afternoon."

"It's always going to be hot. We're on Oahu."

"I know that, Pam, I just think there's a way we can mitigate our heat exposure."

"Heat exposure? You're not going to melt."

"I might"

"Ladies," Edward interjected. "Why don't we play it by ear? The area your dad used to live in isn't just a small village anymore. There are lots of shops and cafés. If we get too hot, we can take a break. But I think this is a pretty good plan."

Edward again waited as their faces contorted into their thinking masks. He crossed his fingers under the table.

"Fine," they said, nearly at the same time.

This was a new world for Edward. One where he was making the decisions. It was working so far. He couldn't help but think to himself, *Maybe I should keep my fingers crossed for the whole trip.*

As they toured the USS *Arizona*, Judith watched as Edward paced back and forth. He kept reading every sign he could, every placard. He kept looking around like he had lost his keys. When the tour was over, they made their way back to a boardwalk that looked out onto the memorial, the perfect spot for scenic photo taking. However, Edward seemed incapable of soaking in the view, and from what Judith could tell, was barely noticing his surroundings even as his eyes were darting back and forth across the landscape.

Judith walked over to him. He seemed to jump a little when she touched his arm. "What's up, babe?"

"What? What? Nothing. I'm fine."

"Well, I didn't ask you how you were. I asked you what was up."

"What? Nothing. Nothing's up."

"Eddie."

"Seriously, what?"

"That's exactly what I was about to say."

Edward took a deep breath in. "I wasn't going to tell you this. Because this trip was about you and your sister and your dad."

"Eddie, what is it?"

"I was talking to Carl before we left. And showing him some photos of my dad. And telling him about how my dad was an engineer in the war. And Carl mentioned that I should try to find a way to honor my dad while we were here too."

"That sounds like a lovely idea. Why on earth would you not want to tell me that?"

"Well," Edward hesitated, "I didn't want you to get mad. Like I was trying to steal your thunder."

Judith laughed out loud. "I think there's plenty of thunder to go around. Is that why you're so upset, because you've been bottling this in?"

"What? No. I just. I can't find the place."

"What do you mean, 'the place'?"

"I was sure that if we came here first, I would feel some kind of emotional connection to the war memorial. And that I could say my silent homage. And just get it out of the way. And then focus back on you and Pam. But I've been wandering around all morning, and feel no connection to this place at all. It just hasn't…I just can't find it."

"What are you looking for?"

"I don't know exactly. But you know how you see photos of men standing in front of war memorials, like the Vietnam Memorial in DC, and they place their hand on it crying? I thought it'd feel something like that."

"Well, most of those men were in the war, or saw a name on the wall they recognized."

"Well, I knew someone in World War II. I knew my dad. And I don't feel anything here."

Judith wrapped her arms around Edward's waste and rested her head on his chest. He placed his cheek on the top of her head like he had done a million times before. She looked up at him and smiled. "You will find your place. Whether it is here or when we get back. You'll find it. Don't waste your time looking for it. Something will pop out. Something will grab you. And then you'll know. And you'll be able to make your peace."

"Is that your plan too?"

"Yep."

"You. The person who plans everything. You're just going to wait until something pops out at you?"

"That's exactly what I'm going to do," Judith said with a smile.

"And what if Pam doesn't get the same vibe in the same spot?"

"Well then, we will honor him twice."

"All these years later and you still surprise me," Edward said, staring deep into Judith's eyes. "Suddenly, you're the women without a plan." Edward took a step back and took her hands in his. "Well, if that's the case, then let's get out of here. I came, I saw, I didn't find what I was looking for. No point to linger. Where is Pam anyway?"

"She's right over there," Judith said, pointing to the edge of the pier.

Pamela and Sheila were standing together, arms wrapped around each other. "It's really nice to see them out like that. In public. Not afraid anymore."

"It is," Judith said quietly. "I wish she didn't feel like she had to hide it all these years. It wasn't like it was a secret."

"You know Pam—she just wanted to make everyone happy."

"Yes, that's Pammy," Judith replied.

"Come on, let's go over to them."

"They look so peaceful. Almost like they are praying. Maybe she found her spot," Judith said.

"Maybe, but I doubt it." Edward and Judith laughed at the same time, sharing each other's thought that Pammy had picked her spot long ago and even if they didn't know it, she knew exactly where it'd be. And it wouldn't be here.

The four of them regrouped and made their way to their father's old neighborhood. Edward had rented a car, so he drove while the sisters enjoyed the sun and the breeze. As the GPS guided them toward their destination, Pam started to become agitated. "We must've made a wrong turn," she blurted out. "All of this is wrong. This isn't the right place."

Edward pulled over to the side of the road to check the GPS. "No, this is it. We are just a few blocks away from the address you gave me. We should arrive any second."

"Why are you so convinced we are in the wrong spot?" Judith asked, looking around. She didn't notice anything particularly out of the ordinary.

"Look around, look at all of the signs. None of them are in Japanese. Or even English. They are all in Korean."

Judith looked around for a moment and realized Pam was right. This was definitely a mini-Koreatown. Funny, she hadn't even noticed it. She looked back at Pamela's face and saw the look of confusion and disappointment. It slowly dawned on her why Pamela was upset. In the 1940s there was no way a Japanese man would be living in Koreatown. Even now it'd probably be rare. This neighborhood was completely transformed from when her dad lived there all those years ago. "The neighborhood must've changed," Judith said. "I know this doesn't look like what you pictured in your head, but we're still here where Dad used to live."

"No, it's not okay. This isn't the way it's supposed to be." Pam replied, almost in tears.

"It's going to be okay, sweetie," Sheila said, trying to take Pamela's hand.

"It's not going to be okay. This isn't right. This isn't it."

Edward leaned into Judith. "I think this was supposed to be her 'spot.'"

Judith looked at her sister and realized Edward was right. Pamela had it all planned out in her head, and now her homage to her dad wasn't going to go at all the way she imagined. A small part of Judith realized that she expected to find a remnant of her dad in this neighborhood as well. And that's why she and Pamela had both wanted to come here first. Perhaps there would still be something. She knew they needed to keep driving just to be sure. But her gut was telling her the more likely scenario. This is all they were going to find. And they were all going to have to come up with a plan B.

40 Hawaii Part II

JUST AS THEY SUSPECTED, PAMELA was indeed expecting to find some kind of connection to her dad in his old neighborhood. Judith figured as long as they could find the house he grew up in, they'd still have a chance to give Pam what she wanted, but when they pulled onto the street, she could immediately see that wasn't going to happen. There weren't any single-family homes there anymore. Instead, where they guesstimated their dad's home used to be, there stood a row of connected townhouses. The construction looked new. Sadness washed across Pam's face.

After driving around for what seemed like hours, they stopped for dinner at one of the restaurants that Edward had looked up before they left. It got rave reviews on Yelp, which was all he really paid attention to, but as they sat down, Edward was kicking himself that he didn't put two and two together. This Korean BBQ joint should have been a red flag for him that the neighborhood had changed. But he was oblivious to its implications. How, after all these years, did he still not see the signs sometimes? They all pouted as they looked over the menus, and then started to bicker as they waited for their food.

"Why didn't we talk more about Dad's neighborhood before we left? We talked about every other little thing," Judith said in an accusatory voice.

"I just assumed we were on the same page. Why else would we go to Dad's house? Why else would I say that it was the most important part of the trip?"

"I don't know, because you're you," Judith said as she crossed her arms across her chest.

"Well, where were you expecting to remember Dad then?" Pam snapped back.

Judith didn't reply right away. She didn't want to concede that Pamela was right. But eventually she let out a deep sigh and said, "At his house. Yes. I expected to see his house."

Pamela stuck her tongue out at Judith the way she did when they were kids. When Judith did it back, they both couldn't help but laugh. Edward and Sheila were both doing their best to stay out of it, there was obvious relief that the tension was breaking, and the food was finally arriving. They ate mostly in silence, letting the food hit their bellies and change their overall body chemistries. Sometimes eating could really do the trick, filling voids both real and imagined. And the food was good too. The Yelpers weren't wrong. Even Pamela begrudgingly admitted it was the best Korean BBQ she had ever eaten.

The sun was still high when they left the restaurant but started to drop quickly as they drove. They continued their silent spell as they were driving down the highway back to their hotel, lost in thought or at least too tired to talk.

Just as all of his passengers were starting to doze off, Edward suddenly pulled the car over to the side of the road. The motion jerked them awake but they barely had time to complain as Edward parked the car along the shoulder and quickly jumped out. "C'mon, let's go," he hollered as he ran down what looked like a path but could have just been a random split in the grass.

"What on earth are you doing?" Judith bellowed as she trailed after him. "Edward, have you lost your mind?"

Edward didn't respond. He was taking action again. He'd been watching the shoreline for a while now. The highway they were on had gotten closer and closer to the water the nearer they got to their hotel. He realized that they would soon be back in the city where the buildings would be blocking their view. He wanted to see the sunset. He wanted to salvage this day.

He didn't know exactly where they were going, but he could tell from their drive that if he could get them around the rocks and trees that were around the highway, their view would be spectacular.

It took them a few minutes of hiking, but suddenly the trees and brush opened up, and there it was. The ocean, blanketed from above with the richest colors of purples, pinks, and reds any of them had ever seen. It was breathtaking, but in a way that forced them all to take a deep breath and exhale all of their disappointments from the day. All of them immediately started tearing up standing there. None of them reached for their phones or cameras. It was as if they instinctively knew nothing could ever truly capture the moment.

Edward looked around and noticed there was a flat rock not too far from where they were standing. He guided them toward it and sat down at the far end. Judith followed suit and snuggled up onto Edward's chest. Judith then opened up her free arm and Pamela snuggled up onto her big sister and Sheila huddled up along Pamela's other side. The four of them sat there in a familial embrace and watched and cried as the sun made its way toward the horizon.

Pamela was the first to speak. "Mom. Dad. We miss you. Dad, I'm so sorry I didn't ask you more questions like I did Mom. I'm sorry I don't know all of your story. And that I didn't come here looking for pieces of you sooner. But I carry you with me. I carry your smile and your hugs and your laugh in my heart. And I'm sorry I didn't tell you more about me and my life. Do we ever really know each other? Know the people we love? I will never forgive myself for not making Sheila a part of our family. But I will spend the rest of my life trying to make up for that." She paused and took a deep breath. "Goodbye, Mom. I love you."

They were all audibly weeping now.

"I love you, Pamela," Sheila said. "And I do think your parents knew me. As much as they could. I want you to forgive yourself. I am not a stranger. I am here. And I feel loved." Pamela shifted away from her sister and threw both arms around Sheila in a palpably precious embrace.

Judith was the next to speak. "Mom, Dad, I miss you too. I am already missing you getting to meet our granddaughter. Mom, you were so close to seeing her being born. Mom, Dad, I'm sorry for the pain we caused each other over the years. And for the years of each other's lives that we missed. I love you both. I wish we had understood each other better then. I wish I could tell you now. How proud I am to be your daughter. I…I…" but Judith could say no more.

Edward gave her a squeeze and looked out at the sun. It was so close to the water's edge now. "Dad, I'm here. It's not where I thought I'd be, but I'm here, nonetheless. To tell you that I'm proud of you. And to say that I'm sorry if I didn't honor our family's history enough. I will make up for it. I will tell our granddaughter all about you. And Mom. And our side of the family. I will make sure she knows our stories too. I promise. Thank you for making me the man I am today. I hope you are proud of me."

Judith sobbed loudly as Edward finished and they all held each other tight until the sun nearly set. "I think we did what we came to do," Edward said, both wanting to live in that moment forever and knowing it had to come to an end.

Pamela stood up. "No, no we haven't." Pamela moved to stand in front of Sheila. She held her hands out and Sheila took them.

"Sheila, love of my life," Pamela began. "Sometimes I can't believe we didn't meet until we were in our 40s. I think about all the years before that we could have had together, and it makes my heart ache. But god must have known I wasn't ready for you yet. When I think about these last twenty years, all I can really think about is you. And when I think about the next twenty, it's you. Recently you told me that we need to start living out loud. That it's okay to be us now. And I've been thinking about that ever since. And I've been thinking about what I want the next twenty years to be."

Pamela got down on one knee and pulled a small box out of her purse. "Sheila, my love. Will you do me the honor of becoming my wife?"

Sheila shot forward off of the rock and embraced Pamela, nearly knocking her down. "Yes," she whispered. "Of course, yes!"

As Sheila and Pamela started kissing Edward and Judith sprang off the rock and started clapping and jumping up and down. Soon, the four of them were in a tight embrace. "That was the most beautiful thing I have ever seen," Edward chimed.

They stood there for a long time, holding each other. Soon, even though it wasn't much colder, they all felt a chill as the sky became darker. They stayed there for a moment longer, as day officially became night, not wanting to let the moment go.

When the chill became unbearable, they got up and laughed when they realized they would not be able to see their way back. Thankfully, they all had their phones and turned on their flashlights and made their way safely to the car. As they climbed in, they didn't say much of anything, but the silence, the overall mood, was palpably different.

As Edward starting driving, he felt an indescribable sense of gratitude for his life. And pride that the decisions he made brought them to catharsis. They had the moment they were looking for. And no matter what else happened on the rest of their trip, they could go home knowing they had accomplished what they came to do. And that their family was finally exactly the way it was supposed to be.

41 Aiko

(CLICK)

Pamela: Okay, Mom, I think that's it. I don't have any more questions for you.

Aiko: Yes, you have asked me ALL of the questions.

Pamela: (audible sigh)

Aiko: What?

Pamela: What? What?

Aiko: You sighed.

Pamela: Did I?

Aiko: Yes. What are you sighing about?

Pamela: I guess...never mind.

Aiko: No. We have come this far. You tell me.

Pamela: (silence)

Aiko: Pamela...

Pamela: I guess...(long pause). I guess I still feel like I don't know you very well.

Aiko: That's crazy. You know everything about me now. Not even your father knows this much about me.

Pamela: But, like...

Aiko: But, like what?

Pamela: What about YOU. Like, what are your dreams for yourself?

Aiko: I have no dreams for myself.

Pamela: That cannot possibly be true. Everyone has dreams for themselves.

Aiko: What are your dreams for yourself?

Pamela: So many things. I want to be a writer. I want to be in love. I want to travel the world. I want to have someone stop me on the street and go "wait, are you THAT Pamela?" but you know, like in a good way. I want to be asked to be an expert witness. I want to know what the color pink tastes like.

Aiko: What the color pink tastes like?

Pamela: Yes. I mean, think about it. Bubble gum. Cotton candy. Pepto Bismol. We've made these things all pink. For no particular reason. Because somehow, we have it in our heads that this is what pink tastes like. These things. Which leads me to think that there must be something that ACTUALLY tastes like pink.

Aiko: That is a stupid dream.

Pamela: It's not a stupid dream.

Aiko: Okay, stupid isn't the right word. But it is not a dream for an adult.

Pamela: Well, then I don't want to be an adult. Not fully at least. Don't you have any dreams, Mama. Even if they aren't "stupid" ones like mine. I mean, what did you think your life would be like?

Aiko: I don't remember.

Pamela: (frustrated) I don't believe you.

Aiko: What difference does it make? You heard what my life became. My dreams were impossible the moment the notice for evacuation went up.

Pamela: That's not true. So many people have come out of the camps and lived remarkable lives.

Aiko: Are you saying my life is not remarkable?

Pamela: Argh! Mom, no! Your life is incredible. I just mean, like, if you could have anything, be anything, what would that be?

Aiko: Well, I wouldn't waste my dream on what pink tastes like.

Pamela: Well then, fine...pick something else.

Aiko: (long pause) I guess...I wish that I had been a dancer.

Pamela: A dancer? What kind of dancer?

Aiko: A tap dancer?

Pamela: Like Gene Kelly?

Aiko: No. Not like Gene Kelly. Like Ann Miller.

Pamela: Who's Ann Miller?

Aiko: You need to watch more old movies.

Pamela: Sorry. That's beside the point anyway. Why didn't you ever learn to tap dance?

Aiko: I had a job. And a husband. And children. Who has time for these things?

Pamela: Well, you do. I mean you do now. Why not learn now?

Aiko: I'm too old for these things.

Pamela: Mom, no you are not. You're not too old.

Aiko: This is a pointless conversation. Are we done now?

Pamela: Yes, Mom, we're done. (sigh)

Aiko: What is it? You're sighing again.

Pamela: I just wish you'd let me help you.

Aiko: Help me what?

Pamela: Help you make your dreams come true.

Aiko: Why in the world would you want to do that?

Pamela: Because, everyone deserves to know what pink tastes like.

42 Angela

THE TWO WEEKS HER BOSS had given her to produce her segment flew by in a split second. She had never worked on anything so hard in her life. Every ounce of her energy went into finishing the piece. Every spare minute she had she was at work. Despite their arguments, Carl and Angela seemed to be at some type of an impasse. Carl kept muttering under his breath, "Two more weeks," as Angela tried to keep him updated on her schedule. Then it was, "One more week," and then "Three more days," and now here it was, she was about to turn it in, and she still wasn't quite sure where they stood.

The worst part was she knew this wasn't the end of it; soon there would be a whole new bucket of work in front of her. As the segment producer, she was going to be intimately involved in the lead up to airing, which was scheduled for next week, so she would really have to tell Carl to add a week to his countdown. Then there would be press follow-up.

The juxtaposition of her work life and her home life could not have been starker. At work, the energy was electric. People were pumped to be working on something they thought was meaningful, and the positivity was a huge driving factor in that. So many times people said to her, "I love working on something that's not just about how terrible this all is," or "I am so inspired by the people we are featuring in these packages!" It was exactly how she hoped it would be.

At home, it was like she had entered into a zombie land. She and her husband were down to communicating via Post-it notes, his becoming more passive-aggressive with each passing day. "Pamela asked your mom to be matron-of-honor at the wedding. But you must've known that already." She did. Her mom had texted her, but she got the point.

When the time finally came, it was a difficult decision, where to watch her segment run. Her instinct was to watch it live on air with her colleagues. To gather together in one of the production offices with the video on one screen and social media feeds on all the others, gathering real-time feedback on what people were thinking and feeling about the piece. In fact, that was a big part of her job. And then, for a piece as big as Angela's, champagne would most likely be involved, and the camaraderie level would be high. It had been such a group effort to get the segment on air before her due date. They had all spent the last few weeks jumping through every hoop imaginable to finish it. She had never been prouder of her colleagues, or of herself.

But the pull to watch with her family was also overwhelmingly strong. After all, it was about them. And the sacrifices they had made, not only in the past, and throughout their lifetimes, but also in the last few weeks, months really, while Angela put herself and her work ahead of them. For a while she toyed with the idea that she might invite them to her office, but when she tried to picture her parents and Carl in the production room, she realized it would be a failure. They wouldn't get swept up in the excitement. They would just feel left out. There would be no way she could split her attention between her two worlds adequately enough for either.

The morning of, she still hadn't made up her mind. She flipped a coin. Heads she'd stay at work. Tails she'd go home. She got tails three times in a row. The universe was telling her something. There was also somewhat of a thaw. The latest Post-it note from Carl said, "Good luck today. I'm proud of you." It was such a change of tone that she wondered if someone else had broken into her house to write it. She left one in reply that simply said, "I love you," and made her way into work.

When she told her coworkers she wasn't going to stay for the airing, it wasn't total shock, but it was close to it. It was like they were at mile 25.5 of a marathon and she opted to sit out the final leg of the run. She assigned out all the work she would have normally done herself. She took a leap of faith that Malcom would be so pleased with the results that he wouldn't fire her because she wasn't there. And, she told her team, sincerely, that she owed it to her family to be home with them. Given everything they had learned about her family in the making of the segment, they seemed to understand.

And, just to make sure she covered all her bases, she played the baby card. In truth, it was an easy card to play. She was incredibly uncomfortable and tired all the time. Like every expectant mother, she felt the push and pull between wanting the baby to go full term and wanting the baby to come early so it would get the f out of her already. Her colleagues told her that they would still send her updates and photos from the production room. That they had it covered. That they would cover for her. She was eternally grateful as she internally conceded that would have to do.

As she was preparing to go home for the evening, she did a little light packing too. She had less than two months before the baby was due, but she knew that it would be totally consumed with follow-up from the segment. She had a few canned post-production articles for their website and blog ready to go, but there'd be requests for interviews and pitches for follow-up pieces to field too. She didn't have to pack much, since she was only taking 8 weeks of leave, possibly 12, but it still felt like she was leaving for a long time.

She texted her family before she left work. They had all assumed she was coming home to view it. She had never told them it was a possibility that she wasn't. So, her text was a friendly "See you in a few," but for her that was the seal on the deal that she was going to go through with leaving the office. That she'd chosen them over her work.

On her way out, she thought about saying goodbye to her team. To wishing them good luck. To giving each of them a hug or a high-five. To thanking them all. But she knew if she did that she'd just end up staying. She had thank you notes and gifts for each and every person all ready to distribute the following day. That would have to do.

As she walked in the front door of her home, she could smell the unmistakable aroma of her mother's donburi. Her mother rarely, if ever, cooked Japanese food, but this was one of the recipes that she knew how to make. She wasn't expecting her mother to be there yet, let alone cooking, so she was still quite stunned when she walked toward the kitchen.

"Mama?"

When she turned the corner, she saw that it was not only her mother, but her whole family. Her Auntie Pamela was rolling maki. Sheila was preparing a charcuterie plate. Her dad was making a fruit salad. Carl was prepping some skewers of teriyaki beef to toss on the grill. "What's all this?"

"We thought that tonight deserved a proper celebration," her mother said, in a sweet and calm tone that Angela had almost never heard before.

"We are so proud of you, sweetie," her dad chimed in.

Carl put down the plate of skewers and walked over to her. "Go upstairs. Change into sweats. Let us take care of everything."

"But…" Angela was truly at a loss for words. "But…you've been taking care of everything for weeks. I've been working nonstop; I haven't had time for anything. For any of you."

"We know how important this story was to you," Edward said.

"And it's become important to us too," Pamela chimed in. "Every great moment in life requires sacrifice."

Carl forced a smile, "We can't wait to see what you've worked so hard on."

Angela saw Edward give Carl a nod of approval. Carl really had gotten close to his family in the last few months. Angela burst into tears. Her dad walked over and wrapped his arm around her. She stayed snuggled into her father for a moment. This might be the best few moments Angela had had in months.

"Okay, just a quick shower and then I'm coming downstairs to help finish getting dinner ready."

"You're seven months pregnant, babe. There's no quick anything for you right now," Carl teased.

Were they back to teasing now? Was that another passive-aggressive Post-it note in human form? Was it too much to hope for that she and Carl were suddenly okay? "Hardy har har," Angela replied, attempting to bring some levity to the tension between them. She kissed him on the cheek and made her way to her bathroom. As she showered and the warm water poured over her, she rubbed her hands over and over again across her belly. "If I do one thing in my life, let me make you feel as happy every day as my family just did for me now."

When she emerged back into the kitchen, the food had already been carried into the TV room. They had set out TV trays so that they could eat in front of the TV and not miss a second of what was airing that night. They were recording the hour before, the hour of, and the hour after, just in case something (who knows what) happened.

When the hour arrived, Angela didn't think about her coworkers at all. She didn't think about what she was missing back at the office. She felt her stomach full of delicious food and she felt the warmth and love of her family surrounding her and she sat back with wide eyes and watched as her work flashed across the screen. This was it. At that very moment, she took Carl's hand in one hand and her mother's hand in the other and squeezed.

43 Angela

HER SEGMENT AIRED SECOND IN the hour. They had to sit through an excruciating eight-minute-long segment recapping the latest tweets and their fallout. But she had segments two and three. By the end of her packages, they were all in tears. She had been wondering if she'd be able to watch it objectively without thinking about every production decision she made, but there was something about being there with her family that brought her out of her own head and made it seem like she was seeing her work for the first time. The footage they had from the war days mixed with the documentary-style footage she and Carl took painted a picture of how easy it was to not only forget people in the moment, but also to forget our past. Angela's commentary about how her grandmother's story affected her present-day life were words her family had never heard before. The story of her family felt so alive and vibrant in the room, it was almost like her grandmother was there with them.

The ending came out just like she wanted it to. It was a montage of marches from across American history. Soldiers marching in Vietnam, women gathered for the March for Women's Lives, Parkland students marching for gun control, freedom marchers from the civil rights movements. The footage culminated with old newsreels of Japanese Americans being marched onto trains with her own grandmother's voice narrating, "We did not protest because we wanted to show we were loyal. We wanted to show we were loyal Americans." As the footage of the marches came to a close, the montage shifted to news clips about the current presidency. Demands for loyalty. Demeaning comments about various races or groups of people. Footage of white supremacists from

Charlottesville. Each one followed by a story on someone who was fighting back. Someone who was trying to make things right.

The voices of the new commentators morphed into a mix of a gospel choir singing "We Will Overcome," a traditional Japanese lute, and the call to Allah from daily prayers. The music was pieced together in such a way that it sounded like the different melodies should have belonged together from the start.

The last moments of screen time were a cascade of faces and people of all different ages, colors, and genders, overlapping one on top of the other, each image becoming progressively more optimistic as they went on. People hugging. People arm in arm. People helping each other out of natural disasters. People smiling at 4th of July parades and bake sales. Angela's aim was to invoke a palpable feeling of hope. The images ultimately came together and formed one word, "America," and the segment faded to black.

Through her own tears, Angela could see the visceral reaction her family had to the entire piece. Hearing Aiko's voice again. Walking through the parallels between the Executive Order to evacuate the Japanese and the Muslim ban. Hearing racial slurs from everyday Americans against Asians, blacks, and Muslims, juxtaposed with inspiring speeches from politicians across the decades and the words of everyday people pushing back on hate. A shared story.

Before she had time to process how she was feeling, her phone started blowing up. Texts, tweets, posts from all across social media. Her parents' phones, Carl's phone, Pamela's phone all started beeping and vibrating just the same. When Angela saw that one of the calls was from her boss, she picked up. Her boss's phone was on speaker and all Angela could hear were the cheers of her colleagues coming from the production room.

Over the yelling, Malcolm said, "You did it, Angela. You really did it. Rest up tonight because tomorrow we dive in to follow-up. We have a lot of people wanting to talk to us already."

Angela hung up the phone and turned to Carl. He hadn't said anything yet, his face almost stoic. She could tell he had been crying. She waited for what seemed like eons to find out what he was going to say. Were these last few months worth it? Was she worth him?

Finally, he turned to her and said, "I'm so sorry."

"Babe, what could you possibly have to be sorry about?"

"I didn't want this. Not for you. Not for us. I didn't get it. As much as you told me about it, I didn't see your vision. But what you just put together. It wasn't just TV. It was a statement. Maybe THE statement for our time. And if had been up to me, you would have never done it."

Angela curled up into Carl's lap, as much as she could at her size. "Sweetie, I literally couldn't have done this without you."

She kissed him. Passionately. Without a care in the world that her parents, Pamela, and Sheila were right there.

Edward stood up. "Ladies, I think it's about time we head home."

Angela pulled away from Carl. "No, it's okay. Don't go."

"Angie…" Judith replied, "…we're leaving."

Sheila smiled and said, "Do you need any help cleaning up?"

"I think they have other plans," Pamela teased.

They all laughed and without a word turned and went into the kitchen to start cleaning. Angela stayed suction cupped to Carl, fearful he might detach again. He seemed just as keen on holding her as she was with him. Sheila turned and came back into the room.

"Listen, Pamela told me not to do this tonight because she didn't want to take away from your big night, but we wanted to tell you we set a date. We're getting married in a few weeks." Sheila pulled an invitation from her purse and handed it to them.

"Not wasting any time, are you?" Angela teased.

"Of course," Carl said, taking the envelop. "We wouldn't miss it for the world."

As everyone helped clean up, the conversation shifted back and forth between their thoughts on the segment and wedding planning. It was the perfect symphony of old and new. Angela almost collapsed when it hit her how much she missed being around her family.

"Congratulations again," Sheila said as they were walking toward their cars.

Edward walked toward Angela again. "Sweetie, I am so proud of you."

"Thanks, Dad," Angela said. She held her dad a little too long, worrying about what she'd be facing when she went back inside with Carl. Had the magic of their PDA faded? Or was he okay with her again?

She turned toward Carl and as they walked back into the house, she pulled him to the couch. "Okay. I'm listening. With my whole heart I'm listening. Tell me what I've missed."

"Ang, I don't know if it's as simple as that."

"It may not be. But, I'm here now. I get it. I get it now. I do. Just start. Just start telling me, and we'll take it from there."

"Okay," Carl answered. "Well, if you hadn't heard, your Auntie Pamela is getting married."

Angela threw her head into a pillow. "I did know that one!" She lifted her head up. "Okay. Aside from that. Keep going. I'm here. I'm listening."

44 Angela

JUST AS ANGELA EXPECTED, THE next two weeks flew by. Her segment won the timeslot and was re-aired across several channels, which was a total coup to have her station's logo on other station's airtime. Then it was broadcast nationally. They also posted the segment in full on the station's website and it had been viewed millions of times. She was getting job offers from all over the country, from Hollywood to the major networks in New York, but she turned them all down. She was very happy working in Chicago. And she had a baby on the way.

The time also flew by because Angela had re-entered her own life. She made a commitment to Carl that she'd be home in time for dinner every night and she stuck to it. She also became quite involved in the wedding planning for Pamela and Sheila, helping in all decisions large and small. She and her mom were both full of papercuts, trying their best to make 1,000 paper cranes by the day of the wedding. She'd even figured out the perfect wedding present for them. She commissioned a quilt to be made that had a mini family tree on it, the branches of one side with names of Pamela's family and the branches of the other with the names from Sheila's family and their names in a heart carved in the trunk of the tree. She had seen it on Etsy and knew right away she had to order one; she just hoped it arrive in time.

The wedding itself could not have been more beautiful. They reserved the Horticulture Hall in the Garfield Park Conservatory. The fall skies shining through the greenhouse ceiling were absolutely dazzling. Angela had never seen her auntie so happy. It was a small wedding, mostly filled with people that Angela did not know. Pamela and Sheila had a life together that was completely foreign to her, friends that were clearly as close as could be to the couple, but whom Angela had never met. She couldn't help but marvel at the idea that there really is only one person in the world that knew every part of her. And without thinking, she turned and reached her hand over to hold Carl's.

"How are you doing?" he asked. Once she got within three weeks of her due date, he asked that about every five minutes. Now that she could give birth any day, it may have escalated to every two.

"I'm doing okay. Tired, but okay."

"Do you want to dance?" he asked her.

"No one else is dancing," she replied. "It's more like a dinner party."

"That shouldn't stop us." Carl turned to Edward and Judith. "Come on you two. Join us so Angela won't feel so uncomfortable."

Edward smiled. He would never turn down a chance to dance with Judith.

As the four of them danced under the sparkling reflections streaming off the glass ceiling, Angela felt a tug on her stomach. And then a wetness started to trickle down her leg. She froze.

"What, what is it, hon?" Carl asked. Angela stayed frozen. "Seriously, Angela, what's going on?"

She turned to her mother. "Mama. Mama, there's something running down my leg. Mama, what's going on?"

Judith took one look at her daughter and Carl and jumped into action. "Oh my god, oh my god, Angie, your water just broke!"

"What? My water can't break now. We're at a wedding!"

Carl was already on the move, running to get the car to pull around to the front.

Pamela, seeing the commotion, came over. "What's happening?"

"Sorry to steal your moment," Angela said.

"What does that mean?" Pamela asked. By now, the whole dinner party had turned their way. Sheila walked over and took Pamela's hand.

"Looks to me like our niece is about to have a baby!"

All of Pamela and Sheila's wedding guests immediately started clapping and cheering.

Pamela gave Angela a hug as best she could. "It's okay, Angela. It's kinda cool. She clearly didn't want to miss out on your big night. She's going to be the center of attention. Just like Mama was."

The idea that her daughter might be just like Obachan brought a smile to her face. And she started breathing in and out. She wasn't even having contractions yet. Is this how it was supposed to happen?

Carl was soon by her side, swooping her into the car. Edward and Judith followed in a car close behind. She began texting her boss. She was set to do an interview on NPR the next day, one of her last big assignments before her maternity leave. But, as often happens in life, her moment was not to be outshined by the wants and needs of her daughter. So much for being in the office tomorrow. Malcolm would have to handle the interview on her behalf. Normally that would have killed her, tormented her that someone else would be speaking on her behalf. But as she rode to the hospital, she realized she didn't care. She was about to meet her daughter and a whole new chapter of her family's history was set to start.

45 Judith

June 3, 1984

I'm sorry, my dear journal, that it's been so long since I've written in you, since I've taken the time to update you on my life. I wonder if I even know how to journal anymore. I'm so tired right now, I didn't even know this level of exhaustion could exist. Or that I could be so happy about it. Today, in the wee hours of this morning, my daughter was born. I gave birth, can you believe it? We named her Angela because I was too chicken to name her Angel which is what she is. She's such an angel. From the moment she was born I looked down at her face and it was like a halo was shining brightly on top of her head.

The birth itself was just as horrific as you'd think it'd be. Maybe more so. The pain was so intense I thought I was going to pass out. Childbirth is such a sick joke. But Eddie was there with me every step of the way. Holding my hand. Rubbing my back. Bringing me ice. He insisted on being in the delivery room when she was born. I love that about him. But I insisted on being the first one to hold her. My little angel. My Angela.

Now it's so late in the night, it might even be June 4 already. I'm not quite sure. Angela is asleep on Eddie's chest and I dug this out of my bag. I found you, journal, a few months ago when I was "nesting." It was quite the journey to flip through the pages, to read my own thoughts from so long ago. It's hard to think there was a time when I thought I would never see my mother again. Especially now looking at my own daughter. (Ack! I have a daughter!) I've known her for 12 hours and I can only imagine how heartbroken I'd be if we ever stopped speaking. All those years wasted. All those angry feelings clouding our way.

Now though, now we are better. Or at least getting there. Pammy has insisted upon it. And tomorrow mom will come to see the baby. And we will be a family again.

The baby. My baby. I still can't believe it. It's taken us so long to conceive. Years of trying, of wanting to be parents. I had truly given up hope. Maybe I should have named her Miracle.

And all this time, wondering how she would look. If she would look more like Eddie or more like me. And she doesn't look like either of us. She looks exactly like herself. An entirely new creation, unique to this world. Maybe I should have named her Unicorn.

I wonder if I'll even be able to read my own handwriting tomorrow. It's pretty dark in here, and I am so tired. But I can't sleep. Not yet. I'm not ready for this day to be over. This day when Angela was born. This day I became a mom. This day that Eddie became a dad. This day that we became a family. No, I'm not ready for today to be over. So, I will sit here and write and try and keep my eyes open for as long as possible.

I wonder if Angela will ever journal one day. What will her life story be? I wonder if she'll ever...I don't even know. I want her to know it all and do it all.

My journal, I'm so glad I have found you again. There will be so many thoughts and dreams to share.

My god, I'm so tired.

I'm just going to close my eyes for a second. I want to be alert for when my angel needs me. My angel. Angela. Angela. Angela.

46 Angela

EIGHTEEN HOURS OF HARD LABOR, three hours of pushing, lots of screaming and swearing, and their daughter was brought into the world. Angela had never experienced such agony or stress in her life. It seemed as if it would never end and that the pain would never go away. She had wanted an epidural, but the timing did not work out and she had to go without one. She could almost hear herself tearing as the baby's head emerged from her body.

And then suddenly, after all of that, the doctor was holding up this little person, and what happened next was a blur. The cutting of the chord. The afterbirth. The quick weighing and rinsing off of her daughter. Her daughter's screams. Her daughter's little footprints being placed onto a keepsake card, the residual ink used to make little footprints across Carl's forearm. The look on Carl's face as his daughter's feet touched his arm for the first time. The warmth of her daughter as the nurse placed her on Angela's chest. It was truly the most surreal moment of Angela's life. It was hard to believe this happened every day. To so many women. This horror and miracle of childbirth.

Angela gently placed her hands around her daughter who was curled up in a little ball on top of her and tried to get a good look at her face. Her eyes were half closed, half opened. She looked like Carl. And she looked like her. Mostly Angela thought she looked like her Auntie Pam, if that was possible.

The baby had stopped crying almost the instant she was skin to skin with her mother. Angela noticed this immediately. She clearly knew who her mother was already, at just a few minutes old. But how did Angela feel? Did she even feel a connection to this little person now laying on top of her? Angela glanced down at her little fingers and within an instant she knew that she did, a sense of familiarity that was unlike any other she had ever experienced.

Angela peeled her eyes away from her little bundled and looked at Carl, who was now close to weeping. With tears streaming down his face, Carl leaned down and kissed Angela on the top of her head and then gently kissed the baby too. "I've literally never been this happy before," he said.

Angela tried to check her emotions too. Happiness was there for sure, but overwhelming exhaustion was clouding it. Pain too. Discomfort. Wasn't she supposed to be over-the-moon like Carl was? Instead, she started to feel guilty that her arms were feeling too tired to keep holding her own daughter, although there was almost nothing in the world that could ever make her give her up. Almost nothing. Carl was practically twitching with glee. "Do you want to hold her?"

Carl's face lit up and he said, "Of course," with his eyes as he gently scooped her up, rocking her in his arms, introducing himself to her. "Hello, my little one. I'm your dad. I've been praying for you for a long time. And look at you. You're perfect. Just like your mom."

Angela smiled and sunk back into the bed. She felt grimy all over. The nurses and doctors had just finished buzzing around and were giving them a moment to themselves. She wondered when she would be able to shower, but the idea of getting up and moving was so overwhelming she decided she'd rather be dirty.

She looked over at Carl, rocking this tiny little life back and forth, and tried to comprehend what was going on. She had a daughter. She was a mom. Carl was holding their baby. He was a father. That tiny little person was now their responsibility. Years of lessons flashed before Angela's eyes. There were so many things to teach her…like what undergarments to wear in the summer so her inner thighs didn't blister as they rubbed together, or how to be a good friend—present but not pushy, or how to be a good listener, or how to stand up for yourself at school or at work.

"I think we're going to have to finally settle on a name," Angela said, yawning.

"I think our last top choice was Julia," Carl said, never taking his eyes off of the baby.

"That is pretty. But we keep picking names that are too close to the names of people we already know. Julia is too much like Judith." Angela paused. She had been thinking about a different name for a few weeks now but hadn't told Carl about it yet. "What about something like Hanae?" Angela asked quietly. The name had been tumbling about in the back of her brain, but she had never said it out loud before.

"Hannah is okay I guess."

"No, not H-a-n-n-a-h," Angela replied, "What about the Japanese girl's name H-a-n-a-e? It sounds more like 'han-nigh' than Hannah."

"For the middle name?"

"No," Angela answered, "for the first name."

"I thought we ruled out Japanese names for the first names?"

"We did, but I thought this one could be nice. It almost sounds American. People may even think it is, and people do all sorts of weird spellings of names these days. But for people who know Japanese names, they would know right away," she paused. "It means 'flower' in Japanese."

"Hanae," Carl said. He repeated it a few times, even looking up on his phone how to pronounce it. "I think I like it," he said after a while.

"I think I do too," Angela replied.

"But, if we do that for the first name, what would her middle name be?"

"That is still up for grabs," Angela said. "But honestly, I'm leaning toward Pamela."

"Your aunt's name?"

"Yes. She's the one who kick-started this whole thing. She made the tapes. She kept the family history. And our little girl clearly wanted to be there for Pamela's big night. I want to honor that."

"I bet she would like that a lot," Carl said.

"Hanae Pamela," Angela whispered.

"Hanae Pamela Campbell," Carl whispered back.

"Hey, little girl," Angela said to Hanae. "I think you might just have a name now."

After a few more times of saying it out loud, she realized how right it sounded to her. Like her daughter was meant to have that name. She allowed herself a few moments to go down the inevitable spiral…about how she was going to explain to Hanae why her name was different and why she'd never find it on those keychain racks in gas stations or gift shops, or why her grandmother looked so different from her. But then her thoughts shifted to more the more mundane worries of any mom. She thought about how many friends

Hanae would have over her life, and how one day she would break someone's heart, or have a broken heart herself.

Without even thinking about it, she reached her hands out, needing to hold her baby in her arms again. Carl smiled and passed Hanae back to Angela and they suctioned together like magnets. After all the time Hanae had spent inside of her, Angela realized she wasn't ready to be detached from her baby, not yet.

Soon enough their room was busy again. The nurses were going to take Hanae for a proper wash and switch out the bedding so Angela could have fresh sheets. There was a lot of cleaning to be done and the hospital aides were jumping to it. Carl followed Hanae with the nurses and after the latest flurry of activity ended, for the briefest of moments, Angela was alone in the hospital room. The quiet was almost deafening. She was a mom.

She thought about how crazy her life had been these last few months. How Hanae's whole existence was bookended by the story of her Obachan, with Obachan's death and then the discovery of how Obachan actually lived. She allowed herself a few tears as she thought about how Obachan and Hanae would never meet, and then recouped. Obachan was strong. Strong enough for all of them. And Hanae would know all about her. She would make sure of it.

She reached for her phone and sent texts to Carl's parents and a group text to her closest girlfriends announcing Hanae's arrival. Then she did the same for people at work. She would post it to Facebook later. She was putting her phone down when her parents walked into the room. Her mother was absolutely glowing. Judith walked over and gave Angela's hand a squeeze. Edward leaned down and kissed her cheek. She was happy they were there. As she was about to say just that, Carl walked back into the room, holding their baby in his arms.

"Ed, Judy, there's someone I'd like you to meet."

47 The Family

JUDITH FELT HER ARMS RAISING before her mind could catch up to what was happening. The idea that she was about to hold her own grandchild was something that she could barely comprehend. As she took the baby from Carl and cradled her in her arms, she couldn't help but think what a miracle each new life was. "She looks like Pammy," she said through a smile.

Almost on cue, Pamela and Sheila materialized in the doorway. "I little birdie told us that our great-niece was ready to meet us," Sheila said. Sheila looked down at the baby. "She does look like you, Pam."

Pam's eyes opened wide, glowing with delight.

"Wait until you hear her name," Edward chimed in.

"Auntie Pam, Auntie Sheila, I'd like to introduce you to Hanae Pamela Campbell."

Pamela looked over at Angela with such surprise, and with such love, that the whole room immediately burst into tears.

"You..." Pamela started, not able to keep speaking. She tried to catch her breath. "You named her after me?"

"I couldn't think of any better way to honor our family than to name Hanae after our premiere family historian."

Pamela raced over to Angela and gave her the best hug she could while Angela was still in her hospital bed. "I don't even know what to say."

"Don't say anything, Pam," Judith said, walking over to her. "Just hold your namesake."

Pamela took the baby and held her delicately, still in shock over the unexpected gift of the name. After a few moments, Judith couldn't help herself and took the baby back. Judith began rocking the baby back and forth, muscle memory kicking in from decades earlier when Angela was a baby. Back and forth, back and forth. Before she knew it, she was crying. "What is she going to call me?' Judith asked.

"What do you want her to call you?" Angela asked in return.

"I don't know. Obachan doesn't seem right. I know that's what you called my mom. And that's what I called my grandmother. But it just doesn't seem like the right fit."

"How about just grandma then?" Carl suggested.

"I've always been fond of Nana myself," Edward chimed in. "That's what I called my grandmother."

"Nana. I could get used to Nana," Judith said through a smile, her eyes never off of Hanae's face.

"Nana it is then," Angela replied.

Judith continued her rocking, rolling the word Nana over around in her mind. For the rest of her life, that would be her identity to this little girl. She wouldn't be Judith or Mom or Judy or Mama. She would be Nana. Eddie might even call her that in front of Hanae. How often in life do you get a whole new identify that comes with a new name included?

"Come now, you're hogging her," Edward said, hands extended.

As Edward took Hanae into his arms, his eyes welled up immediately. Flashbacks to Angela's birth came rushing at him fast and fierce and he realized just how long it had been since he'd held a baby. "She's gorgeous," he whispered.

"What do you want to be called, Ed?" Carl asked.

"Papa," Edward said immediately. It was what he called his own grandfather. He wanted to be called the same.

"Nana and Papa it is then," Angela said as she rested her head back down on her pillow, yawning loudly. "This giving birth thing is no joke."

Edward smiled but didn't look away from Hanae. There was so much that was about to happen. So many firsts. So many milestones. All leading to another moment just like this. "I wish our parents could be here to see this," Edward said, almost to himself.

No one responded, letting that thought float around the room and fill the moment. Then Edward started to sing, "This little light of mine, I'm gonna let it shine. This little light of mine, I'm gonna let it shine. This little light of mine, I'm gonna let it shine. Let it shine, let it shine, let it shine." He used to sing that to Angela over and over again to get her to sleep. He marveled at how it came back to him in that moment. Like no time had passed.

When he was done singing, the room was all on the border of weeping. Carl was now sitting on the bed with Angela, holding her hand. Judith and Pamela were locked in another embrace. Edward was standing in the center of the room, his singing had changed to humming, completely engrossed in the face of his new granddaughter.

The moment was only broken by a nurse coming into the room. "Hello there, folks. I'm your nurse for the next few hours. My name is Hannah. I'm going to do a few quick checks, and then mama, we're going to see if we can get your baby girl to latch."

"Your name is Hannah?" Judith asked.

"Yes, ma'am," the nurse replied as she started checking Angela's vitals. Judith and Pamela smiled at each other. Their mother did not believe in coincidences. "You're going to be in good hands," Sheila said to Angela as they were passing across the room. "We'll be right outside. I get to hold Hanae next."

"Hanae?" the nurse asked? "So close to mine. She will like having that name."

Everyone smiled. As they all stepped out of the room. Edward and Judith couldn't help but turn back and give the new little family one last look. Carl was still sitting on the bed as Angela was sitting up, trying to get into position. The nurse was explaining the different holds Angela could use to breastfeed and was explaining to Carl a few ways he could help stimulate milk. It was an incredibly intimate moment, but all her parents could see was that this new life was already full of love. That their choices had been good ones. And that their baby had a baby who they would love with all their hearts.

After a few moments, they made their way to the waiting area and joined Pamela and Sheila. They were flipping through magazines but obviously weren't really reading them.

"I still can't believe it," Edward said as he sat down. "What a night."

"It's daytime now, isn't it?" Judith asked.

"Almost night again," Pamela replied. "We had time to finish the party, go home, get some sleep, and shower before we came over here."

"Hell of a way to start our honeymoon!" Sheila added.

"I'm so glad you are both here," Judith said, smiling.

"I am too," Pam replied.

Judith sat down next to Edward and rested her head on his chest. It felt as warm and comfortable and familiar as ever. Before she knew it, she was asleep. When she woke up, Edward was looking at her smiling. "You were out for a good 30 minutes," he said as he gave her a kiss on the forehead.

"I was about to say I've never been this tired before in my life, but I guess we have. Just think of how tired Angela is about to be!" They both laughed and stood up to go back into Angela's room. They stopped again in the doorway. Pamela had the baby now and was quietly talking to her. Sheila was talking to Carl as he organized some things in their suitcase. Angela looked fast asleep on her bed. She looked just like she did when she was a little girl. Peaceful. Resting.

"We are so blessed," Edward said, putting his arm around his wife. "We are so blessed."

48 Pamela

Dear Diary,

I took Sheila to the cemetery today. It was time to introduce her to Mom and Dad. I should have done this a long time ago. I should have told them the day I met her that I loved her and wanted to be with her forever. A big part of me hopes they knew. They were not stupid people. But I wasn't brave. And I wasn't bold.

We walked to their headstone and set up a picnic in front of them. Part of me thought it was sacrilegious to be eating in a cemetery, but Sheila convinced me it would be okay. We brought some of Mom and Dad's favorite foods. I even made Dad some Spam sushi.

I talked to them like I would have. Like I should have. I told them how we met. When we decided to live together. I told them about the wedding. About how magical it was. About how much I wished they could have been there.

Then before I knew it, I was talking about how I wanted to get back to writing. I didn't even plan on it. I just started talking. Sheila took my hand and listened. I said, "I have always thought that your story was your story. That it wasn't mine to tell. But my own niece has taught me recently that all our stories are connected. And that we have to tell them. Because if we don't, we will never learn just how beautifully connected we all are."

So, I basically asked my dead parents' permission to write our family history. And, diary, I swear to god they answered. I don't know how I know, but they said yes. There was no sound. No sign. No breeze. But maybe the absence of rejection was a sign in and of itself. So, soon, my writing won't just be in journals. It will be out there. Out loud. For all to see.

I'm so scared. I've never written a book before. But Sheila says I can do it, and I believe her. I believe her because she believes in me.

I will never live down the regret of not being my true self to my own parents. Of making the love of my life feel like she wasn't invited or allowed. I should have brought her to Mom's funeral. Hell, I should have brought her to Dad's. But, I guarantee, she will be at every family event from here on out. She's already planning a book launch party and I haven't even started writing yet. God, I love her for that.

I won't forget about you, diary, though. My lifelong loyal friend. We are in this together.

XOXO,

Pam

49 Carl

CARL ADJUSTED THE COLLAR OF his tux and reached in his pocket again to pull out his phone. Still no messages, which he told himself was a good thing. Of course, it was a good thing. No messages meant that nothing was wrong. He put his phone back in his pocket and nearly immediately pulled it out again and placed it face up on the table. Just in case. When he was about to pick it up again, he felt Angela's hand on top of his. "She's okay," Angela whispered in his ear.

It was the first night they were both away from the baby. He knew Hanae was in good hands with Judith and Edward, but he couldn't help but feel anxious. For the past six months at least one of them was with Hanae in the evenings. They even brought the baby out with them on rare "date nights," which now entailed eating dinner at 5:00 p.m. and being home by 6:30 p.m. so they could put Hanae down to sleep. Their main source of couple time was during the hours of 8:00 p.m. – 10:00 p.m. when they sort of fell into each other from exhaustion and struggled to watch TV. Sleep was getting better as the months went on, but really, Carl never complained because he never felt he had to. During their time as a family of three was the happiest he had ever been.

But tonight was not a night for domestic bliss. Tonight was a special occasion. Angela's news segment had been making the rounds of awards shortlists, winning several along the way, and rumor had it that it was a shoe-in for a Peabody. Tonight, at her company's annual banquet, she and her team were receiving an award for outstanding programming with Angela receiving the award for the company's MVP. She was the youngest person to ever receive the award, and certainly the first to do so in the same year as having a baby and going on and coming back from maternity leave. Carl was so proud of her. Only the thoughts of Hanae could distract him from what a big moment this was.

When the time came and they called Angela's name, the entire hotel ballroom stood up and clapped. Angela rose to her feet, Carl standing up a split second after her, so that when she went into to kiss him, she leaned down a little bit and the kiss finished as he was still standing up. He watched as she walked up to the podium with such confidence and such grace. His heartstrings pulled for a moment as he again remembered how angry he was at her for the months of pouring herself into her work, how neglected he felt. He wished he could have seen the import in the moment. All he could do now was be grateful that her stubbornness won out, and that they had made it through as a couple, and to be as proud of her as humanly possible.

She took her place behind the microphone and began to speak.

"I'd like to start off by thanking my team. To Malcom Greer, who allowed me the room to make this happen and then pushed it up the chain. To Teresa Mendez, the best production assistant a person could ask for. To my entire production team, so many people helped with this that the list is too long to read here. You know who you are and there are already handwritten thank you notes awaiting you in your inboxes.

"Beyond our team, I want to thank the studio for taking a risk to go outside the box and air not only one segment, but two, that focused on education, history, and positivity. In a time when it's best to get your news in 280 characters or less, 11 minutes was pure luxury. To all of the broadcasters who picked up the piece and helped share it, I thank you for your selflessness. To me, that shows there is a deep appetite for changing what we produce. For showing the world that the headline-grabbing bad news is not the real story. The real story is how everyday people love and are loved."

Then she took a breath and turned and looked at Carl. "But most of all, I want to thank my family. My parents. My grandparents. My Auntie, now Aunties. I have been shaped by a colorful tapestry of people, people who have overcome seemingly insurmountable roadblocks for the simple right to live their lives as equal Americans.

"As some of you may know, I used to struggle with my own identity, trying to decide if I was more Japanese or more white, or more of a hyphenated

American. What was my label? How should I describe myself? Working on this project made me realize that I can call myself anything I want. You can call me anything you want.

"Our identities are more than what we call each other. They are more than one part or the other. They are more than this half or that half. Our history shapes us, our upbringing shapes us, our lifestyles shape us, and at the end of the day we all just want to be seen for who we really are—people who wake up and try their best.

"I could not be my best without my life partner. My rock. My everything. I dedicate this award to my husband Carl, without whom I would not have my beautiful daughter Hanae and without whom I would not have had the confidence or the wherewithal to bring this work to the light of day. He came with me on my trip to Amache. He read the books with me, he jumped into the project with me. He is an uncredited partner on this production, but he is the lead partner of my life. Thank you, Carl, for always being there for me. And for the sacrifices you made and continue to make for me and for our family."

With that, Angela stepped back, held up the glass MVP award and made a small bow with her head and the ballroom exploded with applause again.

Carl sat speechless, unable to even clap at first, tears streaming down his face. Angela had never said those words to him before, at least not quite in that way, and he was blown away that in the middle of her moment, she took the time to appreciate him. He didn't even realize he needed it until it was over. As the applause died down and the ceremony came to a close, people started approaching him and patting him on the back, passing along congratulations to Angela. Directly after her speech, she had gone backstage to do some press interviews and to take photos with the other award winners that night. It was like the Oscars in miniature. He felt an overwhelming sense of connectedness to her while simultaneously missing her and longing to be with her.

It was nearly an hour before she returned to their table. In that time Carl had talked to so many people and checked his phone so many times, his nerves were frayed. He was about to text her to see how much longer she might be when he again felt her hand on top of his. She was standing behind him, leaning down, resting her head on his shoulder. "Put your phone down. I'm sure she's fine."

His whole body relaxed. It was like he was being plugged back into his battery charger. She was back by his side and he was whole again. "I was going to text you to see if you were ever going to come back."

"I will always come back," Angela said with whimsy. She smiled at him. It was a classic Angela smile. Full, bright, soft. He was so desperately in love with her.

She sat back down in her seat. "This is pretty much over. Do you want to go?"

Instead of answering her, he simply kissed her. "Thank you for your speech."

Angela placed her hand on his face. "Thank you for being you."

With that, Carl stood up, offered her his hand, and led her out of the room. They collected their coats and he hailed a taxi. Angela leaned her head on his shoulder as they drove, fingers tracing the box that her award was in. "I'm proud of you," Carl said.

Angela didn't respond for a few moments. "It's funny. I'm getting an award for something my family went through. For something other Americans are going through. I know it's the role of a TV producer to expose and to narrate and to report. But it almost doesn't seem fair that I'm getting this. What did I actually do?"

Carl sat up straighter so that he was looking directly into Angela's eyes. "When will you ever know how amazing you are?"

And with that, they kissed again. And continued kissing all the way home.

50 Angela & Judith

THE BREEZE HIT THEIR FACES with welcome gusto. It was a hot day, but you would never know it looking at Hanae. She was as happy as could be, gliding back and forth in a park swing, her smile showcasing that she was in the middle of the best moment of her life.

Angela was standing in front of Hanae as her mom pushed, trying to get the perfect photo of Hanae's intoxicating smile. "I think I got it," she said as she scrolled through the snapshots on her phone.

"I'm not even sure Hanae knew she was in your photoshoot," Judith said with a laugh.

"I take so many photos of her, I'm pretty sure she thinks that being on camera is an integral part of life," Angela quipped, only half-joking.

Angela glanced up at her mother. Over the past year, their relationship had really changed. Judith had taken to being a grandmother like a fish takes to water. She was gracious and helpful and warm. Angela couldn't help but think that this must have been the way her childhood was too; she just couldn't remember the small, lovely moments. Her mother was full of love. Bursting with it. The way she looked at Hanae and the way to she cared for her proved that. It almost made Angela's heart ache that she had spent so many years being annoyed with her mother instead of learning more about the woman she truly was.

Hopefully, that was now all in the past. This new chapter they had started together was seemingly sticking. And she was determined to do her part to make their relationship as strong as possible.

Really her mom had been a godsend over the past year. As the news kept getting more and more grim, and Angela's segment became more and more prescient, her segment turned into a full-blown series. As her career climbed, she turned to her mom for advice about balancing work and family and she found herself listening. Two years ago, she would have never listened to her mother's advice on work. What else had she missed by being so stubborn?

"Hey, you okay over there?" Judith called as she pushed Hanae for the hundredth time. "You looked like you were somewhere else. You feeling okay?"

"Yes, Mom. I'm feeling great." Angela walked toward Hanae. "You ready to go little one?"

As Angela slowed down the swing to lift Hanae up and out, Judith stepped back and smiled. She couldn't help but think about how Angela had taken to motherhood with such grace and aplomb. Her job had never been crazier, and Hanae was a high-spirited little girl, but Angela made it look like this moment in her life was exactly where she was supposed to have been all along.

Judith loved being a grandmother, but she loved how close she and Angela were even more. It was like a switch was flipped when Hanae was born, and she would do anything to keep their relationship "on." She realized that her daughter was really funny, maybe funnier than any stand-up comedian. She was sincere and genuine and even though she was stubborn, Judith now saw that her dogged determination was from a place of love and not anger. The frustration Judith used to feel when Angela just wouldn't listen was replaced by an appreciation that Angela was paving her own path and that she *was* listening, just in her own way. Judith watched as Angela leaned forward and gave Hanae a kiss on the forehead, walking her back toward their stroller. Another generation of strong women.

"So, should we head back to the house?" Judith asked, joining them.

"It is very hot," Angela said, "but I think maybe we should walk just a little bit more. It's not so bad in the shade."

"Sounds good," Judith replied as she took her place alongside her daughter.

Neither of them spoke as they walked, save to occasionally point something out to Hanae who was perfectly content in her seat, soaking in the sights of the world like each one was brand new. "Maybe you should come over for dinner tonight," Angela offered.

"I'd like that a lot. Your dad is working late tonight, so it'll save me from a meal by myself in front of the TV."

"You know Mom, any time Dad is working late, you're welcome to come over."

Judith looked over at Angela. "I know," she said quietly. Smiling.

Angela looped her arm through her mom's and kept walking. "I think we can go a few more blocks before we turn back toward home, don't you?"

"Yes. Let's."

"Yes!" Hanae yelled from the stroller. It was her first word. Angela and Judith both stopped dead in their tracks after she said it. They turned to each other, tears filling their eyes.

"You heard her," Judith said.

"Yes!" They both bellowed as they walked down the street, arm in arm. Mother and daughter. Yes.

51 Hanae

Name: Hanae

Grade: 3

Book Report Title: An American Family

Author: Pamela Oshiro

My name is Hanae and the book I read was *An American Family*. The author is my great-auntie Pamela. She wrote a book about my family and the stories my family tells. It was a good book. I learned a lot about my family. I learned that my family has been in this country a long time and that many bad things have happened to them. I also learned that many good things have happened to them. I liked this book. I think my mom likes this book too.

52 Aiko

(CLICK)

Hello? Hello? I don't know why I'm saying hello like I'm talking into a phone. I still don't know how this thing works. I hope I'm not recording over something important. Although these tapes are just about me, so nothing important. I just wanted to send you this message, Pam. And for some reason I couldn't say it while we were talking. It's just not the way we do things. But I wanted to thank you for interviewing me. It meant a lot to me to know that you cared and to share my story. I am sorry I am not a better storyteller. I will leave that to you. You always tell great stories. One day, I do hope you will share this story. Not for me, but so that we don't repeat the mistakes of our past. So that you and Judith can have a better future. Follow your dreams, Pam. Let me know when you find out what pink tastes like.

(CLICK)

○○○

Acknowledgments

There are always so many people to thank, and for that I am grateful.

To the women of Windy City Publishers—I thank you for helping me reach my dreams. A special thank you to Dawn McGarrahan Wiebe. You are a true pleasure to work with!

To Laura Alsum who helped edit this book. Her inputs are always invaluable, and she points out so many things I don't catch (like in this book how often people take showers…I tried to take some of them out, but that's just what the characters would do in that moment, so I had to keep a lot of them in!).

To my dear friend Glenn Steward who created the first cover for this story, when it was called "Amache's America" and was hosted on channillo.com.

Speaking of which, a huge thank you to everyone at channillo.com, a wonderful platform for writers that allows us to be creative in a safe, collaborative space. I love writing for channillo and will continue to do so.

To all of the channillo readers and writers that got to hear this story first (in a much different version!), I thank you. A special shout out to supporters like: Bill McStowe, Joe Prosit, Brian Dykeman, Sharon Clark, and Ibrahim Oga. Your encouragement and support mean the world to me.

An extra special shout out to Kerri Curtis—who I met via channillo and has become one of my best friends. Kerri, you inspire and support me every day. I am so grateful you are in my life.

To Margaret Hahn for her bottomless well of support and friendship.
I do not know what I would do in this world without you.
I love you so much.

To my partner in crime, John DiCello, for your never-ending support and interest
in every facet of my life. I could not do the things I do without you.
And for taking me on the incredible journey we've been on
the last few years at the Arch. I value you every day.

To Matt Riel, the best friend a girl could ask for.
I'm glad we find each other utterly delightful.

To Sara Wiemer for always being there for me.
And for "happy thoughts" texts whenever we need them.

To the amazing women in my life…and forgive me I can't list them all,
there are so many, but here are a few…Julie Kasper, Eileen McWherter,
Rhonda Weiss, Tricia Weiss, Angel Weiss, Sara Russell, Angie Cooper,
Keely Schoeny, Ciara Mentzer, Emily Rotta, Sara Lukkasson, Blake Rose,
Amy Trang, Lorena Mora, Yentl Love, Elizabeth Schirick, Cindy Glennon,
Alex Anderson…I love you all, forever and always.

To Laura Weiner, for often believing in me way more
than I could ever believe in myself.

To my LSAC boxing crew—thank you for keeping me sane, in shape,
and for always encouraging me every step of the way.

To everyone at the Chicago Writers Association and CWA's Windy City Reviews—
I am proud to be a part of an organization where writers support writers.

To everyone I work with at the Arch. I am so proud to serve in this IT department
and I learn from you each and every day.

To our families at Waters Elementary, Luther Memorial Church,
and Walter Payton College Prep. We love the communities that hold us up.

To my dear friend Greg Emmett—because I know your name has two tt's.

Thank you to Mike Williams and Richard Cahan for providing me the high res image
of my family in front of the train to use in this book and to have for our family
archives. I have truly appreciated corresponding with you.

To everyone in my family. We are on this amazing journey together.

To my husband, Aaron, and my daughter, Cora.
I am nothing without you. Heaven is being with you.

To my sister, Julie—who helped raise me. Who supports me.
Who is there for me every time I call. Who loves to travel and see the world.
And who pushes me to be a better person. I love you so much. Always.

To my mom, Sharon—I will never fully understand the sacrifices
you have made for me and Julie, but I thank you for them.
You are a strong, independent, smart, sassy woman and I am honored to be your
daughter. Thank you for being brave. Thank you for being you.

To my Grammy, Mary—I will never forget the day you came
to my high school to teach my class about your experiences in the camps.
And how it opened up our eyes and minds to history in a way that we never knew
possible. I thank you for always sharing your story with me.
And for making me laugh.
And for being feisty and stubborn and rude
and lovely and sweet all at the same time.

And thank you to all the survivors of the Japanese incarceration camps.
From my family to yours. Thank you for persevering.
We will do our best to honor what you endured
and ensure it never happens again.

About the Author

KELLY FUMIKO WEISS is a member of the Chicago Writers Association and the author of the novel *The Cube*. She is also an author on channillo.com and co-host of the podcast *Women Know IT*. Kelly's career has centered around IT management in the education/nonprofit sector. She lives in Chicago with her husband and daughter.

@kellyfweiss
#TheCubeNovel
#TheStoriesNovel

Made in the USA
Monee, IL
20 February 2021